TRY BEFORE YOU TRUST:
TO ALL GENTLEWOMEN AND OTHER MAIDS IN LOVE

Constance Briones

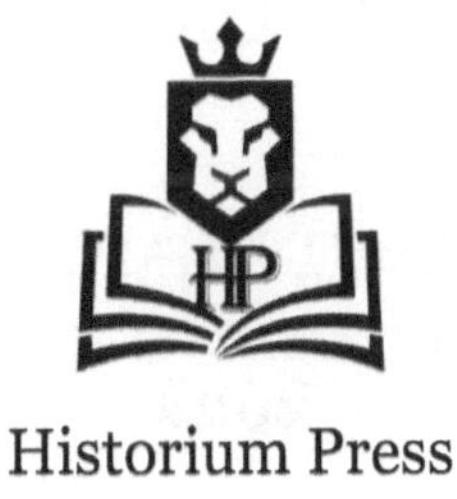

Historium Press

Ebook published in 2023 / Historium Press

PAPERBACK ISBN 978-1-962465-54-0
EBOOK ISBN 978-1-962465-17-5

HISTORUM PRESS

MACON, GA, USA

2024

TABLE OF CONTENTS

Part One

Housewifery for Women and Nothing More

*At the age when the girl seems ready to learn letters and
gain some practical knowledge,
let her begin by learning things that contribute to the care
and management of the home.*

Juan Vives, *Education of a Christian Woman*

*I know you housewifery intend,
Though I to reading and writing fall.*

Isabella Whitney

1

Bramwell House
London, 1567

On a brisk September morn in the ninth year of Queen Elizabeth's reign, I arrived at Bramwell House, a grand London estate of Lady Bramwell, a widowed baroness, and my new mistress. The fiery brick facade made the house seem indestructible as it stood proudly on the bank of the Thames. It boasted eight chimney stacks and forty mullioned windows with diamond-shaped glass, reflecting the sunlight in a dazzling array. I mused whether I would find friend or foe within.

As I gazed at the gables and corner turrets, my sisters' sweet laughter reverberated in the cool breeze that swept across my cheeks. How they twirled and giggled with delight when my mother promised that, like me, when they reach the age of eighteen, they too will venture from home to work for a grand lady, acquiring superior housewifery skills that would help them snag a well-bred gentleman. Being the eldest girl, it fell to me to be the exemplary model they would strive to emulate. 'Prove your worthiness to Lady Bramwell,' my mother advised me when I first received word I would work in her house. 'Perform your duties with due diligence and obedience.'

I adjusted my cloak to sit squarely on my shoulders and pulled my gloves tight over my fingers. "Proceed steadily," I muttered, and with calm deliberation, took that first step down the stony path that led to a magnificent marble portal. An elderly footman with a dour expression answered the door.

"And you are?" he asked, leaning forward. His bulging eyes and slouched stance reminded me of the toad my brother had recently snatched from the riverbank near our house, infuriating my mother that he dared bring the hideous creature into our Godly home.

"I am Isabella Whitney, the new maidservant, arrived from Nantwich," I said clearly and with confidence.

"This way, Miss Whitney," he said with a curt nod and not the slightest hint of a smile.

He led me into the long gallery on the first floor. "Wait there," he instructed, pointing to a stool with a curved seat that cupped my hips in a snug embrace.

My eyes followed him as he ascended a marble staircase. When he disappeared from view, I turned my attention to the silk tapestries that adorned the wall facing me. I wanted to rise and examine the stories told in the details of the exquisite needlework. Still, I resisted the impulse; a better first impression for Lady Bramwell to find me seated as directed. Shifting my gaze to the closed doors in the long gallery, I wondered which one might lead to the master library.

Cousin William's breathless descriptions of the libraries in the country estates of his university friends left me yearning to experience one. 'All splendid,' he had said, 'with domed ceilings painted gold and stain-glass windows that seemed to soar upward to the heavens. And with hundreds of books on myriad subjects that would satisfy the musings of the most curious mind.'

It was my fervent wish to continue reading the kinds of books I secretly read with William whilst he tutored me these last few years: ancient tales of history, adventure, and romance. I banished any nagging doubt that, like my mother, Lady Bramwell would limit my reading to holy scripture, conduct, and housewifery books. Every night hence from receiving her letter, I prayed that her husband, whilst alive, had amassed a book collection that equaled William's descriptions of those he had seen and that she would be receptive in allowing me to choose books from the library.

The approach of Lady Bramwell descending that glorious marble staircase jolted me from my thoughts. My fingers nervously straightened the few wrinkles in my russet-colored skirt, not of silk, yet made from the finest broadcloth. As she drew near, I noticed she was slight in stature. Still, she cut an impressive figure clothed in silk, striking in her indigo-colored gown. Gold chains in concentric circles hung about her neck, and a bejeweled belt encircled her tiny waist. Her tawny-colored hair was swept up into a caul adorned with pearls. She was the vision of an aristocrat.

Rising to greet her, I said, "Your ladyship, I'm most fortunate that you have chosen me to be your maidservant for the year, to learn all that I can to one day be an exemplary mistress of my own house."

She inclined her head as she observed me, appraising my worthiness to live and work in her household. Her gaze settled on my round hat, from which my mother very wisely had me remove its long purple feather and replace it with a small metal hatpin. 'A less ostentatious accessory is better,' she had advised.

With a tepid smile, Lady Bramwell sat on a cushioned stool beside a tapestry of a woman and two children. In the top corner was a blue and gold shield with a bear standing on its hind legs in attack mode, its curled red tongue jutting out of its mouth. It was likely the family's coat of arms, for I knew that the bear represented a fierce protector of families. A choice place for her to sit to impress upon me the honor of working and living in such an eminent home.

"You have been blessed with fine weather, Isabella. I trust that it was a smooth journey with few delays?"

My ear took a moment to adjust to her clipped tone. "Aye, my lady. It was unhindered."

"In his reference for you, Reverend Tisdale of your local parish said you enjoy reading."

Joyful anticipation coursed through my veins. This fine lady was about to thrust the door open to her deceased husband's library and allow me entry. "Indeed, my lady, I enjoy reading."

She drew her shoulders back. "You may then make use of my personal collection of books."

No mention of her husband's library. Still, my curiosity was piqued. "Your personal collection, my lady?"

"I have a fine collection of books suitable for your training here. Books that will reinforce the virtues of womanhood and housewifery skills. What say you? Are they of interest to you?"

My disappointment caused a surge of resentment to well inside me. *Nay, they are not. I have a hunger to read books that are deemed unsuitable for our sex. Do you really believe that women need men to control what we read because of our weak nature? Will we be unduly influenced by romantic tales, leading us astray from the path of virtue? I don't believe that — no matter how vigorously the church fathers preach it from their pulpits.*

Zounds! I wish I had said that. Instead, inculcated by the teachings of my mother and father, I followed proper decorum. "And the reading of scripture is also important, my lady."

Her smile became more inviting. "How is your hand with the needle, Isabella?"

The needle — how I hated it. Did she expect me to devote the little leisure time I would have to needlework and not read or write poetry? I didn't wince but smiled, "Quite competent, my lady."

My mother stressed the importance of making an excellent first impression with Lady Bramwell. I was no fool. Had I given her any reason to think I could be willful, she would have deemed me an eye-servant, someone to watch with a hawkish gaze. For the moment, the whereabouts of the library would remain a mystery until an opportune moment presented itself. Lady Bramwell beckoned me to follow her, and I did, in silence, up the staircase to another long gallery on the second floor.

At the top of the stairs, a young woman greeted me. "Isabella, I am Mistress Walden, cousin and gentlewoman to

Lady Bramwell."

Her winsome smile softened the sharp, angular features of her face. The youthful radiance of her skin placed her age at not much older than my eighteen years. She wasn't as ornately dressed as Lady Bramwell but wore a pleasing sunny yellow gown complimented by a heart-shaped bonnet.

"I have instructed my gentlewoman to give you an orientation of the house," Lady Bramwell said. "When you finish, we shall reconvene in the little chapel on the third floor to begin our afternoon recitation of the psalms. Do you have a favorite, Isabella?"

I didn't have to think long on my answer. "The psalms of praise and gratitude are my favorites."

"Which one in particular?" Lady Bramwell insisted, her lips pressed tight —she was testing my piety.

I met her stare with an unwavering smile. "*Psalm 100*, my lady. 'Shout for joy to the Lord, all the earth. Worship the Lord with gladness; come before Him with joyful songs.' I have a gift for words but not for composing music. Had I the skill, I would compose a ballad extolling the beauty of nature created by God's hands."

"What a lovely sentiment," Mistress Walden said, with a sideward glance at Lady Bramwell.

There was a glint of approval in Lady Bramwell's eyes. She crooked a finger for Mistress Walden to begin the house tour. I was relieved that my orientation was to be conducted by Mistress Walden, who had a far more pleasant demeanor than Lady Bramwell.

As we made our way down the long gallery, all the doors except one were closed. A vibrant garden mural on the wall opposite the opened door caught my eye, its colors seeming to come alive in the soft light. I poked my head into the room and smiled when I spied an open chest filled with toys. Laying on top of all the rest were wooden Bartholomew dolls.

My youngest sister enjoyed playing with the same wooden dolls my aunt gifted her when she returned from Bartholomew's Fair in London last year.

"This must be the bedchamber of Lady Bramwell's daughters."

Mistress Walden nodded. "Presently, they are elsewhere in the house, busy with their studies, and are not to be disturbed."

"Do they conduct their studies in the library?"

She didn't utter a response but shook her head no and proceeded to close the door. Before she did, I looked at the sampler on the wall near the door. One sentence, beautifully stitched, read, 'Reverence thy father and mother as nature requires.' Alas, I thought, how sad for Lady Bramwell's young daughters that their father was no longer with them. Oh, how the plaintive cries of my sisters and mine would have pierced the air if we, too, had lost our dear father; such a dreadful thought caused me to shudder.

The first stop on the house tour was the magnificent Great Chamber. Mistress Walden dubbed it the crown jewel of the house, reserved for formal meals and the center of entertainment for Lady Bramwell's family and their guests. The room's rich décor was a feast for the eyes. The walls were made of oak wood, gilded with real gold, and topped with a ceiling of red and white diamond-shaped tiles.

I bent to touch the floor and was surprised it wasn't cold. "How deceptive. It's not a marble floor."

"Merely a trick, borrowed from our queen's father, the great Henry. He had the oak floors at Hampton Court covered with plaster and painted to resemble marble."

A large, intricately carved medallion over the fireplace beckoned me with its tale of familiar characters. In the middle of the idyllic scene, a young man, dressed in ancient clothing played the lyre. He was surrounded by nine women, their ethereal beauty and grace captured in the delicate lines of the carving. I reached out and touched the medallion. "Look here, what a lovely depiction of Orpheus and the nine muses."

Mistress Walden starred with equal adoration. "I, too, enjoy gazing upon this scene, for I love music and dancing. Orpheus could charm all living things with his music."

Merry thoughts of this past summer spent with William reading tales about Orpheus elicited a warm smile. "Aye. When the followers of Dionysus threw stones at Orpheus whilst he played, the stones deliberately missed their mark, so enchanting was his playing of the lute."

"Is it not a fitting image to hang in this great room, where music and dancing occur on special occasions?"

"Indeed, Mistress Walden, this room calls out for much merriment." And then to my pleasant surprise, she moved to the center of the room, whereupon she gracefully executed four hops and one leap. I clapped in delight. "Bravo, Mistress Walden."

She beamed. "The Gillard is Queen Elizabeth's favorite dance. Would you like to try?"

Marry! I couldn't believe my ears. "Most certainly," and bounded over to her.

She took my hand and led me through the steps she had just performed. We laughed as I stumbled on the third hop, but she was most patient in guiding me through the steps. After two tries, I finally got it right. I playfully curtsied to her when we completed the last step of the dance. She rested her hand on my shoulder, "Well done, Isabella."

Her amiable manner convinced me I could ask her anything about Lady Bramwell and the house, and she wouldn't think me impertinent. "Mistress Walden, will we visit the master library on our tour?"

Suddenly, her countenance turned solemn. "Lady Bramwell has kept the library locked since her husband died, and only she has the key."

My heart sank. Looking down at the floor, I muttered, "Oh. I see."

Sensing my disappointment, she added, "However, I can show you where it is. Would that help satisfy your curiosity?"

I mustered a weak smile and nodded. We descended a back staircase, clanking our heels on the stone steps, filling the silence. At the first-floor gallery's far end, we stood before a thick oak door adorned with gilded moldings. A fitting décor for the treasure trove of books inside. My hand rested on the shield-shaped keyhole, and I gently slid my finger through it with a wistful smile.

"Have you ever been inside?"

"Only once. Baron Bramwell had a sharp and curious mind. Whenever he traveled, he always returned with books and had managed to build an extensive collection."

"And no one except Lady Bramwell can enter?" I asked, hoping to hear a different answer this time.

"There is one other who makes frequent use of the library. Lady Bramwell's young nephew."

"Nephew?" My curiosity heightened. "How old is he?"

"He is five years younger than me – twenty-one now and a law student at the Inns of Court."

"And his name, Mistress Walden?"

"Robert Barrington."

I whispered his name under my breath, stressing every syllable to commit it to memory.

That night, I wrote to my cousin William, who has served me well as a friend and tutor.

To my dear cousin,

I remember well your words the day we parted at the ruins of Nantwich castle. 'Let's hope, Izzy,' you said, 'that your baroness will be forward-thinking. I hear tell some allow their maidservants who can read access to their libraries.' Alas, William, Lady Bramwell is not one of them. She forbids my entry into her husband's library, which I hear has a collection as great as those you have seen. I can't believe my expectation of Lady Bramwell was so misguided. I was sure that in her position as baroness, she mingled with courtiers and ladies of Queen Elizabeth's court and would appreciate the ancient classics with their tales of adventure and romance, as does our fair queen. Instead, she offers me her dreary collection of books that would only delight my mother. I fear that my progress with you in reading and writing will be stunted without access to books that will sharpen my mind. But all is not lost. I might have found a way into the locked library, which rests upon a young gentleman and law student, Robert Barrington, Lady Bramwell's nephew. I tell you now – I intend to have my ears attuned for the utterance of his name the next time he comes to visit his aunt. For now, I bid you a hearty farewell. From Lady Bramwell's house in the Strand, London, on the twenty-second day of September 1567.

Your assured, loving cousin, Izzy.

2

A Most Formidable Mistress

In the six weeks that had passed since my arrival at Bramwell House, the name of Robert Barrington was absent from all talk. I went about my days, attempting to perform my assigned tasks with the utmost diligence, careful not to err because I daydreamed about befriending the scholar, Robert Barrington. I didn't have to prove my worth to my mother, but I did to Lady Bramwell. 'Take great care in being dutiful and respectful to Lady Bramwell. 'Tis she who will govern you in my absence,' my mother reminded me the morning I left home. I promised her I would, but Lady Bramwell had proved to be an intimidating mistress, most fastidious on how chores were to be done, and woe to the servant who did not meet her expectations.

I well remember my first try making sweet water for perfuming Lady Bramwell's clothes. It was a dismal failure. After waiting ten days for the flowers and herbs to settle in the rose water-filled jar, I strained the liquid into a bottle and anxiously presented it to Lady Bramwell. Both she and Mistress Walden were engaged in needlework and gossiping about families they knew. Lady Bramwell took one sniff, crinkled her nose, and waved it away.

"The scent is off," she snapped.

"Perhaps, my lady, the lid was not fastened tight enough," Mistress Walden suggested, coming to my aid. "A common mistake for a first try."

"Or perhaps Isabella did not assiduously measure every ingredient. The smell of musk and clove overpower the scents of lavender and jasmine," Lady Bramwell countered without looking up from her needlework. "Mistress Walden will observe you as you try again."

"Aye, my lady, I promise to do better at my next attempt."

Lady Bramwell laid her needlework frame on her lap and locked eyes with me. "See to it that you do. It has been a hot October, and my daughters nor I can afford further delay in scenting our clothes."

"Aye, my lady," I repeated in my best conciliatory tone.

I couldn't begrudge Lady Bramwell's dismissiveness, for I had not done the job correctly. I left the room, silently cursing the kitchen maids, for it was their jibes about their amorous encounters that had distracted me. The still room adjacent to the kitchen made it possible for me to hear every word. 'I tell you truly, he delights me not,' I heard one of them say, 'when he pressed his lips against mine with his hand on my bosom, my valley was dry.' Her candor made me laugh heartily. And was most likely when I added more than a teaspoon of musk and an extra drop of clove oil to the rosewater, thus resulting in a medicinal scent.

"Do not worry. All will be well," Mistress Walden remarked assuredly when she joined me later in the still room.

"I fear Lady Bramwell thinks me incompetent," I said, fetching the jars of jasmine, lavender petals, and the required herbs to begin the process again. "I don't know if I can ever execute my duties with the precision she requires."

"Bear in mind, Isabella, my cousin wishes no one ill will," she began to explain as she placed the bottle of rose water and an empty glass jar on the table. "As a widow, she must prove herself an efficient mistress of her household. She expects every staff member to perform their duties to perfection. Otherwise, her brother would say she lacks control in managing her household and demand that she remarries at once."

An exasperated sigh escaped my lips as I opened the jars of flower petals and herbs. "If she's under pressure to prove herself to her brother, I see no reprieve for my anxiety in trying to please her. Think on it, an accidental slip of my hand can damage the woolen cloth I'm assigned to brush. And if one pesky moth hides within the folds of gowns and skirts, Lady Bramwell will say I didn't vigorously shake out the clothes before storing them."

Mistress Walden fell silent, observing me as I carefully measured the ingredients to add to the rose water. I paid particular attention to measuring one teaspoon of musk. When it came to adding clove oil, I counted aloud five drops. I watched in anticipation as the drops of oil formed beads and lost their shape as they spread out upon the scented water.

"Take heart, Isabella, the year will pass quickly," she offered with an encouraging smile and gave a final twist of the jar's lid to ensure it was securely closed. "As a maid of all works, you will surely find housewifery tasks in which you excel. In time, you will please Lady Bramwell. Be thankful you do not have to earn your keep as a washerwoman whilst here."

I returned the jar of rosewater to its sunny spot on the shelf. Mistress Walden's words rang true. As Lady Bramwell's washerwoman demonstrated, performing the same prescribed duties day after day, hour after hour, would be a cheerless existence. The middle-aged woman, her body weary from standing and bending, spent her days meticulously folding large linen sheets one by one. She took great pains to position each one at the right angle in the tub, knowing that placing them at the wrong angle would allow dirty water to get trapped within the folds, leaving dirty marks, forcing her to wring the large, damp sheets and start the process again. It was admirable that she always got it right the first time, despite the toll it took on her body. I oft observed her walking toward the gate with her hand pressed against her lower back, her gait much slower than when she arrived in the morning.

That night, in my prayers, I asked forgiveness for my ingratitude. How peevish of me to wail to Mistress Walden about the hardships of working for Lady Bramwell. When my term was done here, I had a comfortable home to return to with a mother who readily forgave my flights of fancy whilst I did my chores. 'Rid your mind of foolish dreaming,' my mother would say, 'go for a brief walk in the garden and resume your work with a clear head.' Henceforth, whenever I spied the washerwoman leaving at the end of her workday, I uttered a blessing to keep her well and wished for her safe return the next day. And when my work day was done, I welcomed the sweet night. My mind, finally at liberty to drift away with fanciful thoughts of befriending the elusive Robert Barrington.

☙❧

One dreary November afternoon, whilst I was assisting Mistress Walden in storing Lady Bramwell's velvet gowns in an oak chest, she sighed, and a frown settled on her features.

"This year, my cousin will be hosting the Twelfth Night celebration. Her brother will attend with his family. Be prepared, Isabella, for her hawkish attention to every detail in preparing for the festivity."

Although I found that prospect daunting, it couldn't diminish my joyful anticipation at finally meeting the mysterious Robert Barrington. "Will the whole Barrington family be here, then?"

She confirmed with a quick nod.

"What's the name of Lady Bramwell's nephew? You spoke of him the first day I was here. It begins with an 'r' —Rafe? Richard?" I inquired with feigned forgetfulness.

"Robert," she smiled wryly, aware of my pretense. "Now, hold the end of this gown. Be careful with the beading at the hem."

The gown bore the colour of my favorite flower, violet. Once it was appropriately put away, I followed Mistress Walden to the highest table in Lady Bramwell's bedchamber. Sitting on stools with embroidered cushions, each depicting a different songbird, we commenced our inventory. She removed two leather-covered coffers from under the bed and gave one to me.

"Is there a special reason Lady Bramwell wishes to host the celebration?" I said, opening the lid of my coffer, which held gold and silver hairpins.

"Her brother thinks 'tis time she considers remarrying. He has invited many eligible bachelors of high rank to attend. Such men seek a wife who can host grand affairs for visiting dignitaries and courtiers. Of course, her beauty is a bonus."

"Does she wish to remarry?"

Mistress Walden remained silent whilst I counted and recorded the number of items in my coffer box. She then gave me another box with ribbons and bows to adorn the hair. After she entered her total count of pin cushions, she said, "It has been twelve months since the baron died, a respectable passage of time to contemplate potential suitors for marriage. She is but thirty-six. I know of widows older than she and not as pretty who have remarried within six months of their husband's death."

"Was her marriage to Baron Bramwell a happy one?" I said, gliding a rose-coloured satin ribbon through my fingers.

"She was married off to the baron when she was twenty years of age. Her father encouraged the match, for it elevated the Barrington name into the ranks of nobility. He was much older and widowed with no children. I cannot say with certainty that she was in love with him when she married, but her affection grew for him. He doted on her and the two daughters she bore him."

"She must have been overcome with grief when he died."

Mistress Walden closed her eyes and nodded solemnly as she recalled that sorrowful day in her cousin's life. "She took to her bed for a week. Her mother was summoned and managed to rouse her out of her miserable state. Since then, my cousin has worked tirelessly to remain a grand lady, well respected for her virtues and charitable work with the poor."

I picked up a tiny bow, the color of a robin's egg, and held it to my hair.

"Aye, 'tis a pretty colour," remarked Mistress Walden, who began separating the long needles used for stitching and hemming in her coffer. "Now, Isabella, we must work in silence. If we continue our chatter, we will be late for church. And you know my cousin is conscientious about getting to church on time."

Indeed. Lady Bramwell was most insistent on being among the first to be seated in church, which puzzled me. She would never have to search for a place to sit as her husband had purchased a family pew when he was alive. And I oft wondered why Lady Bramwell chose to wear Queen Elizabeth's favorite colors of black and white to church. Perhaps she hoped others would see the queen's celebrated virtues in her.

Whilst counting, I recalled the first time I attended Lady Bramwell's parish.

I thought it was strange not to sit in one of the pews as I did with my parents. But servants had to stand at the church's sides or the back. Lady Bramwell preferred that we stand across from where she sat so that she could turn her head ever so slightly to keep an eye on us.

"Take heed, Isabella. She'll watch us," Lady Bramwell's day servant, Sybil, advised. "Don't speak to me, not even in a whisper. Just keep your eyes on the priest. Many busybodies lurk about and won't hesitate to tell Lady Bramwell they saw us talking during the service."

Alone with no husband, Lady Bramwell was responsible for ensuring that her staff of maidservants upheld the virtues of silence, obedience, and chastity.

"I wonder, Sybil, how these busybodies consider themselves pious when they're not minding the sermon but are instead looking about the room for the ungodly behavior of maidservants."

She silenced her laugh. "Indeed, Isabella, many of us share your sentiment. But take heed. The sermon's about to begin."

I followed Sybil's advice, for I had no wish to be labeled an eye-servant in God's house. My gaze never left the pulpit, but my mind strayed whenever the sermon touched upon the duplicitous Eve, whose actions thrust us out of the Garden of

Eden and made sin and hardships our constant companions. Our lives are made difficult in recompense for Eve's disobedience and unrelenting curiosity – a guiding principle that the church ceaselessly reinforces.

I shifted my attention to counting and recording the ribbons and bows that lay in the coffer upon my lap. The circumstances of Lady Bramwell's marriage made me think about my prospects for a husband. She married not for love but out of duty to her father. Nay, not so for me. My father harbored no plan to raise above his station by arranging an advantageous marriage for one of his daughters. He was serenely content to live on the small estate that had been in his family for centuries.

My mother had her merry dreams. She yearned for me to marry a wealthy gentleman who would provide me with a grander home with more servants than she had. Unlike Lady Bramwell, I was free to set expectations for the man I would marry. I sought a well-learned gentleman with an appreciation for a woman's wit who would nourish my love for reading and support my forays into writing poetry. With eight months remaining, I prayed I would find such a gentleman before my contract with Lady Bramwell ended.

3

Blessed Days, Home for the Holiday

As the days of my housewifery training dragged on, the eminent arrival of Christmastide, with all its good cheer, buoyed my spirit. Even Lady Bramwell was full of good humour, granting me an early leave to return home twelve days before Christmas Eve. On the day of my departure, I bid a respectful farewell to Lady Bramwell and warmly embraced Mistress Walden, my heart brimming with gratitude for an early leave.

The journey home was tiring, requiring travel by road and waterway. It was near sunset on the twenty-third of December when the wherry I was traveling in approached the stony embankment of the River Weaver. My heart leaped as I caught sight of a tall, lean figure of a man wearing a hat with the back turned up, making the front resemble a duck's bill. It was my father, unmistakably so.

"Father!" I shouted, waving my hand high up in the air.

When the boat reached the embankment steps, my father rushed to meet me. "Welcome home, my dear daughter," he said, his voice filled with fatherly affection, as he readily extended his hand to help me off the boat. The boatman hastily placed my belongings on the platform.

"My thanks for securing a safe passage home for my daughter," my father said, giving him a few silver coins.

The boatman tipped his hat, took hold of the oar, and gleefully shouted, "Good tidings to you this Christmastide," as he pushed away from the embankment.

With an approving nod, my father held me at arm's length.

"London agrees with you, Izzy, for you look well." He leaned toward me as if he was about to impart a secret. "Now, we must gauge what effect living in London has had on your character," he teased.

"Father, I assure you, I have experienced very little of the delights of London to induce a change in my character. Lady Bramwell keeps me on a busy schedule six days a week," I replied, picking up my small bundle whilst my father took hold of my satchel.

"Patience and hard work are prized virtues, Izzy. With a testimonial from Lady Bramwell, you'll reap the rewards – mark my words."

As we walked home, my father expounded on the benefits of securing a good reference. "When your year is done serving Lady Bramwell, you may choose to remain in London with her or work in another fine home along the Strand. Or perhaps you may consider something closer to home. Many mistresses in Cheshire live in houses nearly as grand as Lady Bramwell. They would outbid each other for the domestic service of a local girl who gained experience in the London home of a baroness."

"Or I can remain in London married to a wealthy gentleman."

"Faith," he chuckled, "one who has far more money than me. Marry! That would surely please your mother."

And that would please me too, I silently agreed. Although not for the same reason as my mother. Girls are told it's their destiny to become wives and mothers. Even the queen, in her exalted position, cannot dodge that expectation. Hence, that being my calling, I pray to fall in love and marry a London gentleman whose status and money would grant me a life uncommon to most women. I would join that small, exclusive group of literary-minded women such as the Cooke sisters, Anne and Mildred. Ensconced in their London mansions along the Strand, married to learned men of the queen's court, and supported by a large staff of servants, their lives are not circumscribed by domestic duties. They are afforded the luxury of time to pursue their interests in scholarly reading and writing. What bliss it would be to augment that small membership of intellectually active married women by one more, namely me.

I held on to my father's arm tightly. "God willing, Mother's wish will come true."

My father smiled, drawing my hand into the fur that lined his cloak. As we approached home, I caught sight of my two younger sisters, Mary, age fourteen, and nine-year-old Dorothea, peering out from the window. They giggled and darted away when I waved at them, only to reappear in the doorway moments later with my mother. My heart quickened, and I hastened my steps to warmly embrace my mother first.

"Look, my tender lambkins, all is well now. For you see, Izzy has returned to us. Our Christmas wish is fulfilled."

My sisters cheered and pulled me inside. The furnishings of our main sitting room seemed smaller and less ornate than I had remembered, for my eyes had grown accustomed to the grandeur of the rooms in Lady Bramwell's house. Nevertheless, what I missed the most was still present. My family's love abounded in the air, permeating every pore of my body.

"And where's Brooke?" I asked loud enough for him to hear. "Hiding no doubt."

My sister Mary signaled that he was rolled up inside the carpet beside the fireplace. In an instant, the rug began to undulate.

"What! Ho Father! We're bewitched!" I screeched. "For don't you see the carpet is moving. What devilry is this?"

My father gave a mischievous smile and shouted, "Then I shall purge our house of the evil spirit trapped inside this rug by throwing it into the fire."

"Izzy, Izzy. 'Tis I coiled up so tightly here," my brother yelped.

My sisters ran to the carpet in a fit of giggles and unraveled it, and out popped my red-headed brother, newly turned eight years old, sitting upright with a scowl.

"You missed my birthday celebration!"

"But not on purpose. That's one of the problems with working so far away from home. Come see what I have for you, Brooke," I coaxed, pulling a toy soldier from my bag. "I have brought you a lovely birthday gift from the toy chest of Lady Bramwell's daughters."

He took it from me and examined it. "From a girl's toy chest?" he asked in disbelief.

"Their chest is overflowing with toys. When I told the younger sister it was your birthday, she rummaged through her chest until she found this wooden soldier. She said her boy cousin enjoyed playing with it when he was your age."

He held the toy close. "Tell her I'm happy with her choice and thank her for me." I kissed him on the forehead, and off he went clutching his new toy.

Turning again to the same bundle, I announced, "And now I have brought something we can all enjoy eating after our evening prayer." With outstretched arms, I held my gift for all to see.

"Manchet bread!" my mother exclaimed. "Oh! It has been a while since I had this bread. We can have it with butter and quince marmalade. This is a welcomed treat, especially now that Advent has ended, and we're free to eat whatever pleases us."

"May we eat it now?" Brooke implored from his spot on the carpet.

"You must wait, Brooke, till after our evening prayer," Mother said.

We all gathered together, sitting in a tight circle, by the warmth of the fire for evening prayer. My ears rejoiced to hear my father's rich baritone voice as he read his favorite passages from the Holy Book. A welcomed change from Lady Bramwell's monotone readings of the psalms. After the conclusion of evening prayers, we eagerly retreated to the kitchen, filling our bellies with morsels of manchet bread.

"Did you bake this bread, Izzy?" my mother asked.

I held my head high with pride. "I did, Mother. It was a

laborious chore, for I had to shift the flour through the cloth at least three times."

My father patted his stomach. "A man enjoys a wife who can satisfy his stomach," he remarked with a wink at my mother, which she acknowledged with a ready smile.

"And now, children, let's get ready for bed," my mother commanded so gently that not even Brooke objected. He trotted happily to bed, still clutching his toy soldier, whilst my sisters and I helped clear the table. When that chore was done, no sooner had I stepped into my bedchamber than Mary bounded in and began pestering me with questions.

"How often do your duties take you into the center of London? Is it true that the very rich have exotic pets? Are the young gentlemen in London more handsome than here?"

Her curiosity about London didn't surprise me, for it loomed brightly on the horizon for us country maids, beckoning us to pass through its city gates and experience the vibrancy of its streets. She was fourteen, and our mother would allow her to leave home to hone her housewifery skills in a grand house in just four years. Although I was weary from my long journey, I indulged her.

"Well, now, where shall I begin?" I pondered aloud as I sat on my bed. I didn't want to lessen her enthusiasm by telling her the truth. Lady Bramwell wasn't keen to venture out into the streets of London. She was happily ensconced in her neighborhood, which lay outside the city gates, a tiny enclave of mansions along the Strand. But occasionally, I did accompany Mistress Walden to Cheapside to purchase accessories for Lady Bramwell's wardrobe, such as ivory combs and colourful silk lace. There was plenty to say about Cheapside. Thus, I started there.

"There's no other street in London that offers more to delight the eye, Mary. 'Tis the widest avenue in all of London, with endless rows of merchant stalls. The last time I was there, I saw an exotic bird with shimmering green feathers and a spectacular tail resembling the flowing train of a wedding gown."

"Was the bird for sale or just for show?"

"Most definitely for sale. The Spanish had brought it from the New World. Although it seemed a shame that something so exquisite should be confined to a cage."

"Only in London can you see such wonders," she uttered wistfully.

Having told my most impressive tale about London, I was grateful when my mother appeared in the doorway with Dorothea.

"Mother, Izzy has been telling me all about Cheapside, the broadest street in London and the marvels you can see there," Mary enthused.

My mother smiled but spoke firmly. "There will be plenty of time to hear stories about London, but no more tonight, for 'tis late, and there's much to be done on Christmas Eve tomorrow. Now bid Izzy goodnight, Mary, and take Dorothea to bed."

"Do Lady Bramwell's daughters wear velvet slippers lined with satin and taffeta?" Dorothea asked, bending down to remove a speck of dust from the brown woolen slippers Mother had made her.

"They do, but they must take exceptional care, for their mother would be very vexed if they got even the slightest stain on them."

"How now? Lady Bramwell doesn't forgive like Mother?"

"Nay, she doesn't. Lady Bramwell's daughters are not as fortunate as us." Pleased with this affirmation, she readily took Mary's hand and left.

As I undressed, my mother prepared the bed. "Does Lady Bramwell treat you well?"

"Well, enough. But she's stern, at times harsh. Not mild-mannered the way mistresses are encouraged to be."

"Try to be more understanding of Lady Bramwell's situation. She's a young widow with two daughters to raise and a household of servants to supervise herself. That's enough pressure to cause anyone to fall into periods of ill humour."

"I'm very fortunate that her cousin Mistress Walden, her waiting gentlewoman, is very kind to me. She convinced Lady Bramwell that I should sleep in a little room near the kitchen where sacks of grain are stored instead of with Lady Bramwell's daughters. I'm grateful for the privacy."

"And are you eating well?"

"Aye, Mother. We all partake of the same meals the cook prepares for Lady Bramwell and her daughters."

She nodded, pleased by my account. She tucked the ends of the linen sheets under the mattress and quickly steered the conversation back to Lady Bramwell. "Is Lady Bramwell oft ill-tempered with you?" she asked with concern.

"Enough times to make me cautious when I'm around her. She's very exacting and quickly becomes irritable when something is not done to her liking. Fortunately, Mistress Walden knows what to say and do to calm her, and then she's in good spirits again."

"And how old is Mistress Walden?"

"I believe she's twenty-six."

"Then she's of an age to consider marriage proposals. As her kinswoman, I'm sure that Lady Bramwell is presently in the process of finding a suitable match for her."

Her prediction unsettled me, for Lady Bramwell's manner was only made tolerable by Mistress Walden's calm and steady presence. My mother placed my favorite red woolen blanket on me and retreated to the chair opposite the bed.

"Listen well, Izzy, if you prove your worth to Lady Bramwell, she may advance you to Mistress Walden's position when she marries. Or, when your year is completed, she may recommend you as a waiting gentlewoman to one of her friends. Hence, you'll accompany your new mistress to social events where you'll be seen by eligible, prosperous gentlemen," my mother predicted, beaming.

"Perhaps what you say will happen. But, for now, I wish Lady Bramwell was more mild-mannered," I sulked, pulling the covers to my chin. "It would ease the burden of returning to the Bramwell House."

"I'm glad Mistress Walden has become your friend and mentor. Observe her ways and all she does as Lady Bramwell's waiting gentlewoman."

She went to the window to check that it was securely locked, and before she left the room, she tenderly placed her hand on my head. "Good night, my good daughter," she whispered and blew out the candle on the side table.

As I lay in bed, I realized I hadn't thought about Lady Bramwell's nephew since I arrived home. As I felt my eyelids grow heavy, I willed myself to dream of Robert Barrington as I drifted off to sleep in the stillness and silence of the country night.

❧

Early Christmas Eve morning, my father and Brooke had set out to find the perfect yule log that would illuminate our house during the remaining days of Christmastide. Dorothea stood by the window, keeping watch for their return whilst Mary and I were helping mother prepare the table decorations for the Christmas feast.

"There's Father," Dorothea squealed. "Look, Mother. Father has found a huge tree root," she laughed. "And Brooke is sitting astride the tree root as if it were a horse. He can barely keep his balance as father pulls it. Mother, come quickly! See how he thrashes his arms about to keep his balance."

Mother peered out the window, narrowing her eyes. "Who is that man helping your father bring it to the house?" As they drew closer, my mother instantly recognized my father's helper. "Bless his good soul, 'tis Samuel, helping your father on what should be a day of rest for him."

Mary ran to get the box of brightly coloured ribbons. "We should be able to use all of them this year. Tying them on a tree root will be easier than a log. Remember how the ribbons kept slipping off the log as we rolled it to the fireplace?"

My father and his longtime trustworthy worker, Samuel,

whom we all called by his first name, struggled to get the tree root into the house. Brooke expertly offered suggestions on the best ways to get it inside. We patiently waited many minutes for the tree root to make its way through the doorway. Finally, with a resounding thud, my father and Samuel dropped it onto the main hall floor.

"We did it. We did it. 'Tis the best yule log we ever had!" Brooke shouted, merrily prancing around it.

My mother insisted that Samuel stay to enjoy a glass of wassail we had prepared that morning.

"Just one drink, Mistress Whitney, and then I must be off. My two little boys will be expecting a special delivery, too," he said, winking at Brooke.

"But I fear we got the most perfect tree root," Brooke said, resting his hand on Samuel's arm to offer comfort that he usurped the best tree root from his sons.

"No matter Brooke. My brothers and I will find another. Rest assured of that." He raised his glass and gave a toast. "To your family's health," and downed his glass of wassail. He smacked his lips. "Oh, that's good," he said, looking at Mary and me. "Well done, girls," he said with an affectionate smile.

As soon as Samuel left, we turned our attention to the tree root and tied our colorful ribbons on it.

"It certainly looks less monstrous now done up in those colourful ribbons," commented Mother as she cocked her head, observing our handiwork.

After supper, we gathered 'round the ribboned tree root. My sisters and brother took turns sitting on it as we sang our favorite Christmas carols. We began with my mother's favorite, *She Must be Called a Sovereign Lady*, and ended our caroling with Brooke's favorite, *The Boar's Head Carol*. When we gathered last Christmas Eve, my cousin William told us the story of the carol's origins. The story goes that one day, an Oxford student was walking in the forest during Christmastide. Whilst reading Aristotle, a wild boar attacked him. Unarmed, he rammed the book down its open mouth, thus killing it. Every year, during Christmastide, a little ceremony is performed at Oxford where a decorated boar's head is borne into the hall on the shoulders of two students, followed by a choir. Hence, Brooke insists on attending Oxford when he comes of age.

Once our caroling was done, we attempted to roll the gigantic tree root into the fireplace with our feet. The thrusting twisted roots caught our feet like claws, which caused us to trip over each other, and we all fell to the floor in a fit of unrestrained laughter. With Father's help we rolled it over the hearth and into the fireplace. Then came the momentous moment of setting it ablaze.

"Oh, please, Father, let me light it!" Brooke pleaded.

"That task is better left to your father," my mother advised.

As hard as Brooke tried not to, we could see the slight emergence of a pout. I retrieved the urn that was resting beside the fireplace. "Here, Brooke, why don't you be the first to scatter the charred remains of last year's yule log around the tree root before father sets it on fire."

He yelped joyfully and thrust his hand into the urn, followed by Mary and Dorothea.

When Father put the flame to the ashes, a burst of light lit up the room, eliciting a mighty cheer. Mother brought in the yule cake and bowls of frumenty with bits of honeyed stewed apples. It had been another memorable Christmas Eve and thoughts of my last few months at Lady Bramwell's house had been far removed from my mind. If only the same could be said for her nephew.

4

A Memorable Christmas Day

The yule log was still burning on Christmas morning with as much intensity as the previous night. Our day servant, Martha, had come promptly at five to revive the flames. She had prepared a simple but sturdy morning meal of pottage, providing much-needed nourishment for the lengthy church service that awaited us. My sisters and brother descended the stairs shortly after me. Brooke roused himself out of bed without coaxing from his sisters. He had taken to heart our parents' belief that rising early in the morning is one of the best ways to keep healthy and holy.

Mother placed her arms around us, pulling us close to her, so pleased to see us neatly attired and patiently waiting for father to lead us all to church. My father observed our smiling faces and cheerfully commanded, "And now, children, to church where we'll pay homage to our Lord on this holiest day of Christmastide."

We silently fell in line behind my mother and father. I looked forward to sitting with my family in our parish instead of standing in the aisle under the watchful eye of Lady Bramwell. Once the church service was over, we eagerly returned to our house to enjoy our first elaborate meal of the season. A sumptuous feast of meat and vegetable dishes, including many of our favorites, was laid on the table.

Our feast was made more enjoyable by having my cousin William and his family join us at our table. There was his mother, my aunt Lydia, my father's sister and her husband, my uncle Donald, William's sister, Marjory, who was the same age as Dorothea, and youngest brother Lawrence, Brook's agreeable playmate. We all cheerfully took our designated places at the table. The chatter came to a halt when Father said Grace, and then it commenced again as we picked up our knives and helped ourselves to whatever food was within our reach.

"Eat smaller morsels of meat, Brooke, and chew softly with your mouth closed," my mother admonished him.

"Nephew, how is Oxford this year?" my father asked William.

"Thus far, all is well, Uncle. This year, the emphasis is on reading the classics of the Roman and Greek philosophers."

"We are fortunate that our William gives himself more to learning than pleasure," his father said proudly.

"We are fortunate indeed. There are many tales of disorderly youths at both our leading universities, Cambridge and Oxford," his mother added.

"But the antics at Oxford and Cambridge still pale to the ones at the Inns of Court," William reminded his mother.

The mention of the Inns of Court pricked my ears. Lady Bramwell's nephew, Robert, was a student at one of the Court schools, but which one was it?

"There are four Inns of Court, William. Which one are you referring to?" I asked.

"Why to all of them. But the most riotous sort is found at Gray's Inn. 'Tis a playground for the privileged sons of the wealthy. They have no desire to learn but are mainly there at the behest of their fathers."

I lifted my spoon and slowly finished the remains of my spice custard, mulling over William's comment. When Mistress Walden said that Robert Barrington frequently visits his aunt's library, I imagined him a serious scholar with aspirations of becoming a barrister. If he be one of those mischief-makers that William described, I doubt he would be much impressed with my clever mind. I shoved my spoon into another sweet dish of plum pudding to dispel such a dreadful thought.

"Izzy, what a ravenous taste for sweets you have today," my aunt observed in amusement. "Are you in love, my dear?"

"I assure you, Aunt, I'm not," I responded, scooping up the last morsels of the pudding's raisins and currants from the bottom of the bowl.

"But Aunt, what does love have to do with Izzy filling her belly with sweets?" Brooke interjected in a somewhat irritated tone. "Does God not intend for us to eat all that is here? 'Tis Christmas after all!"

There was a ripple of quiet laughter at the table. My mother signaled for Brooke to approach as he licked the sugar from the sweet wafers off his fingertips. She gave him a napkin and held him close. "Of course, God intends us to joyfully partake of the bounty before us on this table. But we mustn't forget those who are less fortunate. Our Lord wants us to share what we have with families in need. And in doing so we strengthen our bonds of love and compassion."

"Amen," confirmed my father. We all bowed our heads and uttered the same.

Our meal ended around the hour of two. We helped my mother pack the remains of our meal for Reverend Tisdale, who every year hosted a charitable Christmas supper for parish members in the early evening hours. My father, William, and his father prepared the horse and wagon for transport. When all was ready, we all helped load the wagon with our goods. William and I, being the eldest, were to remain behind, keeping watch over the younger children whilst Mother, Father, and William's parents went off to Reverend Tisdale's parish. I was thankful for the time alone with William. There was much to discuss. Luckily, my sisters and brother were well engaged in playtime with their cousins.

"Aren't you overjoyed, Dorothea, that you have twelve days of no spinning?" I heard William's sister Marjory declare as she did a joyful jig around the spinning wheel decorated with flowers.

Dorothea's response caused Marjory to stop dancing. "I wish Mother didn't make us decorate the spinning wheel. We can't use it, for twelve days now, and I so wanted to finish the wool I was spinning. Mother was going to help me make a cloak for Father's New Year's Day present."

"Knowing your mother, she'll find a way for you to finish your spinning. My mother doesn't decorate our spinning wheel. I'm sure you'll come to our house to use it."

Dorothea flashed a wide smile, and off they went to play with her wooden Bartholomew baby dolls. She had a vivid imagination and could dream up housewifery tales to act out for hours. Meanwhile, Mary was sitting at the kitchen table, patiently stringing chestnuts. She threaded most of the chestnuts Brooke had collected during the past few months to make pendulums for a game.

"Take care, Brooke," Mary advised. "Do you remember what happened the last time we played? You tried to smash Dorothea's chestnut with such vigor that you missed and hit her knuckles instead. Mother was furious. Poor Dorothea's knuckles were swollen and red for days."

William and I retreated to my mother's sitting room. Sipping from our glasses of spiced wine, we spoke of our recent events: William's return to college and my turn as a maidservant in Bramwell House.

"Tell me about your studies this year, William, for I am most eager to hear," I prompted, my curiosity piqued by his earlier mention of the increased rigor in his academic pursuits.

"To be sure, 'tis more rigorous this year."

"Pray, how so?"

William paused to take a sip of wine. "There are more disputations this year. I spend long hours carefully constructing and defending my argument. Still, I prefer the disputations to the lectures." He placed his glass on the table. "But enough talk of me. Not a day goes by that I don't wonder how you're doing. Have you managed to make use of the library?"

I shook my head no. "Alas, I'm still confined to using Lady Bramwell's personal collection."

"You haven't yet met her nephew, as you stated in your letter?"

"I imagine he's too busy with his studies at the Inns of Court to visit his aunt."

William grinned and squinted his blue-gray eyes. "Ah. That's why you were curious to know which of the Inns of Court was most notorious for unruly students. And what else do you know about this young law student besides his name?"

"That's all for now, just his name – Robert Barrington." I walked about the room, slowly enunciating his name, counting each syllable of his name on my fingers. "Is it not the perfect sounding name for a sonnet?"

He raised his eyebrow. "All you know is his name and nothing more?"

"Anon, I should know more, for he'll attend Lady Bramwell's Twelfth Night celebration. I hope he'll retreat to the library, where I'll accidentally stumble upon him."

"Ha!" William blurted, picking up his drink. "He's to be ambushed then!"

I laughed. "I suppose you could say that."

William signaled me to sit by him. "Seriously, Izzy, you should unearth more about Robert before you attempt to trap him in the library. Try to ascertain something of his character from those who know him well. Is he a serious or a rakish sort of fellow? If he's studious and free of vice, it might interest him to show you his deceased uncle's library collection. But, if he's not, he might lead you astray by making all sorts of promises only to have a bit of fun with you for the night."

Before I could respond, Brooke shouted that our mother and father had returned home. I scampered out of the room when Mother called for me.

"How fares it here, Izzy? All well?" my mother asked as she made her way into the large parlour, my father and William's parents trailing behind.

"All's well, Mother, quiet as can be."

Thankfully, she wasn't greeted by a flurry of complaints. Brooke didn't whine about being mercilessly teased by

Dorothea and Marjory, nor did Dorothea complain of being endlessly ordered about by Mary. Instead, she witnessed Brooke and Lawrence engrossed in counting and examining chestnuts with strings attached that Mary had prepared for their game.

"Izzy, fetch your sisters and cousin to help us prepare for supper. My brother and his family will be joining us shortly."

I was halfway up the stairs when I heard William call my name. I turned and found him waiting at the bottom step. I came back down to meet him.

"We might not have another moment alone tonight," he said in a low voice. "So, I'll speak directly to my point. There could be perils in meeting strangers on Twelfth Night. Everyone's in good cheer, and there is free mingling amongst all kinds of people. Wealthy gentlemen will offer a cup of wassail to scullery maids and exchange pleasantries with daughters of tradesmen, all for the sake of engaging in a bit of pleasure just for that one night. And then these same gentlemen forget their pleasantries and promises once the night has passed. Try to learn more about Robert Barrington before meeting him in the library."

I was touched by his concern and grateful for his council. I gave his arm a gentle squeeze. "Fear not. I shall take your advice to heart, dear cousin," and bounded up the steps.

As Mother had predicted, her brother, my uncle Trevor and his wife, my aunt Jocelyn and their two young sons, Martin and Andrew, and daughter Emma, arrived at our house within the hour. When Uncle Trevor stepped into the house, he laid his large hands on his distended belly and exclaimed it was ready to burst open, which caused everyone to laugh. Mother's prudence in preparing a Christmas supper of simple but tasty delicacies was met with hearty praise.

"I'll wager that no woman in town can rival my sister's superior cooking and baking. Year after year, she always conjures savory dishes for all to enjoy on Christmas," Uncle Trevor proclaimed.

"Indeed," my father concurred. "Many townsmen have

threatened to kidnap her for her fine skills in the kitchen and leave their wives in her stead."

My mother smiled modestly at my father's and uncle's flattery, but I knew she savored their compliments. Repeatedly, she told us, 'A skilled hand in preparing dishes is the best way to serve and keep one's husband content.' I oft wondered if I could ever match her skills.

With my Uncle Trevor and his family's arrival, we now had enough children in the house to satisfy Brooke's eagerness to play a game of Conkers. This was the only time of year when Mother and Father tolerated excessive noise in the house. Brooke insisted on playing five rounds. Despite only winning one game, my mother's praise made him happy.

"I'm pleased you listened to Mary's advice and played with greater restraint this year. Good lad, no red, aching knuckles for Dorothea this year."

William's father decided to join in the next game of Shoe the Mare. William and I watched in amusement as his father dashed around the room with the children chasing him. When they implored my father to help, he willingly blocked William's father so they could shoe him. After two rounds, William agreed to take over from his father. When the games were finally over, tranquility was restored. William played a game of cards with the men whilst my mother and aunts retreated to the kitchen, engaged in local gossip and discussing upcoming church events. Brooke and his boy cousins were allowed to play in his room. As for me, I indulged my sisters and cousins by joining them in their bedchamber for a fortune-telling game of who our future husbands would be.

Emma, who was just a year younger than Mary, gave me a bag of marbles and instructed me to toss them onto the floor. She observed with quiet intensity the pattern that the fallen marbles had formed.

"This rectangular shape," Emma began, pointing at the marbles, "indicates a large house. And this set of black marbles clumped together represents a man who lives in the house, a man with whom you'll have a strong connection. Could there be such a man living in Bramwell House?" she asked, her voice filled with interest.

"The lady I serve is a widow. Some men tend the grounds, but they are day laborers."

Emma shrugged her shoulders. "Well then, perhaps another sort of man frequents the house often."

I grew intrigued but remained indifferent, not wishing to reveal Robert Barrington's name. " No one comes to mind."

"Maybe someone who's yet to appear," Mary concluded, growing more enthralled with the idea. "Of course! You will meet a man at Lady Bramwell's Twelfth Night celebration. Someone who will be a potential suitor for your hand - a grand gentleman." She clapped her hands. "Oh! Won't Mother be thrilled?"

"You'll be in London for Twelfth Night?" Emma asked, her voice tinged with envy.

"I must leave tomorrow to help Lady Bramwell prepare for her celebration."

"You're indeed lucky to attend a Twelfth Night celebration hosted by a baroness. What a grand extravagance it'll be," Emma said, her gaze returning to the pattern on the floor. "I believe Mary may be right. You'll meet someone at your mistress's celebration."

My sisters and Marjory stared at me, no doubt mulling over fanciful thoughts of my being pursued by a well-bred gentleman. For a moment, I, too, was entranced by Mary's prediction.

The room suddenly grew hot, and I felt flushed. Wanting to divert the attention away from me, I gathered up the marbles and handed them to Mary. "Well, enough about me. You toss the marbles now to see who you'll marry." I feigned a yawn. "I feel a bit tired. I think I'll go to my room to rest."

Mary followed me out into the corridor, taking hold of my arm. "Izzy, have you told me everything about your stay in London? Your cheeks grew flushed at Emma's prediction. Is there a potential suitor waiting for you at Lady Bramwell's house? I understand if you don't want Emma to know, but surely you can confide in me. I'm your sister, after all."

I embraced her tightly and said, "Believe me, Mary, had I a love interest in London, I would have told you. And when there is one, I promise to write you straight away."

She smiled, satisfied by my promise, and scampered back to hear Emma's prediction of her future husband. As I settled in my room, I thought about the day's events. It was a memorable Christmas day filled with unexpected revelations and good counsel. As I prepared for bed, I didn't wish to conjure a dreamlike visage of Robert Barrington whilst I slept. Instead, during that Christmas night slumber, I dreamed that I was standing at the closed door of the library in the Bramwell House, and a young man's voice kindly bid me enter.

5

Robert Barrington — Well Met

The day before Lady Bramwell's Twelfth Night celebration, a surprise awaited me, shrouded in the secrecy of Mistress Walden's excitement. She whisked me away from the bustling kitchen, leading me up a flight of stairs into her room. There on her bed, lay an embroidered floral silk gown of the most exquisite shade of lilac, spread out in all its glory. She peered into my face as I examined it.

"Give me your honest opinion of this gown, Isabella."

"'Tis a work of astonishing workmanship. Look at these sleeves topped with purple and white bows and ribbons at the shoulders — so beautiful."

"The gown belonged to my sister." She paused and squeezed my hand. "I wish you to wear it at tomorrow's celebration."

I was rendered mute, and tears welled up in my eyes. It was too generous a gesture. "I'm speechless. You must have family members who are dearer to you that you can bestow this gown."

She rested her hand on my arm. "But I have chosen you, Isabella. I think you will turn many heads tomorrow evening. But, I daresay there is one special gentleman you wish to make an impression upon," she said with a knowing smile.

Upon her reference to Lady Bramwell's nephew, I seized the opportunity to do William's bidding and learn more about him. I sat beside my precious gift on the bed, fanning the gown's wide pleats.

"Mistress Walden, how would you describe Robert Barrington's character?"

I anxiously awaited as she pondered her response.

"I would say that he is a very affable young man. He is also very benevolent. I dare say, at times, to his detriment."

What a curious remark. "How can possessing a benevolent nature cause harm to anyone?"

She laughed. "'Tis a rather contrary comment, to be sure," she said, carefully picking up the gown. I followed her to the cabinet and opened its doors, whereupon she laid it on the middle shelf. I couldn't perceive how benevolence was an unfavorable trait. Thus, I repeated my question.

"Let me see if I can provide an example of what I mean," Mistress Walden said, contemplating her response as she sat at the window seat. "About a fortnight ago, Robert's father complained to my cousin that Robert drew his rapier on another student to defend his friend's honor. Fighting is forbidden at Gray's Inn, so Robert was fined forty shillings, which his father had to pay. He was not pleased with paying yet another fine for a school rule Robert disobeyed."

I leaned against the cabinet and breathed a sigh of relief. "Thus, Robert fought in defense of his friend. I say loyalty is a good virtue." I paused, hesitant to ask my next question, but ask I did. "Do you think he might venture into the library tomorrow evening?"

Her eyes flickered with a glint of recognition of my deep-seated yearning. "Little wonder that you would inquire about the library. You have wanted to see it since the day you arrived here." She smiled. "Robert might retreat to the library to escape his father. Since the fines were imposed, their relationship has been strained."

I sat beside her. "What would Robert make of me if I suddenly, by chance, stumbled upon him there? Would he welcome such an intrusion?"

"I do not think he would refuse the company of a bright young woman like yourself."

I gazed out the window with a dreamy smile, the garden path to the Thames visible through the bare trees. "That's comforting to know," I whispered.

Mistress Walden gently took my hand, bringing the two of us to our feet. "Tomorrow, you will come here and dress for the celebration. But now we must make haste to meet Lady Bramwell in the kitchen, where she will oversee the final preparations for tomorrow's banquet."

I cupped her hands in mine. "Many good thanks to you, Mistress Walden. I never imagined I would be dressed in such finery in all my dreams of celebrating Twelfth Night here tomorrow."

⊗

After what seemed like an eternity, Lady Bramwell's Twelfth Night celebration finally arrived, bringing my long-awaited chance to meet the elusive Robert Barrington. But to my dismay, I had lost sight of Mistress Walden early in the evening. I desperately needed her beside me to identify the face of Robert Barrington. Fie upon Lady Bramwell for insisting that Mistress Walden stands with her as she greeted her guests.

It wasn't until the cutting of the Twelfth Night fruitcake that I saw Mistress Walden again. She looked as grand as Lady Bramwell in her goldenrod-coloured brocade gown, hair, and neck adorned with pearls. She was paired with a handsome red-haired gentleman, elegantly attired in a cream-coloured doublet with a fancy ruff just below his chin. As she bit into her piece of cake, he leaned and whispered something in her ear, which made her laugh. Amongst the nearly one hundred guests, I prayed that Mistress Walden would find the bean in her piece of the fruitcake, thus proclaiming her queen for the night.

A thunderous cheer erupted from the middle of the ivy and holly-decorated Great Chamber. I stood on tiptoe to see who was the lucky recipient of the bean. A man about my father's age with a long golden feather in his black cap and tiny silver bells hanging from his beard raised his clenched hand. He hushed the crowd and proclaimed, "'Tis only fitting that the bean has fallen to me. For I'm the proud brother of the lady of this house who has masterfully executed tonight's celebration." Generous applause followed.

Heavens above – Robert's father! But where was Robert? I saw no young gentleman about him offering congratulatory slaps on the back, only middle-aged bearded men. Lady Bramwell bestowed a congratulatory kiss upon her brother and placed a crown on his head. She cast a glance in the direction of a gentleman, mustached and short-bearded, dressed in black, with a heavy silver pendant on his chest. He bowed his head in recognition of her and beamed when he raised it quickly. Judging by her radiant smile, he was likely one of the courtiers she was seeking to impress tonight.

"What now, brother? What entertainment do you suggest we begin with?"

Robert's father looked at the children's smiling faces, including his nieces sitting on the benches near the stage assembled early that morning. With a flourish of his hand, as if wielding a sword, he shouted with glee, "Let the pageant of *Saint George and the Dragon* begin." The assembled children clapped jubilantly whilst the musicians gathered on the side of the stage and played the prelude.

"Robert has retreated to the library," Mistress Walden whispered in my ear. When I turned to face her, she was beside her gentleman. She gave a knowing smile and, with a nod of her head, signaled me to leave.

I tried to control the speed at which I left, not wishing to arouse suspicion in Lady Bramwell as to why I was hurrying out of the Great Chamber. Accompanied by gales of music and cheers from the audience viewing the performance, I descended the stairs. I stepped slowly down each step, afraid of taking a tumble in the heeled shoes Mistress Walden lent me. When my feet touched the floor, I quickened my pace down the long gallery to the last door, which, to my surprise, was left ajar. How strange to see it thus, for it has always been locked. Like Eve's snake, the sliver of golden light streaming through the gap between the wall and the door beckoned me to enter the forbidden room of books and knowledge. I hesitated and then eased my body into the room, quietly closing the door behind me.

After months of waiting with anticipation, my eyes fell upon the gallant Robert Barrington reading a book by the blazing light of the fire. He didn't notice my quiet entrance into the library. I nearly jumped with fright when he abruptly slammed the book shut and let loose a loud yawn as if bored. With a serendipitous toss of his head in my direction, he locked eyes with me. The muscles of my heart tightened. His stare burned hot like the roaring fire.

But I quickly realized I had nothing to fear, for he flashed an inviting smile, and when he spoke, his mellifluous voice dispelled my apprehension.

"Has my aunt bid you to fetch me, Isabella?"

"Y-y – you know my name?" I pinched my thigh to have stammered.

"Are you not the new maidservant in training who hails from Cheshire?"

I nodded, like a simpleton so disconcerted that he knew about me. He gestured to the chair across from him, and I readily obliged to join him. His face had a rugged handsomeness, made gentle by a warm smile, and his deep brown eyes were framed by delicate black lashes. In truth, his good looks captivated me like no other young man I had met before him.

He began his inquiry with a confident smile. "I know your name, but do you know mine?" he asked, deliberating arching his brow in jest to express indignation, which made me smile.

"You're Robert Barrington, nephew to the lady of this house."

He extended his hand. "I'm pleased to meet you, Isabella."

I was indeed startled by the ease of his manner. He lifted my hand to his lips, and he bestowed a respectable kiss—quick but tender. I didn't suspect, as William had warned, that Robert's behavior might be knavish. Nay, his gentle manner was reminiscent of my good cousin. I leaned back into the chair.

"How do you know about me, Robert?"

"I noticed you as soon as I entered the Great Chamber with my family at the start of the celebration. I asked my cousin, Mistress Walden, who's the girl with the honey-colored hair? She gave scant information about you. Whereabout in Cheshire is your family's home?"

"We live in Nantwich on a small estate that's been in my family for years."

"I have never been that far north to the west. What's it like there?"

"Peaceful. I enjoy long walks by the river Weaver, especially during spring and summertide."

"I imagine living in a river valley could be pleasant, but not much there to stimulate the mind, eh?"

"It does pale to London, to be sure." I paused, then tried a feeble attempt at interjecting some humor. "But every Wednesday, the town is bustling when the farmers from neighboring towns converge in the town center for the cattle market."

He clapped his hands in mock excitement. "And I'm sure you await that day with bated breath."

I smiled, pleased that he responded to my dull humor politely.

"Thus, 'tis by chance, you stumbled upon me here, for I know now you were not sent to fetch me." His eyes narrowed as he attempted to comprehend why I was there.

Naturally, he would suspect a motive for my sneaking into the library, especially since his aunt forbade it. I had to guard the truth until I detected a sign that he would be receptive to my true intent of being there. My mind raced for a quick and convincing response, but I couldn't think of any. Thus, I reversed the speculation onto him.

"Are you hiding from someone, Robert? There's much revelry happening upstairs. Don't you want to be with your family amid all that merriment? When I left, a performance of

Saint George and the Dragon was about to begin. And your father was made king of tonight's entertainment."

He dismissed that last bit of news with a wave of his hand. "Pish. I'm sure he knew which piece of cake contained the pea, or my aunt arranged for him to get it. And if you leave anon, stand at the bottom of the grand staircase. You'll undoubtedly hear my father's boisterous laughter as he encourages others to join him in the *querelle des femmes* debate."

A foreign phrase—sounded French. "What does that mean?"

"In English, we refer to it as *the woman question.*"

I was intrigued. "What's *the woman question* debate about?"

He shrugged. "A trite rhetorical exercise in which men debate about a woman's true nature. Is she virtuous or a sinner, rational or irrational, a worthy or unworthy companion for life? When my father's full of drink, he regales others with his colourful views on the subject, whilst my mother and sister must remain tight-lipped as he disparages their sex."

"And what's your view on the subject?"

He pulled in his legs and leaned forward in his chair. "None of us are saintly. In my view, women, like men, fall somewhere in between. We need to acquire a more balanced view of the sexes for harmony. My father would do well to broaden his view of the world and the people who inhabit it."

God-a-mercy! That was my sign. "I'll be plain with you, Robert. My encounter with you here was no accident but deliberate. I have wanted to catch you in this room for months."

"Whatever for?" he asked, genuinely surprised.

I walked over to a bookcase filled with books and glided my hand over its mesh doors. "For these."

An incredulous laugh escaped his lips. "How now? You have a passionate desire to read my deceased uncle's books?"

I unleased my fierce desire. "Aye, I do! I must find respite from the monotony of household chores. Surely, there's more to stimulate a woman's mind than reading conduct and housewifery books. Here, there's a treasure trove of books."

He fell silent, observing me at length. What did he make of me? Perhaps I was too bold in my candor, but I wasn't to blame, for my remark stemmed from his unbiased comment about women. He rose from his chair without a word. Fear gripped my heart. Was he going to order me out of the room and report me to his aunt, whereupon I would be branded an eye-servant for breaking a house rule? To my immense relief, he picked up one of the candelabras on the writing desk and announced cheerfully, "Let's see what treasures we can find to entertain your mind. Shall we?"

I nearly squealed with delight. Still, decorum prevailed, and I walked in my most ladylike fashion to join him. He led me to the center of the room and, with a grand sweeping gesture, announced, "Choose a bookcase, my fair maid, and I will unveil their contents."

I marveled as I looked about the stately room with its golden oak paneled walls and deeply colored oriental rugs. Wood beams with floral motifs decorated the ceiling, and a carved staircase with spindles led to an overhanging balcony. Most likely, it was where the late baron kept his most treasured books.

I pointed to a bookcase next to a tapestry of a fox resting in a garden. "That one," I commanded.

Approaching it, Robert began his summary. "There you'll find books of general knowledge. Are you interested in the celestial sciences – learning about the operations of the planets and constellations? On the bottom shelf, you'll find almanacs, past and present, and a catalog of all the market towns, fairs, and roads in England and Wales. Perhaps one of them will mention your town's illustrious cattle fair."

I hoped my next choice would contain books with a more enticing subject matter. "Shall we explore the bookcase by the alabaster medallion? I have a feeling it holds something truly captivating."

Robert nodded. "Historical books - let's proceed."

I recognized two kings etched in the medallion's center. "Isn't that King Arthur and Charlemagne of France?" I asked, hoping to impress him with my knowledge of past kings, even though I didn't know the third one.

"Quite right, and the third king is?" He paused and then added with a wink and a smile, "That, my dear, is Godfrey of Bouillon, the leader of the first crusade."

"Of course. How foolish of me not to remember," hoping he believed it was merely a simple lapse in memory.

He opened the mesh bookcase doors, and my eyes fell upon a book of enormous size. "Marry! This book must have close to one thousand pages."

"One thousand four hundred pages, to be exact. I know, for I read it whilst studying at Cambridge."

"What's the name of this book?"

"A very apt title that hints at its voluminous size, *A Chronicle at Large and More History of the Affairs of England and Kings of the Same.*" He touched a book on the third shelf. "This is titled *The Union of the Two Noble and Illustrious Families, York and Lancaster.* There are more books here, almost equal in length. Does your interest lie in reading history, Isabella?"

"Not all historical accounts make for dull reading. I must say, it's inspiring to be in a place where I could acquire so much knowledge on the making of our country."

Eager to discover more, I spotted a lovely wall hanging of men fishing and hunting in the countryside that reminded me of home. "There, Robert, let's go there."

He stood in my way, raising one hand. "Proceed with caution, Isabella," he teased. "For in that bookcase beside the wall hanging you so admire are the forbidden romance tales. How would you explain yourself to my aunt if she found one of those books in your possession? Would you call me a knave who tried to compromise your virtue?"

"Don't worry. You can follow Adam's example and say that I coerced you," I replied.

He laughed. "I wouldn't think of doing anything so

ungallant. Come. Let's defy the venerable Juan Vives, for 'tis he that men owe their distaste for women reading books of romance." He quoted Vives's words from *The Education of a Christian Woman* with little effort, "*A woman cannot follow her own judgment in the choice of reading but must be directed by wise and learned men.*"

"I consider myself well-learned," he continued, "having graduated from Cambridge and now in my third year of law at Gray's Inn." He opened the bookcase door. "Hence, I allow you to gaze upon these forbidden titles to your heart's content, for I'm certain their contents will not taint your morals."

My fingertips tingled as they touched the books, considered a pestilent infection for my sex. I pulled *Lancelot of the Lake* from the shelf and slowly turned the pages, pausing to admire the beautiful colored pictures. The one that tugged at my heart was the first time Sir Lancelot laid eyes on Queen Guinevere. The page was tinged with a golden pigment that shimmered under the candlelight, giving that romantic moment an almost ethereal quality.

Robert glided his finger along the top row of books, naming more titles: *Le Morte d'Arthur, Bevis of Hampton, Tristan and Isolde, Guy of Warwick, Romance of Sir Degrevant, Troilus and Criseyde*, to name a few. He tapped his finger on the last one he named. "I read this when I was fourteen. Prince Troilus was desperate to win back his lady love, Criseyde. He wrote her a letter saying only she may command him to life or death."

"Did he win her back?"

"Alas, nay." He leaned toward me, resting his hand on the open bookcase door. "What say you, Isabella? Don't you think I deserve a reward for allowing your eyes to feast upon the romance books in this bookcase?"

I peered into his eyes, made warm and lustrous by the candlelight. "What reward do you seek?"

He grinned. "A simple kiss, perhaps?"

His kiss would have to wait for there were more bookcases to uncover. Still, I doubt I would have kissed him on this night when kisses and embraces between a bachelor and a maid meant nothing, only to be quickly forgotten the following day.

"There's more to see, Robert," I said as I approached a bookcase under a diamond-shaped window.

"There, you'll find books by the ancient Greek and Roman poets. More forbidden titles for women," he said as he followed me.

"But those are the very books I had longed to find," I said, rushing to the bookcase. "Last summer, I read with much pleasure Plutarch's *On the Virtues of Women* with my cousin William, a student at Oxford."

"A harmless book, one my aunt would approve of, even for her daughters to read. Tell me, which of his virtuous women did you favor the most?"

"Telesilla, the poetess. For she had a way with words. They stirred the women of Argos to take up arms against the invading army. Poetic expression is a powerful tool, and a woman can do it just as well as a man, don't you agree?"

My words reduced him to silence for a brief moment and then, in the next breath, roused him to proclaim, "Poetry has the power to sway emotions no matter which sex wields the pen. I take it that you enjoy poetry?"

"So much so that I have attempted to write a few verses myself."

"Write, you say? How come you by the skill? It's rare to find a woman who writes, much less one who attempts to write poetry."

"My mother continued teaching me writing when I finished petty school, but my cousin William truly advanced my skills."

"Why, then, you and I share a common love," he declared with a broad smile. "I, too, enjoy reading poetry immensely and confess I write verses too." He bent down to retrieve a book from the bottom shelf. "I want to give you a book. It'll be our secret. Here, take this book by the Roman poet Virgil."

I gasped. "Oh, Robert! I read Virgil's pastoral poems with my cousin this summer."

"This is very different. 'Tis a romance called *The Aeneid*, my favorite work by Virgil."

I held the book with care and unlocked the clasp. On the first page was a gold-colored impression of Virgil's profile. And on every page that followed, a shimmering blue line guided my eyes from the first line of text to the last. I closed the book, my fingers resting on the raised bands of the spine.

Robert edged closer. "Where do you sleep?" And then added quickly, to my relief. "Did my aunt provide you with your own bedchamber where you can read this book undisturbed?"

"Aye, I sleep alone in a little room adjacent to the kitchen. And your aunt gave me a chest with a key."

"Good, I'm glad you have a secure place to keep this book. And now, Isabella, I think it wise to return to the celebration before my aunt truly sends someone for me."

He cautiously opened the door, and I heard high pitch music played on pipe instruments and the thumping of feet overhead, such as the likes I have listened to at county fairs. He drew his face close to mine. "Look for me here in a fortnight. I'll leave the door as you found it tonight. I'm most anxious to hear your thoughts on *The Aeneid*."

Before I scurried out, he kissed my cheek with as much tenderness as he did my hand earlier in the evening. "You'll be in my thoughts till we meet again."

His sweet farewell nearly left me breathless, but I quickly regained my composure. "And you shall be in my thoughts as well. Thank you, Robert, for this," I said, pressing Virgil's book to my chest. We parted quickly; I sped to my room whilst Robert hastily mounted the stairs.

When I returned to the Great Chamber, Robert's father led a line of men and a few brave women in a merry dance. All were raising their legs whilst holding their arms out to the side. I spied Robert near the musicians, talking with Lady Bramwell and her suitor. I caught Robert's eye and wiggled my fingers to show that the book he had given me was securely tucked away in my room. He gave a knowing smile. Lady Bramwell turned to follow Robert's gaze, but I nimbly escaped her eye. The household staff looked on in amusement as many of Lady Bramwell's notable guests danced the country dance we call The Whip. I stood with them, thinking that Twelfth Night truly brought wondrous surprises.

Once Lady Bramwell's festive celebration was over and the house was again at rest, I dashed off a note to William.

Good Cousin,
I'm happy to write your misgivings about Robert Barrington were all for naught. All went according to plan. I met him in the library, and he was the perfect gentleman, mild-mannered, albeit a bit cheeky at times, but all in good fun. He graciously spent ample time with me, showing me the library's extensive collection. Brace yourself for staggering news. He lent me Virgil's *The Aeneid.* You said you were reading works of ancient poets at school, and now I will be. Although, I'm afraid Robert, not you, will be the first to hear my thoughts on the book. He wishes to meet me again in the library in a fortnight as he is most anxious to hear my views. I'm beginning to believe that he may be a kindred spirit. Rejoice in my news as I do. Thus, I commit you to God's good protection. From Lady Bramwell's house in the Strand, London, on the fifth day of January 1568.
Your assured friend and cousin, Izzy.

6

How He Kept Me Waiting

I have had a recurring dream since my encounter with Robert in the library on Twelfth Night. We are enounced on the cushioned bench in the library, discussing the book Robert lent me to read, *The Aeneid*. During our conversation, Robert keeps edging closer until our thighs and shoulders touch. Then he leans in and bestows a tender kiss on my lips. The moments of silence that follow are consumed with deep kisses.

I am loath to say that my second encounter with Robert did not unfold as prettily as I had dreamed, and a fortnight waiting for him to return to the library led to another fortnight and then another and another. I began to fear that my cousin's warning of fleeting encounters on Twelfth Night was indeed true. Robert, the grandson of a knight and second heir to an estate of three hundred acres, may well have considered our time together as just a bit of Twelfth Night fun and nothing more. I was reluctant to ask Mistress Walden to confirm my suspicion. Go to! She would think me naive to believe that Robert's attentiveness was anything more than a passing flirtation. Still, his failure to keep his promise did not harden my foolish wish to see him again. I still saw every inch of his handsome visage when I closed my eyes at night.

And then everything changed one blustery March afternoon. I was sent to the kitchen to assist Mistress Andrews, the head cook, and spied fruits, nuts, cheese, and a goblet of wine on a silver tray ready to be served. Lady Bramwell must be expecting a guest, for she never strayed from her rigid meal schedule. Perhaps her brother, Robert's father. He oft made unexpected visits to his sister's house, demanding to be fed his favorite dishes. "Isabella, bring the tray to Lady Bramwell's nephew, Robert," Mistress Andrews ordered. "He's at work in the library and has asked for a small meal."

"Lady Bramwell's nephew? Here?" I cried, nearly dropping the meat pie in my hands on the floor before placing it on the cooling rack. After such a long absence, I believed Robert was lost to me forever.

She observed me with a quizzical brow. "And why do you stand there so amazed? He's Lady Bramwell's nephew, isn't he? Now go, girl, and quickly bring this tray to him, for he asked for something to eat a little over fifteen minutes ago."

Despite my knotted stomach, I readily seized the moment to see him again. I carefully picked up the tray and made my way out of the kitchen. I dared not hasten my steps for fear of spilling the wine. It would too embarrassing to return to Mistress Andrews, my incompetence in delivering a food tray to a guest on full display. I approached the library adrift with misgivings. Would Robert show me the same kindness as he did the first time? The library door was ajar, as it had been on Twelfth Night. I hoped Robert had left it so, a silent invitation for me to enter. Despite my apprehension, I stepped into the room with as much composure as I could muster. Forsooth, I would have made a fine actor had I been a man.

Robert was sitting at the desk strewed with books, his head hung low as he wrote. He looked every inch a law student, dressed in his dark blue silk robe with crimson velvet stripes around the hem and collar. Sunlight streamed through the tall window behind him, adding a brilliant luster to his mass of raven-colored locks. I stood transfixed by his presence and moved only when the tray wobbled in my hands. When his eyes met mine, he flashed a beaming smile and swiftly rose from the chair.

"Isabella, 'tis fate. For you have found me once again." He took the tray and set it down on the desk. "Tell me, how have you fared since I saw you last?"

The question struck me as a trifle, and the cheerful smile that accompanied it irritated me. His gaze upon me was unshakable as he began to nibble on the fruit and cheese between sips of wine. Looking at him, eating contentedly without even the slightest hint of remorse for breaking his promise to me, made my blood boil.

"How fare I, Robert?" I huffed. "I have dwelled quite happily in your aunt's house since I last saw you, forcing myself to feign interest in the books she bade me read. I have learned much from her required reading." I laid my hands on the edge of the desk, bringing myself closer to him. "For example, if you happen to spill some of that wine on your lawyer's gown, I know how to remove the stain," I said in mock enthusiasm.

He placed his hand on mine. "I wouldn't dream of putting your lovely fingers to such tedious work because of my carelessness. We have laundresses at school for that purpose."

I swiftly withdrew my hand. His dismissive words caused my ire to soar. "Robert, you promised to return within a fortnight. What made you break your promise? Surely, not your studies. For I hear students at Gray's Inn prefer carousing to studying. I read the first volume of *The Aeneid* in less than a week and was anxiously awaiting your return to read another. But nay. I had to content myself with your aunt's insipid books." I stepped back and held my arms tightly across my chest. "Now – tell me, Robert, how have you fared since last we met?"

He cocked his head and narrowed his eyes. "I detect a bit of resentment in your tone, Isabella."

"Just a bit? Your perception of the depth of my feelings falls short."

He paused, contemplating with great care what to say next. "Don't think, Isabella, that you have not been in my thoughts since our encounter on Twelfth Night. I had every intention of keeping my promise if not for my father, who ordered me to return home."

His stare was met with my gaze, devoid of emotion, as

empty as a stone. I quickly removed the dishes from the tray and turned to leave. Robert swiftly grabbed the empty tray from my grasp, returning it to the desk. Clasping my hands, he implored, "Isabella, I speak the truth. If not for an urgent family matter, I would have returned to see you within the promised fortnight. Despite your impression of students at Gray's Inn, when I returned, I couldn't pull myself away from my studies till now." He then smiled. "Why wouldn't I want to return to see you? I have never kept such stimulating company with a maid."

Indeed, that's what I wanted to believe. His excuse seemed plausible only because I witnessed his father's imperious behavior whenever he visited Lady Bramwell's house. I could understand how difficult it would be to say no to his bidding. I gently freed my hands from Robert's grasp.

"I believe you, Robert, but I must insist the next time you make a promise, I will behold you to it and not forgive as readily as I do now."

Robert pointed to his forehead. "Your gentle reprimand will be affixed here and here," he concluded, his hand resting on his heart. He walked toward the bookcase that held the classical books. "I noticed the book I gave you is back on the shelf. Please let me give you the next volume of *The Aeneid*."

"I have already read them all," I triumphantly informed him.

He stopped short and turned to face me. "Good God, Isabella, how did you manage that?"

"With the help of your cousin, Mistress Walden. She implored your aunt to allow her suitor to borrow the remaining volumes as he had a burning desire to read the books. She finally relented, making it clear that it was only for that one time and no more."

Raising his goblet, he saluted me. "I'm very impressed that you have read the entire set since we last met."

He moved to the chair by the fireplace where I first laid eyes on him. "Please come sit, I would like to hear your thoughts on what is considered Virgil's masterpiece."

His mind is muddled, for I'm not a woman of leisure. "Nothing would give me greater pleasure, but I'm not at liberty to do so. I must attend to my duties."

He smiled ruefully. "Aye, of course. How selfish of me to want you all to myself at this very moment. But before you leave, just answer me this, Isabella. Why do you think Virgil wanted to tell a love story of two lovers who were so markedly different from each other? It was bound to end tragically, wasn't it?"

Now, by my faith! Snatches of conversations I had with my cousin William sprung to mind. Virgil, cousin William, had said, lived his life adhering to the principles of the Roman Republic. Thus, the actions of the character Aeneas represented the Roman ideal of how a hero should behave.

I began my response slowly but gained momentum as my thoughts became more explicit. "True, the lovers' temperaments are different. Aeneas is very much in control of his actions, whilst Dido is chaotic, her actions volatile, driven by passion. I think Virgil is saying a Roman hero, like Aeneas, must adhere to the Roman ideal of order, duty, and political destiny over romantic love. Hence, their love failed."

I breathed deeply, hoping my answer satisfied the scholarly law student whose contemplative gaze never left me as I answered his question.

"Jove!" Robert said, hitting the arm of the chair. "What a clever one you are, Isabella. We must find you another classic to read. I have a book in mind, but we won't find it here, for it has just been translated into English."

"What's the name of the book?"

"*Heroides* by Ovid."

The name brought a smile to my lips. "Another Roman poet whose work is not considered suitable for us females. Are you attempting to corrupt me?"

Robert laughed, "Have no fear about that, Isabella. You have enough wit to interpret the Roman poets with sound judgment — without my help."

He strode over to me, his presence commanding, and

gathered my hands up again in his, with no resistance from me. "Every Sunday, there's a book market on St. Paul's Cathedral grounds. Will you meet me there this Sunday? I'm sure we'll find *Heroides* in my friend's bookstall."

"Sunday – two days hence? Your aunt does allow her staff to miss church service once a month as long as she approves of our activity for that day."

He leaned into me. "Tell her you wish to find the latest comprehensive book on medicinal herbs. That should please her," he said with a wink.

I laughed. "Aye. She wouldn't object to that." I gazed at Robert with a smile that could have lit up the dim winter's sky, so overjoyed that he was making amends for his long absence. "Nothing would give me greater pleasure than accompanying you to the book market."

"Good. Meet me at Paul's Cross at the hour of eleven."

I looked on unabashedly as he slowly kissed the back of my hands and wondered how his lips would feel on mine.

"Till Sunday, then," he said with an eager smile.

I lingered at the door for one last look at him as he shuffled through some papers and carefully removed a book from the pile of books at the edge of the desk. He looked up at me and winked. I put my hand over my mouth to suppress a giggle before closing the door behind me. What a joyful, unexpected turn of events. Come Sunday, I would be with Robert, away from the watchful eye of his aunt, walking amongst the bookstalls in St. Paul's Churchyard. Contentment and satisfaction washed over me, filling me with a warm glow from within.

7

The Promise of Sunday

Sunday morning swiftly arrived, promising a burgeoning romance for Robert and me. I bounded out of the house and hurriedly made for the quay. Being Sunday, the Thames would be free of cargo ships, ensuring my timely arrival at St. Paul's to meet Robert. Within minutes of my reaching the landing, I heard the boatman's familiar cry of 'eastward ho' as the wherry approached. I quickly settled into my seat, and my pulse raced as the wherry picked up speed. A few swans glided gracefully alongside the boat. Swans are most loyal to each other, and I hoped that, like those beautiful birds, Robert would prove a faithful companion. Perchance, this day would bring special memories of Robert seeking a cozy spot to serenade me with passages from a romantic tale as I cuddled close to him, my head resting on his shoulder.

Despite the slight chill in the air, I was comfortable in the open boat, adorned in my midnight blue velvet cloak and matching-coloured boots. My mother's New Year's gift, a lovely velvet bonnet with gold-coloured leaves embroidered by her skillful hands, sat upon my head. Before I left the house this morning, I caught a glimpse of myself in the mirror. The golden hue of the leaves seemed to make my dark blue eyes appear lighter under the light, a detail I hoped Robert would notice and appreciate.

In little time, I spied St. Paul's Cathedral with its towering steeple perched on the hill above the Thames. The wherry rocked slightly as it drew near Paul's Wharf. I patiently waited as the others seated upfront disembarked and sped up

61

Ludgate Hill when it was my turn.

Throngs of people enlivened the area just outside the cathedral's west doors. I poked my head into the crowded nave where newsmongers were assembled to deliver titillating news to all those who passed. A man with fiery red hair cried out, "The queen has sent an envoy to reopen marriage negotiations with Archduke Charles of Austria." Another standing midway in the nave proclaimed, "The queen has had a change of heart about marrying the boy king of France." Poor Queen Elizabeth was beset with ceaseless speculation on who she would choose for a husband. She has received no reprieve regarding the marriage question since the day she ascended the throne.

I restrained myself from strolling over to the bookstalls in the churchyard, where eager readers were already purveying the offerings of books, pamphlets, and broadsides for sale. With so many publications with tempting titles, I would lose sight of the time and didn't wish to arrive late at St. Paul's Cross, where I agreed to meet Robert. Whilst I waited at our designated meeting place, I began to attract stares from men. A group of leather-aproned apprentices slowed as they passed me. One said loud enough for me to hear, "That pretty young maid seems ripe for the plucking."

I pulled my cloak tightly around me and fixed my stare on the pebbles at my feet until their laughter grew faint. I prayed that Robert would arrive soon. Where was he? I expected him to arrive as I did, promptly at the agreed-upon time. God's blood! He would pay a heavy price if he played me for a fool again and kept me waiting for naught. From the corner of my eye, I spied a tall, slim man craning his swan-like neck, desperately searching for someone. Suddenly, he approached my way with deliberate, swift steps. Not wanting to receive unsolicited attention from another stranger, I rose to escape into the crowd assembled in the churchyard when the young man was suddenly upon me.

"Pray pardon, Miss. Are you Isabella Whitney of Lady Bramwell's house?"

My back stiffened. How odd that this elegantly dressed

stranger, clad in a crimson-coloured velvet cloak and a feathered cap, should know my name and for whom I worked.

"Before I answer, sir, may I inquire who you may be?"

"My name, dear maid, is Thomas Seawall, a good friend to Robert Barrington. He has asked me to relay a message to you. His father called upon him at school quite unexpectedly, as he is inclined to do."

He moved his hands most affectedly like a dull magician desperate to grab the attention of impassive viewers. "Are you well acquainted with Robert's father, Miss Whitney?"

"Aye, only by his face, for the need never arose for me to speak to him."

"Let me inform you that he is not easily dismissed once he arrives at your door."

His description of Robert's father rang true, for his behavior at Lady Bramwell's Twelfth Night celebration revealed him to be a boisterous and domineering character. "Aye, I believe he can be formidable."

"Robert and I board in the same room at Gray's Inn. He enlisted my help in seeking you out and keeping you here until he arrives." He then smiled. "I must say he described you well, for I recognized you instantly."

I was curious to hear Robert's description of me, but as I didn't wish to be perceived as frivolous or vain, I turned my thoughts to the more pressing matter.

"Am I to understand that Robert wishes you to keep me here until his father leaves? That could be hours." A pox upon his father for interrupting our plans, I fumed. I knew it was shameful of me to wish such a dreadful sickness upon his father. Only, I had yearned to have Robert all to myself for the day, away from the confines of the Bramwell House.

"Rest assured, Robert is a master at evading his father's clutches," Thomas chuckled, adjusting the lacy cuff of his shirt. "I'm certain he's making his way here as we speak." He offered me his arm. "Shall I escort you to Robert's favorite bookseller, where we'll eagerly await his arrival?"

Although Thomas was amiable, he was still a stranger.

Amid my hesitation, I heard someone call my name, and I stood on tiptoe to see who it was. Robert was approaching in great haste, waving his arms. When he was within reach of me, he pulled me into an ardent embrace, and his warmth enveloped my body. He fervently whispered, "Many good thanks, dear, patient Isabella, for waiting."

Thomas laughed, pleased to see him. "Well, Robert. Now that you are here, I'll take my leave."

Robert seized his arm. "Is she not as lovely as I said?"

"Indeed, she is," Thomas agreed.

"But you have not had the pleasure of experiencing her wit. Her intellect matches ours. Come join us at Belle Savage Inn."

"At what time?" Thomas asked with interest.

"At the hour of four."

"Is this not the night for singing at the inn?"

Robert nodded in earnest. "Why do you think I choose it?"

"I'll see who else I can rouse to be there." With a reassuring smile, Thomas turned to me and said, "Now, will you entrust your hand to me?"

I gave it to him without hesitation, whereupon he bestowed a respectable kiss. "It was my pleasure to detain you, Isabella."

I was tickled by his jesting and couldn't suppress a tiny giggle. "I was most fortunate, Thomas, that Robert had the good sense to send you."

He lifted his chin and smiled, bidding us farewell.

"He's a most pleasant fellow and has proven to be a good friend to me many times," Robert said. "Did he tell you we board together at Gray's Inn?"

"Aye, he did. But Robert, you said nothing about going to an inn for supper when we made plans to meet. We have already lost close to an hour, and even though spring lurks close by, dusk still comes early."

He furrowed his brow and raised his fist. "Of all the Sundays to make an unannounced visit, my father had to choose this day!"

"Don't concern yourself so, Robert. I know it wasn't your fault." I reassured him, my voice filled with understanding.

The deep lines on his forehead dissipated, and a placid smile rested on his lips. I took his arm. "Now, let's explore the book market."

"We shall make a good day of it, Isabella, despite the late start. Let's search for the book by Ovid, and then we will go to the inn. Don't worry. I'll accompany you home."

Out in the open air, away from the library's interior, Robert loomed larger than life. He was fashionably dressed like his friend Thomas, sporting a velvet cloak slung over one shoulder and a silk scarf tasseled with silver threads around his neck.

Robert observed my bonnet and looked directly into my eyes. "Your eyes have a lovely luster of blue today, Isabella."

I breathed. Oh! He noticed the effect the gold-trimmed leaves had on my eyes. I inched closer to him as we walked to his friend's bookstall in the churchyard.

When I first laid eyes on Richard Jones, an aura of red clung about his head like an angel's halo. His ruddy complexion intensified his rebellious reddish-brown hair, a darker reddish-colored mustache, and a pointy beard. His craggy looks made him appear much older than Robert. "I see you have brought company with you today, Robert."

"I have indeed. This is Isabella. She has the most bookish mind of any young maid I know. Thus, my reason for bringing her today. Isabella, this is my good friend, Richard Jones, printer and bookseller extraordinaire."

"A bookish mind, eh?" Richard mused, eyeing me curiously. "Might I interest you in reading Castiglione's *The Courtier*? Very popular reading these days with young gentlewomen as yourself."

A middle-aged woman wearing a narrow-brim feathered hat, accompanied by her respectable and tidy-looking husband, was in the adjoining bookstall. She smiled and nodded in approval at Richard's suggestion, but her smile soon faded when Robert loudly objected.

"Nonsense, man!" Robert blurted, laughing. "Didn't you hear me say that she has a bookish mind! None of Castiglione's courtly advice for her."

"What was the last book you read, Isabella?"

"Virgil's *Aeneid*."

"Her comments about the book showed much depth of understanding," Robert enthused.

"Did they now?" Richard observed me with a slight tilt of his head. "Are you seeking another book by an ancient poet?"

"Robert recommended *Heroides* by Ovid."

The woman, her disapproval evident in her stare, nudged her husband, directing his attention to us.

"Ah yes, Ovid's *Heroides*, translated into English just a few months ago. Today is your lucky day, for I have that one here." He retreated to the far corner of his stall, where a stack of books was piled in an open shallow crate.

Robert began flipping through a collection of broadside ballads and took a particular interest in one. "How's this one selling?"

Richard turned to look over his shoulder. "Romantic ballads sell very well. I need not remind you of that."

Pleased by his response, Robert nodded and put aside a few copies of the same title. Why would he need so many copies, I wondered.

"I've got it," Richard exclaimed, holding the book up in his left hand and quickly restacking the pile of books with his other hand. "I think Robert is correct in assuming you'll enjoy this book."

Upon hearing Richard's endorsement, the meddling woman marched over. "Master Jones, I am appalled that you would sell such a book to this young woman. 'Tis entirely improper reading."

Robert stepped forward, his jaw tight. "I'm buying the book for her. Hence, direct your criticism to me. Do you even know what the book is about?"

"I know all I need to know by the author's name. His writings tread upon dangerous ground. She will learn nothing of virtues from such a book."

"Now, now, Mistress Clifton," Richard said with a complaisant smile. "I understand your concern, but this book is mild compared to Ovid's other works."

"No matter. 'Tis the author I object to, as well as young women reading Virgil," she said, with a disapproving stare at me.

Robert heaved a sigh of impatience and placed his arm around my shoulders. "I can assure you, mistress, this fine young maid will not have her virtues overturned by Ovid. I'm a Cambridge-educated law student at Gray's Inn, and I would wholeheartedly recommend this book to my unmarried sister. Now, good day to you, mistress."

With that final curt reply, Robert turned away from her and bade me do the same. He then picked up a book at random and asked Richard about it. All the while, I thought about what a champion Robert was, defending Richard and me from Mistress Clifton's critical tongue.

I couldn't resist glancing at Mistress Clifton, her stare filled with indignation. She took hold of her husband's arm and bolted away, muttering loud enough for us to hear. "I don't care if that young gentleman is Cambridge educated —the book is unsuitable for maids' eyes."

"That's one customer you can do without," Robert scoffed as he watched her fade from view.

Richard shrugged. "I doubt my business will suffer without her patronage. I'm moving in a new direction now with my publications. My readers desire more broadside ballads and verses about love and" — he winked at me, "translations of Ovid's works. In *Heroides*, Ovid has penned verse epistles about love in a woman's voice. Are you familiar with the women of the ancient Greek tales?"

"A few. Penelope-wife to Ulysses, Helen of Troy, and Medea."

"You'll be able to name more," Richard assured me as he placed the book in my hand. "There are lamentations about love from twenty-two women."

"You say that the letters are written as if the women wrote them themselves - that's rare and would be a treat to read." I touched the metal clasps that secured the pages of the book.

Although I was most anxious to take a peek at one of the letters, I dared not for fear the pages would be swept away by the gentle wind.

"Let me carry it for you," Robert said, attempting to take the book from me.

"I can easily carry it tucked under my arm," I objected.

"Do you want to risk inviting the comments of another busybody?" Robert said.

I frowned and gave the book to him. "What nonsense. The content of *Heroides* seems harmless enough. What woman, married or a maid, wouldn't want to read the musings of another on love?"

Richard chuckled. "I'm in agreement with you, Isabella. But Robert's right. It's best to keep it our little secret, isn't it?"

I smiled ruefully, for I knew they were both right to conceal the book. "I hope to see you again, Richard."

"As do I, Isabella. You must bring her with you again, Robert," he said with a crooked smile that suited his craggy looks.

"I shall," Robert said as he gently nudged me to walk with him. His hands were full with his purchases – my book and multiple copies of the ballad he inquired about. I again wondered why Robert bought so many copies of the same title. What particular interest did it hold for him?

8

Secret Revealed at Bell Savage Inn

It was a short walk to Bell Savage Inn as we turned into Ludgate Hill and walked within a stone's throw to a half-timbered building. The sign of a savage man standing by a bell greeted us at the inn's doorway. I wanted to sneak a peek at the horses neighing in the adjacent yard, hitched to massive carriages, but Robert was eager to go inside. Upon entering the dining area, a group of young men clustered at a long table at the far end of the room shouted Robert's name.

"Friends from school," he noted.

Amongst them was his friend Thomas, who, upon seeing me, rose and tipped his hat. The young dark-haired woman wearing too much rouge who sat beside him playfully snatched his hat and put it on her head. Thomas tried to get it back whilst she fended him off, giggling between sips of her ale.

"I promise we'll join you later after we sup," Robert said, dismissing their objections with a ready smile and a wave of his hand.

My cheeks grew warm as Robert guided me away. It pleased me that Robert desired to keep company only with me. I took it as assurance that I was special. We sat at a small table for two near the wide hearth, a fire crackling in the grate. I spread my skirt and held my hands to the blaze, feeling the warmth seep into my bones. Two musicians, one with a white kitten on his shoulder, entered the room and set their instruments by a bench.

"Ah, the musicians are here already," Robert observed

gleefully. "I need to talk with them. I will be but just a moment."

He took one of the ballad sheets he had bought and approached the musician with the kitten. There was a lively exchange between them. The kitten swatted at Robert's hand as he pointed to the ballad sheet and suddenly leaped onto his shoulder, rubbing its furry head against his cheek. Unfazed, Robert continued his talk with the musician. Could it be, I thought with enthused interest, that Robert would sing the ballad he had purchased earlier today. He shook the musician's hand and removed the crying kitten from his shoulder, gently stroking its head before handing it back to its rightful owner. It was an endearing, sweet gesture. He returned to our table, much enlivened.

"Robert, are you planning to entertain the crowd gathered here with a song?"

"Possibly," he said, grinning.

"Are you, Robert?" I insisted.

He chuckled. "I won't confirm or deny, but let it be a surprise."

I forced a laugh, to which Robert responded, "Don't you enjoy surprises, Isabella?"

"Not particularly," I replied, half-smiling.

He leaned back in his chair with a boyish glint in his eyes. "Surprises make life more exciting, and I predict that tonight will hold a delightful surprise for you —now let's attend to our hungry stomachs. Shall we begin with oysters?"

"As you wish, but I must warn you - I've never tasted oysters."

"Let's change that, shall we?" he said amusedly.

He snapped his fingers at a serving maid with strands of silver in her ebony-colored hair. She spared me a momentary glance, leaving her coquettish smile for Robert.

"Sweetheart," Robert began, "we will start with oysters. Make sure the cook serves them with a splash of ale and black pepper like he did the last time I supped here. Then bring us roasted duck, some toasted cheese, and sugared wine."

Sweetheart, he called her. I couldn't imagine my cousin William calling a woman he was not serious about, sweetheart. But for Robert, it rolled right off his tongue as if it were a habit.

"Tell me about your parents, Isabella. How have they raised a daughter with a deep passion for reading classical books?"

"My mother, I think, regards it as more of a curse than a blessing. She says it will distract me from reading books that will help me become an exemplary wife and mother. Has your sister never expressed an interest in book learning?"

"My sister read a book by Virgil or Ovid?" he scoffed. "If she had, my father would have put a swift end to it. He feels she has no need for such reading. 'Tis the men in our family, with all our formal learning, that will enhance our family's prestige and wealth. My sister can only accomplish that through marriage. But she's content, for she's well rewarded with gifts for doing my father's bidding."

"The only gifts that would satisfy me would be books, parchment paper, and quills."

Robert howled with delight. "I'm picturing my father's horrific expression if my sister rejected his gifts of jewels and silk dresses for books and writing material."

Robert turned his head in the direction of the kitchen. "Oh, look! Here come our oysters."

A heap of bluish-green shells arrived on a large silver plate, to which Robert readily helped himself. But I sat there perplexed on the proper way to eat them. Robert took notice and thus began his instruction.

"Behold, Isabella, with your knife, move the oyster around in its liquid to detach it. Then bring the shell to your mouth and slurp the oyster from its wide end into your mouth."

In two shakes of a lamb's tail, Robert tossed the shell on the table, savoring the taste of the oyster in his mouth. "Just bite into it as you do a grape and chew slowly. You'll get the full flavor of it."

I followed Robert's example. It was hard to believe that

something so soft to eat could come in such a hard encasement. Robert observed me with an amused smile. When I poked it with the knife, it wriggled like it were still alive. My instinct was to toss it back on the heap, but I fought against it. Perhaps Robert was right. Maybe I would be delightfully surprised by its taste. I winced when I slurped the oyster from its shell in an unladylike fashion.

He cocked his head and grinned. "Well, how was it?"

"Like tasting the sea."

"Now tell me truly, Isabella. Did you imagine you would taste a bit of the sea when you awoke this morning?"

I shook my head no and raised my hand to my mouth. "But how long will the taste of salt and seaweed linger on my tongue?"

Robert laughed and refilled our goblets with more wine.

We fell into a comfortable silence, exchanging warm smiles as we sipped the sweet wine until I broached the topic of his father.

"You spoke of your father's wish for your sister. What does he desire of you?"

Robert shifted his position in his chair. "I'm to finish my education at Gray's Inn and then on to a position in parliament, which my father hopes will lead to royal service," he explained dispassionately. He picked up his glass and downed the remainder of his wine. "My father expects his sons to fulfill his ambition. I grow weary of it."

Within minutes of that revelation, our main meal arrived, and he seemed relieved to cease talking about his father. We switched from familial topics to contemplating which nobleman Queen Elizabeth should consider marrying. We both agreed that the prospective candidate for marriage should be a Protestant.

"I heard today that the queen is reconsidering marriage offers with the Archduke of Austria and the young king of France."

"Nonsense," Robert retorted, "both are staunch Catholics. I know who would be the perfect match for her. Although no one would agree with me." He tore the leg of the duck and took his time savoring the taste of it.

I took small bites of my piece of duck as I waited for him to divulge the perfect match for our queen. After a few minutes, I rapped the table with my knife. "Prithee, Robert, don't keep me in suspense."

He dropped a duck bone onto his plate. "Robert Dudley, the Earl of Leicester. He's a champion of the Protestant cause here and on the continent."

"I have heard his name mentioned at home, but more as gossip among my mother and her friends. Isn't he the queen's rumored paramour?"

He shrugged. "They're in love and have been for quite some time now. He truly understands her, as they have been friends since childhood. She should have ignored the scandal surrounding his wife's death seven years ago and married him then."

The musicians began to play a tune familiar to Robert's friends. When they heard the first few notes, there was a thunderous cheer and shouting of *Mother Watkins Ale* from Thomas's table. Thomas's female companion flitted from table to table, handing out ballad sheets. Robert was unruffled by the frenzy caused by the mere mention of the ballad's title. Thomas leaped from his chair, grinning, and briskly approached the musicians.

"I suppose Thomas is going to entertain us with a song," I said.

"Robert, don't you want a copy of the words?" Thomas's companion asked as she neared our table, still wearing Thomas's hat.

"I know the words well as if I had written them myself, Millicent." She smiled and swayed her hips as she walked to another table.

"But perhaps you would like a ballad sheet, Isabella." And before I gave my answer, Robert called out, "Millicent! A copy for my literary friend."

She beamed when Robert shouted for her and scampered

back to our table. I was pleased Robert called me his literary friend, for it made me feel close to him. My mother insisted that shared interests between men and women make for a strong bond. Gazing into the warmth of Robert's eyes, I hoped he could envision me as more than just a friend. With her hair falling loosely about her shoulders and sporting a low-cut bodice, Millicent didn't strike me as one who would be impressed if Thomas addressed her in the same manner.

Thomas left the musicians and approached our table in haste. I wish I could have been privy to what Thomas whispered to Robert, for it caused Robert to chuckle loudly. "Away with you, Thomas. And sing well tonight," Robert commanded cheerfully.

"Prithee, Isabella, try not to be offended by my choice of song and how I perform it. 'Tis pure jest, I assure you," Thomas said his voice filled with mirth before returning to the musicians.

Without glancing at the words on the ballad sheet, I knew Thomas would perform a bawdy ballad and prayed I wouldn't blush like a simple country maiden in Robert's presence. The musicians struck up the familiar notes of *Mother Watkin's Ale*, this time a touch louder. Thomas lifted his arms high into the air, signaling that he was ready to begin his performance.

Some of his friends pounded the table whilst others continued to chant the ballad's title. Coming to the aid of his good friend, Robert rose and let loose a series of high-pitched whistles to silence the crowd.

"Good people," Robert shouted with a welcoming smile. "Give my friend Thomas Seawall leave to entertain you with his rendition of *A Ditty Delightful of Mother Watkins Ale.*"

All eyes fell on Thomas. And as if by magic, he transformed into a humble country fellow, simply by donning a woolen cap and adopting a slouched posture with rounded shoulders. Thus, he began to sing, his voice carrying the essence of the character he had become:

"There was a maid this other day,

And she would needs go forth to play;
And as she walked, she tarried and said —"

Thomas paused and looked expectedly across the room. All eyes followed his gaze and encountered Millicent, who sauntered toward Thomas, singing:

"I am afraid to die a maid."

At this, all the men laughed, and some made whooping sounds. Robert remained quiet but judging by his broad smile, he was amused, too. Thomas continued singing:

"With that, beheard a lad
What talk this maiden had,
Whereof he was full glad,
And did not spare
To say, fair maid, I pray,
Wither go you to play?"

Replying in a very affected manner, Millicent sang out:

"Good sir, then did she say,
What do you care?"

Thomas gave a devilish smile which prompted his friends, including Robert, to lift their glasses and sing in jovial fashion:

"For I will, without fail,
Maiden, give you Watkin's ale."

Millicent raised her eyebrows, which made her saucer-shaped eyes appear even larger, and she sang out in a louder, almost shrill voice this time 'round:

"Watkins ale, good sir, quoth she,
What is that I pray you tell me?"

Thomas leaned in extremely close to Millicent and slid his arm around her waist:

> *"Tis sweeter fare than sugar fine,*
> *And pleasanter than muscadine."*

Faith! The exchange between them became hotter. I prayed my cheeks weren't flushed and, if they were, not crimson-red so Robert wouldn't take notice. Thomas sang:

> *"Thus they sported and they played,*
> *This young man and this pretty maid,*
> *Under a bank whereas they lay,*
> *Not long ago this other day."*

Thomas took Millicent in his arms and covered them both with his cloak, which caused his friends to hoot and howl as if they were dogs in heat. Robert looked at me and patted my hand. "Remember, 'tis only jest," he said. Then he joined the others in the refrain:

> *"For I will without fail,*
> *Maiden, give you Watkins ale;*
> *Tis sweeter fare than sugar fine,*
> *And pleasanter than muscadine."*

Forsooth, the author of the ballad had one singular aim, mainly to show that women lack temperance and good sense, as was proven by the woman's fate in the end. She became pregnant and was abandoned by the man who had lured her to drink. Indeed, there's no punishment for the man who strolls away happily. Thomas emerged from behind his cloak and sang out the final words:

> *"Fair maids, you know my mind,*
> *Say what you will.*
> *When you drink ale beware the toast,*

For therein lay the danger most.
If any here offended be,
Then blame the author, blame not me.

Thomas took his bow to rapturous applause. His friends rushed to him, overwhelming him with congratulatory backslaps for a performance well done. A gent with blond hair and a beard that ended in two points below his chin, attempted to kiss Millicent. Pressing closer to Thomas, she pushed him away. Foolish girl to put herself on public display merely for sport.

"What say you, Isabella? Time to put this carousing to rest, eh?" Robert said as he downed a glass of ale.

The image of Robert flipping through ballads at his friend's bookstall earlier at St. Paul's flashed through my mind. I had found it curious that he was so keen on knowing how well one ballad, in particular, was selling.

"The ballad sheet you bought today is your work, isn't it?" I said with unbridled enthusiasm, my heart racing at the thought of a shared interest in writing. It was a confirmation of a connection I had hoped for.

With a decisive nod, he said, "Aye, 'tis mine. Will you give me your honest opinion of it afterward?"

"I will," I promised, hoping his song would be praiseworthy, for I had not yet learned to mask my disappointment with verses that I found uninspiring.

Gentle and melodious music permeated the room, infusing everyone with a sense of calm. When Robert sang, his voice was lilting and soothing, the perfect vocal accompaniment to the sweet sounds of the lute. When I heard the first lines of his ballad, I smiled wistfully. Robert had composed a love song based on a familiar tale of a troubled romance between a nobleman and a poor country girl known as patient Griselda.

It was an old tale that my sisters and I had oft enjoyed listening to. I wish they could have been with me, listening to Robert retell our favorite tale in song. What skill Robert showed in his choice of words. I glanced at Thomas's table.

The rowdy young men were silent now, captivated by Robert's singing. Millicent was teary-eyed, holding on tight to Thomas's arm. When Robert finished, there was a quiet hush quickly followed by enthusiastic applause. Robert beamed and took a modest bow.

Thomas was soon by his side and rested his hand on Robert's shoulder. "Good people, may I present law scholar, balladeer, and my friend Robert Barrington, the composer of the piece you just heard."

The crowd continued with their applause.

"If you enjoyed his rendering of *A Most Pleasant Ballad of Patient Griselda*, there are copies at my table that may be bought for one pence," Thomas announced. A good number of eager buyers followed Thomas to his table.

"Isabella, did you like my little surprise?" Robert asked with a shy smile when he returned to our table.

"It was magnificent," I gushed.

"I will confess that I wondered how I could make up for not seeing you sooner after Twelfth Night. And then I thought, why not share the ballad I wrote with you? Did I make the right decision?"

I was stunned by his confession, but I quickly regained my tongue. "I assure you, Robert, you made the perfect choice. I wasn't the only one moved by your performance. I looked about the room and saw women dabbing their eyes, and not one man rose from his seat, but all stayed to listen till the end."

"The hour is getting late. It would be wise to leave now," Robert advised. And then he bestowed a kiss on my cheek, so impassioned it came close to feeling like his mouth upon mine. At that moment, the seeds of passionate love took root in me, and I put my hand in his to leave.

9

Beyond a Simple Kiss

A few paces away from Bell Savage Inn, I nudged Robert as we approached the point where Carter Lane joins Watling Street. "Look, the night watchmen are assembling with their lanterns," I warned him.

He grabbed my hand, his grip firm and reassuring, and we scurried down Poor Widow's Alley, a narrow passageway with me walking behind Robert, my feet nipping at his heels. We scampered past Woodmongers Hall, just a stone's throw from the Thames, and descended the steps to the boat landing. How fortuitous, I thought, that a lone boat was bobbing on the water as if it had been sent exclusively for us.

The oarsman, a reed-thin young man with a wide-gap toothy grin, held up his lantern. He tipped his hat and winked at Robert, a mischievous glint in his eyes, as we made our way to the back of the boat.

"Do you know that oarsman?" I asked as I sat on the patched-up cushioned bench under the canopy.

"You mean Orlando? Of course. His discretion has given him a good reputation among the students at Gray's Inn. He has safely rowed many young scholars, made rowdy from too much drink, back to Gray's Inn."

"He looks young enough to join in on the fun," I observed.

Robert laughed. "Nay. He knows his place and is well compensated to row riotous company after their night revelries have ended."

He signaled Orlando to depart and proceeded to remove a wrinkled, stained linen sheet folded under the seat. I noticed metal hooks on the wooden poles supporting the canopy, which Robert used to hang the sheet. Despite the boat swaying, Robert nimbly secured the last corner of the sheet to the final hook.

"Privacy!" he announced with a triumphant smile.

"It does have a practical purpose as well. Our faces will be shielded from the evening wind that blows westward," I added.

"Among other things." Robert smiled sheepishly and sat down beside me. "I need to ask a favor of you?"

I couldn't imagine what it could be and nodded my consent for him to proceed.

"You must not let it slip to Mistress Walden that you saw me sing my ballad tonight."

"Now, why would you have any misgivings about your cousin," I scolded. "She takes great delight in music and dancing. On my first day at your aunt's house, she brought me to the Great Chamber, where she taught me the queen's favorite dance."

"I don't doubt that she would smile if you told her about my singing, but I cannot risk my aunt hearing about it from her." Mimicking his aunt's haughty tone, he continued his argument. "Robert, what is this I hear about your composing a ballad and peddling it at an inn. We are above such a lowly endeavor. Your father, even your recently deceased grand-father, would not appreciate your debasing the family name." His perfect mimicry of his aunt made me laugh.

"Undoubtedly, my father would get wind of the news and march himself over to Gray's Inn and hurl insults far worse than my aunt ever could," he concluded.

I took his hand in mine. "As you wish, Robert. I will say nothing."

He kissed my hand and held it. "I knew I could trust you."

"You could trust me with anything, Robert. I give you my word."

And then suddenly, he kissed me. A restrained kiss—his way of initiating the start of a meaningful friendship?

"Did you mind that I kissed you, Isabella?"

I smiled. "Not at all."

"Have you ever been kissed?"

"Aye, once by one of the sons of the farmhands that work my father's land, but I pushed him away."

He grinned. "But you didn't push me away."

I gazed into his eyes – so warm and welcoming and was overcome by a boldness to speak what was in my heart. "I'll be frank with you. Since you placed Virgil's book in my hand that first time we met in the library, I have longed to feel your lips on mine. Thus, I allow you to do it again if you desire."

He leaned forward and murmured. "Very well then, my queen. I shall happily oblige."

My pulse raced as I felt the weight of his chest press against mine. He slid his warm tongue into my mouth and explored every inch of it. Heaven and Earth! Where did he learn to move his tongue in such a sensational manner? I became lightheaded as his tongue danced beautifully in my mouth. I would have swooned if I hadn't pushed myself away from his tight embrace. I stood up and breathed in the cool night air, hoping to regain control of my senses, but then the boat dipped and swayed, sending me reeling back to Robert.

"Got you," he said, laughing, positioning me on his lap and leaning in. I closed my eyes and waited in giddy anticipation of what other delectable trick he would do with his tongue.

But nay. He, with a gentle touch, brushed a strand of hair from my cheek and traced the contours of my face with his finger. As the boat bobbed gently on the water, I eased myself off his lap.

"Feeling all right, love."

"Aye, I'm fine," I responded blissfully.

With a serene smile, he leaned back into the seat, his legs stretched out in front of him and hands behind his head. "Tell me, Isabella, what did you like best about my ballad, aside from my melodious voice," he asked with a playful wink.

"You're a master wordsmith. Setting your words to the tune of *The Bride's Good-morrow* was most effective."

"You're not saying that just to be kind?"

"Nay! I tell you the honest truth. There was no awkward phrasing. Your words melded perfectly with the music."

"Sing me the most memorable line you heard," he commanded with a smile.

"I dare not, for my voice is not as honeyed as yours, but I will utter the words into your ear."

I cupped my hands around his ear and whispered, "*She sung full sweet with pleasant voice melodiously which set the lords heart on fire. The more he looked, the more he might; beauty bred his heart's delight.*"

Robert sang the words back to me and kissed me deeply once again. This time, I didn't pull away. And just as he moved his hand to my breast, the boat lurched forward, and Orlando, the trusty oarsman to Robert and his friends, shouted, "Arundel Stairs."

Robert held out his hand. "Come, this is where we disembark."

I held back. "Here? But aren't these stairs for private use?"

He shrugged. "Don't worry, the Earl of Arundel is in Padua, and even if he was home, he knows my family well. 'Tis a shorter walk to my aunt's house if we get off here," Robert urged gently.

Orlando bid us goodnight, giving my privy once again to his unsightly smile. "Hope the boat ride wasn't too rough for you, miss. The current was mild for this time of year." His earnestness to please elicited a smile from me.

"God give you good night, Orlando," I said, taking Robert's hand.

As we mounted the Arundel steps, I grew apprehensive about treading on private property. "Are you sure the earl is not home?"

"Aye," Robert stressed. "And 'tis my deepest wish that the queen devises a plot to keep him abroad."

"Why do you wish that for him? 'Tis a terrible fate to be exiled from one's home."

"I would show him no mercy, for he continues to harbor

strong Catholic sentiments."

Robert drew my attention to the ornate archway that framed the steps, with two majestic lions lying atop the pillars. "Look here. When Queen Elizabeth was deathly ill with the pox, Catholic sympathizers docked their boats here. They gathered in the earl's house to consider supporting Lady Catherine Grey's right to ascend the throne should the queen not recover from her illness. And now, I have no doubt, the earl will return to England to support the Catholic Mary Queen of Scots, who says she is the rightful heir to the throne, not Elizabeth."

How distressing Robert's account was. My parents had hoped that the derision between Catholics and Protestants would ebb under the reign of Queen Elizabeth. Sadly, it remains a grave matter for our queen. We hurried up the steps, turning westward on the Strand, and strolled with our hands tightly clasped. The threat of London's nocturnal ruffians wasn't a concern in this haven of grand stately homes. For they seemed far away, confined behind the city's ancient walls.

"I know little about the Earl of Arundel, but I take a special interest in another house on this street," I said.

"Which one?"

"The York House, home to Sir Nicholas Bacon and his wife, Anne. Sometimes, when I'm out doing errands for your aunt, I deliberately pass their house slowly, hoping to catch a glimpse of his scholarly wife, Anne, but, thus far, I haven't." I sighed with a hint of longing.

"Anne Bacon," he repeated with a curious tone. He folded his arms across his chest in mock irritation and faced me squarely. "Isabella Whitney, have you been misleading me? Anne Bacon devotes her writing to religious translations. Doesn't your interest lay in poetry?"

I nudged Robert forward. I couldn't help but express my admiration for Lady Bacon. "Poetry is my passion, silly. It's just that I admire Lady Bacon's dedication to her scholarly work. How fortunate she is to have a supportive husband. His encouragement assures her that she has a greater purpose in life other than wife and mother."

"So ..." he mused aloud, "that's the kind of relationship you yearn for." He got down on bent knee. "Give me your hand, Isabella." I felt as if the pounding of my heart would pierce my chest.

"I promise you that henceforth, I will be your Nicholas Bacon. Let's vow to support each other's writing in the name of the friendship we have forged tonight. And if, by chance, we were to marry, you need not worry you lack time to write. I will see to it that our house overflows with servants and governesses. And when company comes to sup, afterward, they will listen in rapt attention as you read your poems."

His promise hit me like a gust of wind, nearly knocking me to the ground. Married to Robert Barrington – what a glorious picture of marital bliss he painted! When he stood, I wrapped my arms around his neck and didn't wait for him to kiss me first.

"Then you promise to be my champion, Robert, and silence men who say that a woman's time shouldn't be squandered in reading books of all kinds and writing poetry."

"My enchanting Isabella," he smiled, cupping my face with his hands. "We'll be each other's champions. For many believe that a gentleman's son should not take up the pen to write love ballads for a living."

"But aren't you bound for a career in the law? What is this talk of becoming a balladeer?"

"Well, I can dream, can't I?" he asked, indignant.

I gathered his hands up in mine. "I have a surprise for you, Robert."

"I love surprises," Robert enthused.

I put my arm in his and pulled him forward, laughing. "Let's make haste, for your surprise awaits you at your aunt's house."

When we arrived at the side gate of the Bramwell House, I bade Robert to stay put as I fetched my poem from my room.

"Don't forget this," Robert said, placing Ovid's book in my

hand. His fingers caressed mine as he pulled his hand away.

I held the book close and scampered down the path to the kitchen door. Once inside my bedchamber, I reached for the small chest under my bed where I kept my poems. I quickly sorted through them until I found the one I wrote about friendship. A rapping on the window startled me. I clutched my poem and scurried into the kitchen, where I saw Robert's grinning face at the window. Was he mad? His impatience would arouse suspicion. "Have patience, my love," I whispered as I returned outside. We made our way to the gate. All the while, Robert was playfully grabbing at what I had in my hand.

"What do you have there? Let me see it!"

I gently slapped his hand away and implored him to be still. "Just as you wanted my honest opinion of your ballad, I desire the same of you when you read my poem."

"Are you sure you want my honest opinion? I can be brutal," he teased. And then he turned as serious as a schoolmaster. "I jest. I promise to read it attentively."

"When do you think we can meet again?"

"Why don't we meet two Sundays hence, in the same place—at St. Paul's Cross, at the same hour. We'll discuss your poem and your thoughts on Ovid's book."

"Oh yes, my love, in two weeks hence."

He grabbed me by my waist. "One last kiss, Isabella, to sustain me till I see you again."

Before his lips touched mine, I uttered, "Robert, you may call me Izzy."

"One last kiss, my Izzy," he murmured. I glowed from within as he uttered my name with the same sweet and loving tone as my family.

When he pulled away, I remained at the gate, my eyes fixed upon his departing silhouette till I could no longer see him. God in Heaven! If he had turned 'round and asked me to lay with him, I surely would have. Chastity be damned.

10

Ode to Ovid, Fie on Juan Vives

Two days after my romantic evening with Robert, I found a letter mysteriously slid under my bedchamber door. I hastily broke the seal, and my lips parted into a wide smile when the sender was none other than Robert. He must have gone to great lengths, perhaps even risking discovery, to secretly deliver this note to me. My heart raced when I read his salutation: My sweet Izzy — Merry Dreams! He used the shortened name by which my family calls me, and I read with anticipation the body of his letter:

I cannot believe the good fortune that has befallen me in meeting you. I never thought I would be indebted to my aunt, but it appears I must, for she has brought you to me - albeit unwittingly. Let's keep our burgeoning friendship a secret from all at Bramwell House so that our profound connection to each other will flourish without interference from those who would be keen to end it. Although just a day has passed as I write you this letter, your absence is keenly felt, and the fiercer I grow to see you again. How heavenly fair, Izzy, is your face. And I boldly say the taste of your delicious mouth still lingers on mine. But it's just not your physical self that has so bewitched me. Your wit brings me much pleasure and makes you fair company indeed. Thus, am I not blessed to have found someone who provides me with dual pleasure? I count the days till we meet again and promise to pay due diligence to your poem. Yours will be the first by a woman I have ever read, and for you to have entrusted me with it makes me your humble servant. May God keep you safe till I see you again two Sundays hence. By the hand of him that I trust will behold you again, Robert.

Robert's words anchored my feet to the very spot I stood—so amazed was I by his adoring words. I concluded this was most assuredly a love letter as my fingers gently caressed the parchment it was written on. After rereading it several times, I clutched it close to my heart before putting it in my lockbox. Yes, my love. Our burgeoning relationship will be our precious secret.

When the night had cast its veil, and in the sanctuary of my room, I delved deep into the pages of *Heroides*, the book Robert had bestowed upon me. Shielded from the prying eyes of my mother and Lady Bramwell, I was granted a glimpse into the passion and heartbreak of women in love. I dismissed the caution of the esteemed Juan Vives, who advises mothers to keep such books away from their daughters, fearing it will entice them to stray from virtue. Pish! Thankfully, Robert has more faith in the inherent good sense of women.

I gazed at the portrait of the author Ovid, positioned beneath the title. Clad in the fashion of the ancients, I felt a surge of gratitude as I traced the intricate folds of his toga, the wreath of leaves adorning his hair, and his noble nose. The tenth epistle I was about to read was from the nymph Oenone to Paris. The renowned Paris, in truth, was a mere scoundrel. Away with him! He had abandoned Oenone to pursue Helen of Troy, whom he eventually married. Oenone's opening words of lament read: *Oenone the fountain-nymph, well known in the Phrygian woods, writes these words and complains of the way you—my very own, treat her—*

My reading was interrupted by an urgent knocking at my door.

"Isabella, 'tis I, Mistress Walden. Rouse yourself out of bed."

Heaven and Earth! Something was amiss for Mistress Walden to knock at my door at such a late hour. In haste, I put the book into my lockbox and bounded to the door.

"Mistress Walden, whatever is the matter?"

"Eleanor has fallen ill."

"Is she gravely ill?" I asked apprehensively.

"Her throat is red, and she has a deep cough," Mistress Walden explained in a hushed tone. "It pains her to swallow and speak. Lady Bramwell is unsettled to see her daughter in such an uneasy state. Make haste, Isabella, and meet me in the still room."

Poor Eleanor. I was fond of her, for she reminded me of my younger sister. Like Mary, she too had a gentle comportment: sensitive, courteous, and soft-spoken. I threw my kirtle over my night shift. As I tied the laces, I worried that Eleanor's illness would prevent Lady Bramwell from taking her and her sister to their uncle's house in a few days. With Lady Bramwell gone, I could somehow notify Robert that perhaps we could meet sooner than the date we had set—God forgive me! I was wrong in thinking only of myself whilst poor Eleanor lay ill. As reparation for my selfishness, I would recite *Psalm 119:36, turn my heart towards your statutes, and not toward selfish gain,* every night for a week.

Once my night shift was adequately covered, I hurried to meet Mistress Walden in the stillroom to begin the meticulous task of making medicine. With the scarcity of physicians, even in the thriving city of London, learning the medicinal use of herbs was a vital part of housewifery training. Hence, the heavy burden of correctly preparing medicine for the ill weighed heavily on my mind every time I was summoned to the stillroom.

Mistress Walden directed me to join her at the table. Her hand rested on a page from Markham's *The English Housewife*, the home-remedy book that Lady Bramwell deemed the best.

"Isabella, I have marked the page with Markham's most widely used recipe to ease a sore throat accompanied by heavy coughing. You shall use this one to make a cough remedy."

I took a step back. "You want me to prepare it?"

"Come here, girl," Mistress Walden insisted, taking hold of my arm. "'Tis but a simple recipe. Look and see for yourself.

Do not worry. I am here to help you should you falter."

Upon scrutiny, the recipe seemed simple enough, requiring but a few common herbs of wood betony, caraway seeds, and hound's tongue, but the dried skirret caused me concern.

"Skirret can cause intestinal pain if one has overeaten, can it not?"

"Indeed, it can," Mistress Walden affirmed.

Thinking carefully, I surmised, "Although Markham calls for one dram of powered skirret, we should use half to be safe. Eleanor has a hearty appetite and has already eaten supper and dinner before the onset of her illness."

Mistress Walden nodded her approval. "I see now that you have been paying attention during Lady Bramwell's talks on the effects of medicinal herbs. That pleases me, and it will please Lady Bramwell as well."

Anxious to begin, I spun 'round to the shelf behind me, where there were jars of exotic herbs for which Lady Bramwell had paid a high sum. As I removed the lids of the required herb jars, their earthy smells, a mix of sweet and pungent, permeated the air, tickling my nose. I carefully measured the herbal powders into a small wooden bowl, and mixed them well with honey, the sticky sweetness mingling with the herbal scents.

After a few hesitant moments, I was confident I had prepared the medicine correctly. "All ready, now. Let's make haste to administer this medicine to Eleanor."

When we arrived at Eleanor's bedchamber, Lady Bramwell was by her side, holding her hand. With an encouraging nod, Lady Bramwell bade us to come forward. I looked down at Eleanor and was disheartened to see her lovely cream-colored complexion partially covered with reddish patches. She pointed to her forehead and complained of pain. Lady Bramwell offered words of comfort as she applied a warm cloth to the affected area.

"Mother, I am cold," Eleanor managed to say through a series of coughs.

Mistress Walden hurried to add more wood to the fire. She

returned to Eleanor's bedside with two woolen blankets, which she promptly spread over the coverlet.

I leaned forward, giving Lady Bramwell the vial of medicine I prepared. "Here is the medicine, my lady," I said.

At once, Lady Bramwell dispensed the medicine to Eleanor. She carefully poured the mixture into a small spoon, ensuring the correct dosage. Then, supporting Eleanor's head, she gently placed the spoon to her lips, encouraging her to swallow the bitter-sweet concoction. "Not too bitter, is it, my sweet girl?"

I held my breath, waiting for Eleanor's response, and let out a quiet sigh of relief when she shook her head with a weary smile. Give thanks to God that she swallowed the medicine with ease.

Once Lady Bramwell finished dispensing the medicine to Eleanor, she remarked, "My girl, you took it well." Then, turning to me, she spoke in a hushed tone, "The medicine was well prepared, Isabella."

"I thank you, my lady. God willing, she will have a peaceful night's rest."

Lady Bramwell anxiously looked upon her daughter, who had now closed her eyes and appeared to be breathing with less difficulty. "God willing," she whispered.

It moved me to see the love Lady Bramwell bore her daughter. She must have attended to her husband with the same tender care when he was ill but to no avail. I wanted to place my hand on Lady Bramwell's shoulder and reassure her that Eleanor would remain strong and achieve her mother's dream of securing a place in court as a lady in waiting for Queen Elizabeth.

It very well could happen, for Eleanor excelled in all her music, dance, needlework, and French lessons.

"All went well, Isabella," Mistress Walden assured me once we were in the corridor.

"I'm much relieved that my decision to add an extra dram of honey lessened the possibility of an acrid taste."

"Aye, you have learned well." She stopped midway on the

stairs and asked, "Will you join me in the kitchen for a well-deserved glass of claret?"

I preferred returning to my room to finish reading Oenone's letter. But then I remembered all the kindness Mistress Walden had shown me since I arrived. And hence, I accompanied her to the kitchen.

I fetched the goblets and brought them to the kitchen table. Mistress Walden proceeded to pour the pale red wine into the goblets. As I savored the fruity flavor of the claret, thoughts of the letters I had thus far read in *Heroides* drifted in and out of my mind. It was an extraordinary experience to read such intimate thoughts and emotions from women as if they were whispering their secrets directly to me. I wondered if Mistress Walden would disapprove of my reading the book. The wine made my tongue bold, and thus, I made mention of the much-maligned title. "Mistress Walden, I have been reading *Heroides*. I believe 'tis a book all women should read."

She arched her brow. "How did you come into possession of that book?"

"Lady Bramwell's nephew, Robert, bestowed it upon me—as a token of our newfound friendship?" I added quickly.

She sipped her wine and gave a knowing smile. "I am pleased to hear Robert has become your ally in helping you acquire books that interest you."

I laughed cheerfully. "And you knew he would. For it was you who encouraged me to seek him out in the library on Twelfth Night."

She smiled as she brought bread and cheese wrapped in cloth to the table.

"Truthfully, when I read the first letter in Ovid's collection, from Penelope to her husband, Ulysses, I was astounded by what she said."

"Did you find it offensive?"

I cut myself a piece of cheese. "Nay, on the contrary. I was amazed by Penelope's forthrightness. She made it clear that she was suspicious of her husband's dalliances with other women whilst he was in Troy. And without reserve, she tells him perhaps that was why he didn't return to her sooner. And then Ovid has her say, *I know how fickle men can be*. Imagine a woman saying that about a man in print for all to see," I marveled.

Mistress Walden clutched the stem of her goblet. "Merry dreams! That's a good turnaround. Men never cease to hold that opinion of us. Do all the women in the book speak their minds as freely as Penelope?"

"All of them lay their pain and disappointment at the feet of the men who have wronged them."

"That is indeed astonishing. For are we not told to accept our husband's flaws in silence? Yet, these women, they defy such norms."

I nodded and took another piece of cheese. "Imagine if a ballad was written based on Penelope's letter and, better yet, performed by a woman at a tavern. Can you foresee what would happen?"

"Go on," she urged.

"There would be a reversal of male behavior. Men would slink down in their chairs, cowed by the riotous cheers of women."

"Oh, what I would give to behold that!" Mistress Walden joined me in spontaneous laughter.

I pounded the table with my fist. "'Tis unbelievable that the views of us women held by Juan Vives are still popular despite his death more than twenty years ago. If confronted by his ghost, I would ask him to explain why women should suffer in silence when love has gone awry, for men do not."

Mistress Walden rose from the table. "Aye. The required comportment for women has not altered much in the conduct books." She began to clear the table. "Come now, Isabella. The hour is late, and much work awaits us in the morning. Foremost, we must attend to Eleanor's care. The first thing you will do in the morning is to prepare a steam bath for her with peppermint oil."

"Aye, that will be good to strengthen her muscles."

Mistress Walden smiled at my earnestness to prove I was a

good student of herbal medicine. "We will make medicinal candies from dried roses and violets that Eleanor will take with her when she stays at her uncle's house."

"Thus, you think Lady Bramwell will still travel with her daughters to her brother's country estate?" I asked as I finished wiping the goblets with a cloth.

"Why wouldn't she? Eleanor will be well cared for at her uncle's house. There are plenty of servants to attend to her every need. Besides, Lady Bramwell would want to attend the first formal dinner planned by her brother to welcome her nephew's future wife and her parents. Lady Bramwell is anxious to get to know them."

"I don't understand. The older brother is already married."

"I am referring to Robert's future wife. His father is keen on establishing a pre-marriage contract as soon as possible. His prospective bride, Rose Clavell, is the daughter of a viscount, which pleases Master Barrington very much."

My face burned, and my legs threatened to give way. Robert, to be wed? It was inconceivable! I stumbled into the nearest chair, my mind reeling with the sudden revelation.

Mistress Walden rushed to my side. "How now, Isabella? You've grown flushed." She put her hand on my forehead. "Nay. You don't feel warm."

I gently pushed her hand away. "I assure you, I'm fine."

"You gave me such a fright. The news of Robert's impending marriage seems to have caused you distress." She paused. "Robert has been honorable with you, I hope?"

"Aye. I assure you Robert is nothing more than a good friend." I nearly choked on my words but I managed to continue, my voice strained. "The news of his impending nuptials is a shock, for he had not breathed a word of it. I dread that our friendship will come to an abrupt end, and I will no longer have his generous support in procuring books."

She sat next to me and held my hand. "Pish, do not worry. Robert is a most benevolent young man. He will continue to support your interest."

I smiled weakly. As she praised his benevolence, I silently

cursed him.

I returned to my room, my mind swirling with mixed emotions. I retrieved Robert's letter and read it once more. My heart ached to think it might have been a letter of trickery.

Did Robert believe Juan Vives's words that women are easily deceived by flattery? Hence his flattering tongue with me. Or perhaps Robert was leading Rose Clavell into a merry dance only to please his father. Like Ovid's heroines, I would not remain silent but seek out Robert to uncover the truth.

Part Two

Changes

So fare thou well a thousand times,
God shield thee from thy foe:
And still make thee victorious,
of those that seek thy woe.

Isabella Whitney

11

To Gray's Inn in Search of the Truth

On a clear Wednesday morn, two days after Eleanor fell ill and thankfully had now recovered, Lady Bramwell departed for her brother's home, accompanied by her daughters, the girls' governess, and Mistress Walden. When the wheels clacking on the cobblestone path grew faint, I made haste for the kitchen, where I helped myself to a piece of sweet ginger cake and a handful of hazelnuts from the cupboard. I wrapped them in cloth and placed them in a small basket to take with me on my walk to Gray's Inn.

Robert once mentioned it was a pleasant walk from his school to his aunt's house. Unfortunately, there was no one in the house I dared ask about the particulars of getting there, for they all knew Lady Bramwell's nephew attended Gray's Inn. To be sure, my inquiry would arouse suspicion. Why else would they think I wanted to visit Gray's Inn other than being in hot pursuit of Robert? Instead, I would seek help from strangers to show me the quickest route to Gray's Inn.

Fortune favored me that morning as I set out. At the corner of Little Drury Lane, a group of three maidservants, all of mid-height, darted onto the Strand. The red-headed maidservant, dressed in a tawny-colored livery, stopped to place her basket on a stone wall whilst the other two continued rapidly down the Strand. Seizing the opportunity, I hurried to the red-headed maid before she dashed to join the others.

"Pardon me, miss," I said pleasantly. "I'm on my way to Gray's Inn. Do you know the speediest way to get there?"

She said not a word, being too engrossed in trying to close

the clasp on her cape. Her only utterances were sighs of frustration. I pressed on, hoping she did know the way to Gray's Inn.

"May I help?" I offered cheerfully.

At first, she did naught but stare. My sunny disposition convinced her I was sincere in wanting to help, for she beckoned me to assist her. She waited patiently as I attempted to get the bent ends of the clasp into the tiny loop. All the while, I couldn't help but take notice of her hair. It was the most brilliant shade of red I have ever seen. On the third try, I managed to pull the tricky clasp through and stepped back. "There, all done now," I uttered with a satisfied smile.

She looked at me curiously. "From which house are you?" she asked.

I couldn't tell her the truth for fear that her mistress might know Lady Bramwell. I lied with an innocent smile. "I'm not from here but from the north, where I work on a farm."

"Oh! 'Tis a country maid you are. And your name?"

"Abigail," I lied again.

"I'm Susan from the Lawrence House," she said, picking up her basket and welcoming me to walk alongside her.

"I must say, your hair is quite a dazzling shade of red, as rich a color as rubies."

With a prideful toss of her head, she said, "My mistress thinks the same. She spends a fortune buying saffron to dye her hair the same color as mine. Although, one day, she will come to regret it. For afterward, she always complains of a burning sensation on her scalp that lasts for days. No good can come of it." She stopped suddenly and, peering at my face, asked in a tone of suspicion, "What brings you to the Strand?"

I had a ready response prepared to answer such a question. "My mistress was most generous in granting me a two-day leave to visit my ailing aunt who lives within the city walls. It was my aunt's wish that I deliver a letter to her grandson, a student at Gray's Inn, and bring him a piece of his favorite cake that she baked."

She pointed in the direction of the gate. "You have strayed

far from Ludgate."

"Aye. I fear I lost my way."

"I don't know the route to Gray's Inn, but perhaps one of the other girls does. Lucy! Helen!" she shouted to the others already heading into Fleet Street. She became vexed when they didn't heed her call. "What ho, stop!" She commanded, hastening her steps. I followed close behind.

We caught up with Lucy and Helen, and my red-headed companion angrily stepped before them.

"Did you choose not to hear me?" huffed Susan.

They offered no apology but eyed me. Helen, willowy with honey-colored hair like mine, and a slight crook to her nose, asked impartially, "And who's this?"

"This is Abigail, a country-serving maid visiting her aunt in London. She's seeking the way to Gray's Inn," Susan explained.

"Zounds! A farm maid in our midst," Helen responded with a boisterous laugh. "I was a dairymaid up north until one hot summer day, my mistress's husband came into the barn whilst I was milking the cow. He grabbed me from behind, and forsooth, it wasn't the cow's tit he wanted to tug at."

"Tell what happened later," Lucy, a plump girl with an ample bosom, exhorted with a cackle.

"Later that night, the husband came into my room wanting more, but I squealed loudly like a pig being brought to slaughter, and he ran. The following day, I left for London, without my wages but with my virtue intact."

I laughed along with them. What a merry band of maidservants I had fallen in with. Although Helen told the tale in jest, I knew from other accounts I've heard from friends back home that the life of a country maid could be fraught with problems such as lustful stares from farmhands and even the mistress's husband. That very well could be the subject of a future poem - a warning to country maids of how one dairymaid escaped the lustful attention of her mistress's husband. Despite their pleasant company, I knew I had to make haste for Gray's Inn.

"Can either of you direct me to Gray's Inn?"

"You're in luck," said Lucy. "For this past week, I accompanied my mistress to Gray's Inn to fetch her ailing son. We went by carriage, but I've been told 'tis not a long journey on foot. Right before you get to the tollgate, you'll come to Shoe Lane. Follow the lane up to the top of Holborn Hill. From the Church of St. Andrews, you'll see the walls of Gray's Inn.

"Oh, now be careful, Abigail," teased Helen. "Lucy has been known to confuse street names and has led many astray into a deep dark wood."

"Nay!" cried Lucy. "Pay her no mind. Treading on Shoe Lane is the right path to Grey's Inn. There's no mistaking it. For I remember it well. My mistress was so vexed with her driver because he missed the turn for Shoe Lane after he crossed River Fleet bridge that she took off her shoe and said she would smack him with it should he miss the turn again."

"Faith, I believe it!" shrieked Susan. "For I have seen how quick-tempered your mistress can be."

We were all amused at how the name of Shoe Lane would be forever fixed in Lucy's memory. My confidence, bolstered by Lucy's entertaining story, made parting with my merry band of maidservants a bit easier to bear. I took my leave of them at the toll bridge near Ludgate. Lucy's story proved true, for when I reached St. Andrews Church within the half-hour, I spied the high walls of Gray's Inn in the near distance. Knowing I was close, I sat at the tower's base to eat the ginger cake and nuts I carried. Although what I had to offer my hungry belly was meager, it would have to suffice for now.

⚬⚭⚬

I followed the wall of Gray's Inn until I reached a locked gate. Beyond it were red brick buildings surrounding a pretty courtyard. Perhaps they were the lodgings of students. If so, in which one did Robert reside? The wall continued down the long road, its path disappearing as it turned the corner. It suddenly seemed a daunting task to locate Robert in this vast place.

My head snapped around at the sound of a woman's voice, filled with a mix of delight and surprise.

"Marry! Isabella. 'Tis you," she squealed. "Have you come seeking Robert?"

Faith, I remembered Millicent well but not fondly. She showed little regard for her reputation when she performed a lewd ballad with Thomas at Bell Savage Inn.

"Aye, Millicent. But I'm unsure how to find Robert."

With an air of self-importance, Millicent declared, "Jove! Isabella, since I work here, I can help you."

She grabbed hold of my arm. "Look here. You're at the wrong gate." Locking my arm in hers, she carted me off to the school's main gate. Her silly chatter grew faint, for I was preoccupied with finding Robert and what I would say to him when I did.

"Watch your head here!" Millicent warned as we passed under a low-hanging archway and then made our way down a narrow side street that led to the main gate of Gray's Inn.

"Wait here," Millicent instructed.

I leaned against the stone wall whilst Millicent spoke to the guard. She appeared familiar with him, for he quickly uncrossed his arms from his chest and greeted her by name, smiling. Laughter passed between them. A few moments later, Millicent returned, giggling as she clasped my arm.

"Follow me, little sister," she said loud enough for the guard to hear. "Let's go to work."

She leaned into me and whispered, "Play along with me, Isabella."

I didn't let go of her arm, and as we didn't resemble each other, my eyes were fixed on the ground as we passed the guard. We came to another courtyard just as lovely as the first. But in this second courtyard, pathways sprang out from the center of the yard, each leading to buildings of varying sizes and shapes. I surmised that this was the central hub of the school. But it was oddly quiet with no one in sight.

"Where are the students?" I asked anxiously.

"Where else would they all be but in the Grand Hall eating dinner? And that's where we're going right now," she said.

She pointed to a low gray stone building to our left. "There's the building where Thomas and Robert stay whilst they study here."

"And that grand building ahead with stained glass windows and multiple arches at the entrance is the Grand Hall?" I asked.

"Aye, that's where I work, in the kitchen. And that's where I'll fetch your Robert." She squeezed my arm and let loose a series of high-pitched giggles.

'Tis a scullery maid, she is. I suspected as much. Still, I marveled at how she could toil in such a lowly position and remain in such high spirits. I had to admit I rather admired her for it.

Once we reached the Grand Hall, I scurried to the side of the building whilst Millicent went inside to get a message to Robert that I was there to see him. The wait seemed interminable.

I began deciphering the shields on the stained-glass windows to occupy my mind. When the strain of looking up became too much for my neck, I looked away toward the courtyard and caught sight of someone moving briskly in my direction. It wasn't until the law student got close enough for me to hear the clattering of pebbles under his feet that I recognized it was Thomas, Robert's friend. He was attired in his law school uniform, a sleeveless black gown with a matching black cap. I prayed he was bringing good tidings and not the distressing news that Robert had already left for his father's house.

He greeted me pleasantly. "My dear Isabella, it seems I'm bound to play the herald for you and Robert. First, Robert sent me to St. Paul's Cross to alert you he would be arriving late. And now you wish for me to alert Robert that you have arrived here," he paused to whisper in my ear, "in secret to see him." He pulled back, a mischievous glint in his eye. "The two of you are quite the clandestine couple."

"Thomas, 'tis of the utmost importance that I see him straight away," I implored.

The urgency of my tone changed his playful manner. "Very well, then. Let's not waste time. Come, walk beside me."

With purposeful steps, we made our way into the gray stone building that Millicent had pointed to earlier. Once inside the vestibule, Thomas spoke in a hushed tone, "We must proceed with caution. Maids who don't work on the grounds are not allowed in this building. When I grab your hand, we'll make a mad dash for the room that Robert and I share. Thankfully, it's on the first floor."

He opened the second door in the vestibule and looked briefly to his left. He reached for my hand, "Now, Isabella!" he barked.

Like two scared rabbits pursued by hungry hounds, we dashed out of the dark shadows of the vestibule. Within seconds, Thomas opened the door to the room he shared with Robert and pushed me inside.

"I'll stand watch," he announced to a startled Robert, who had been packing and slammed the door shut.

"Izzy!" Robert exclaimed and rushed toward me. "Tell me, my love, is something amiss?" He stroked my cheek and smiled. "Or have you forgotten that our meeting date was set for Sunday next."

My eyes remained fixed on his travel bag stuffed with his belongings. Oh, duplicitous fellow toying with the hearts of two unsuspecting maids. I brushed his hand away and got straight to the matter that had become a festering wound since my talk with Mistress Walden.

"Your aunt has left for your father's house, and in her absence, I stole away from my duties to see you on a matter of great importance. I have learned that you are to be betrothed to a viscount's daughter by the name of Rose Clavell. "

He remained calm and cleared his throat before he spoke. "Who delivered that bit of news to you – my cousin?"

I remained silent.

A deep line edged itself between his brows. "And during your merry gossip with my cousin, did you mention my singing at the inn?"

God's Blood. I grew hot, for he didn't answer the betrothal question. "Nay, Robert. I didn't reveal your secret to Mistress Walden," I seethed. "I was true when I told you your secret was safe with me, but you were not forthcoming in revealing a major truth about yourself."

"Not so," he asserted, reaching for me, but I wouldn't submit to his embrace. Lying knave. I made my way to the door, but Robert instantly blocked me. "Izzy, I assure you, there's no marriage contract. 'Tis merely foolish talk. My father wishes for me to marry this girl, not I."

I didn't cease my quarrel. "I understand that tonight there's to be a meeting with the two families – yours and Rose Clavell's." I gestured toward the bed. "And from your packed bag, you're also expected to attend. What will tonight's conversation be about in your father's house? Surely, not the weather nor intrigues of the court but planning your wedding to Rose Clavell!" I shouted.

Robert stood motionless against the door. A tense silence followed as we observed each other. Suddenly Robert blurted out, "I will defy my father and not go home." He approached me and placed his hands on my shoulders. "Do you hear me, Izzy? In defiance of my father's wishes, I will not go home."

My heart grew light, for his declaration could only mean one thing. If Robert was determined to thwart his father's plans, he had fallen deeply for me.

He sat on the bed, wearily pushing the remaining items he had planned to pack. "I'll not follow the path of my older brother just to satisfy my father's ambition. Your presence here has made it clear what I need to do."

Robert had not revealed much about his brother before, only mentioning his name – until now. I joined him on the bed. "What did your father bid your brother to do?"

Robert's voice quivered with a mix of resentment and determination as he began to explain. "When my brother was but thirteen, my father arranged a betrothal for him with a nobleman's daughter. Now, my brother has secured his place at court, but bears no love for his wife. What I yearn for, Izzy, is a union founded on love, a concept my father fails to grasp. And I believe, with every fiber of my being, that I can find that with you."

We kissed, and the warm, familiar touch of his lips made me crave more of him. In that moment, a whirlwind of emotions swept over me-desire, fear, and a deep longing for a love that was yet to be fully realized.

"What say you, Izzy, will you stay with me tonight?"

My mother's voice whispered in my inner ear, 'Make Christ and not Cupid govern your emotions.' Her advice was challenging to heed at such an eventful moment as this one.

"I will stay with you tonight on one condition. That we exchange betrothal vows, promising to stay true to one another and that we will soon set a date to marry in my parish church."

I half expected an expression of horror on Robert's face at my bold proposal, but nay, he grabbed my hand. "I faith! Why not?" he declared, most willingly.

He sprang into action, rummaging through trunks filled with his personal belongings. "Now let's see what I can use instead of a ring as a token of my love?" He expressed disapproval of each item he pulled from his trunk before tossing it aside. He seemed to enjoy keeping me in suspense. Just as I was about to voice my displeasure, he cried out, "Aha!" and held up the green silk scarf tasseled with silver thread that he wore on that memorable day we met at St. Paul's.

"My dear, sweet mother gave me this scarf on my nineteenth birthday. I wear it with much pride and joy. For my mother's deep love for me is unwavering." He gently draped it around my neck and looking deeply into my eyes delivered the line I so wanted to hear. "I, Robert Barrington, plight you my troth, Isabella Whitney, to one day be your wedded husband. And now, what is your token of love for me?"

I had nothing as grand as his silk scarf but something of personal significance to me as much as Robert's mother's gift was to him. I pulled a yellow velvet ribbon from my hair. "When I was ten, I recited twenty-five of my father's favorite psalms for his birthday gift. I didn't falter but perfectly spoke every word. In gratitude, my mother gifted me with this ribbon because I made my father so happy." I kissed the ribbon and wrapped it around his wrist. "I, Isabella Whitney, plight thee my troth, Robert Barrington, to one day be your wedded wife."

We sealed our fate with a kiss. "In God's eyes, we're as good as married, my love, and tonight, we'll remain together," Robert said.

Our spontaneous plighting of troths would not have satisfied my mother or father, but it suited me. I had no misgivings about moving forward with Robert.

"One thing is certain, Izzy, we cannot stay here tonight. If we're discovered, we'll have to appear before the school's governing board along with Thomas, who brought you here."

He paused and raised a quizzical brow. "I never did ask you. How did you manage to get onto the grounds?"

"By chance, I met Millicent at the east gate. She got me through the main gate on the pretense that I was her sister, come to replace a scullery maid who had fallen ill."

Robert chuckled as he put on his black robe. "Good 'ole Millicent, full of fun trickery, that one. Then, you must leave with Millicent so as not to arouse suspicion. That means you must carry out your assigned role and assist her with her duties in the kitchen." With an amused expression, he added, "I suppose now you can put your training in my aunt's house to good use."

"Let me remind you, my training was not for scullery maid."

"You'll have to play the part," he teased.

I relented with a sigh. "Oh, very well, since there's no other way."

"Oh, my Izzy, the price we pay for love," he said as he

quickly kissed me. In response to his jesting, I playfully pinched his arm.

"Ouch!" he cried, rubbing his arm with feigned pain. "You shall offer recompense for this offense."

"I'll do no such thing." I laughed, trailing close behind him as he made for the door.

"Listen closely now, my love. I'll go now to relieve Thomas of his watch, and together, we'll arrange for you to meet me in a location away from here in a few hours." He signaled me to be silent as he gently pushed me behind the door.

He leaned in to kiss me, but I nudged him away, "Make haste and return to me quickly."

"As swiftly as dragonflies glide over water, I'll return," he whispered and shut the door behind him.

I felt giddiness from this unexpected turn of events. When I awoke this morning, ready to confront Robert with Mistress Walden's distressing news, I never imagined it would result in our betrothal and that I would spend the night with him. "Oh, glorious day!" I cried out and then clapped my hands to my mouth to silence my joy. I spun away from the door and danced the quick high steps of the Gilliard to Robert's bed. I eyed his bag and pushed it to the floor. Nay! Rose Clavell, you will not see Robert tonight, nor shall you ever see him, for he has pledged his troth to me.

I lay down and began to fill my head with enchanting dreams of our life together. I gave no thought to the dire consequences of abandoning my house duties in hot pursuit of Robert. By my actions, Lady Bramwell could cast me out as an eye-servant, the worst appellation a domestic could incur. Alas, Cupid's fiery arrow caused all my good sense to flee.

Within thirty minutes, Robert returned to his room with a scullery maid's bonnet and apron. "Izzy put these on," he ordered cheerfully. It was time to play my part for the rest of the day.

I cast him a knowing glance. "Millicent?"

"Aye, she has been of enormous help to us today."

Whilst I put on the white layered cap, Robert tied the

apron strings around my waist. He unsuccessfully tried to make the front of the cap go further down my forehead to conceal my eyes to make it difficult for someone to describe me. He stepped back and observed me.

"The most beautiful scullery maid I have ever laid eyes on."

I curtsied. "I thank you, sir, for the compliment," I said in the manner of a shy, demure maiden.

He took hold of my hand, and we scampered out of the room and down the quiet corridor, stopping at a gnarled door with protruding knobs.

"Where are we going?" I asked, my apprehension rising as I wondered where this ominous-looking door led.

He turned to face me and kissed my hand, calming me. "Behind this portal is a staircase that leads outside, away from the main entrance to this building."

Slowly, we descended the narrow staircase. When we reached the bottom, we were confronted by another door that resembled the one at the top. Robert heaved his shoulder against the door, and it thrust open. Thomas was on the other side, waiting with a ready smile.

Robert handed me off to Thomas. "You'll go with Thomas now, Izzy. I must away and work in haste to make the arrangements for our accommodation tonight. Thomas will tell you of our plan."

Robert laid his hand on Thomas's shoulder, "Guard her well, for as you know, she is most dear to me." He kissed me on the forehead, "Till tonight, my sweet love," and dashed to the staircase from which we had just descended, slowly pulling the door shut.

"Come along, Isabella," Thomas urged, "dinner is nearly over, and the grounds will soon abound with students. We must reach the side door of the Grand Hall undetected, where Millicent will be waiting for us."

I edged closer to Thomas and looked down at the ground when I noticed a small band of black-robed students walking on the path opposite us. They were deep in conversation and barely cast us a glance. Still, we quickened our pace.

During our brisk walk, Thomas told me Robert's plan. "Around the hour of four, you and Millicent should finish your chores in the kitchen. Then, you'll leave the grounds the same way you came, passing the same guard who allowed you entry. Once you pass the gate, I'll be waiting for you a few yards away, just around the corner where the stone wall turns. From there, we'll take a short walk to Monk's Tavern." Thomas paused, "Have I explained the plan clearly?"

I nodded, kicking a few pebbles in my path. "Aye, Thomas. It sounds fine."

It all sounded fine, except for the part about playing scullery maid alongside Millicent. The thought of the arduous chores I had to endure for the next few hours was far from appealing. Robert's jesting, 'Oh Izzy, the things we do for love,' was, in fact, a harsh reality. The trials of love, indeed.

Once we reached the Grand Hall, Thomas veered away from the main entrance, stopped at a tiny oval window cranked open near the ground, and gave a series of short whistles. We hurried to the side door adjacent to the window and waited. Within seconds, Millicent opened the door and pulled me inside.

Thomas put his foot on the threshold. "You're a love, Millicent, and I'll show you my appreciation tonight, I promise."

She pulled him in close and smiled seductively. "I expect to be spared very little tonight," and closed the door on his bemused face. She hurried me down a short flight of steps into the dreaded scullery. It was not as tiny as the one at Lady Bramwell's house, and thankfully, there was a small, opened window above a long white wooden table. I was relieved that some fresh air would seep into the room. How oft I have seen Lady Bramwell's scullery maid depart for home, her face flushed for lack of a window in the room.

Straightaway, Millicent insisted on doing the heavy washing. Standing at the large basin with dirty pots and saucepots, she boasted, "The head cook has told me I do a fine job of getting rid of the grease in these pots and saucepans. If she continues praising my work, it'll lead to a better position, perhaps as a kitchen maid. Don't think, Isabella, I'll remain a scullery maid forever."

She need not have worried that I would challenge her on who is the best scullery maid for the day.

"Today's your lucky day-ay," Millicent said in a sing-song manner. "Thomas said that many of the older students are away, doing mock trials. So that means fewer dishes for you to wash."

Relief washed over me like a cool breeze. "That's good news," I sighed, feeling the burden of the day's tasks lightening.

I immediately got to work cleaning my share of dishes, goblets, knives, and spoons. Millicent had every right to boast of her good work, for I did not catch one speck of food when I placed the pots and saucepans she had cleaned thus far on the racks to dry. My next task was scrubbing the work tables whilst Millicent was on her knees, swilling the floor. I felt guilty as I observed her arched back and bent head, her whole body moving across the floor at a turtle's pace. She deliberately gave me the less strenuous tasks.

"Millicent, I want to say that I know what you're doing, and I'm grateful."

"Whatever do you mean- ean?" she sang out again.

Her silly way of responding increasingly became difficult to bear. "Stop singing words and look at me!"

She turned her head with a fool's grin.

"I simply want to say that you're giving me the simpler tasks, Millicent, and I'm grateful."

Millicent sat back on her heels. "Thomas told me tonight will be special for you and Robert. You don't want to arrive at Monk's Inn smelling like a country wench who's been emptying pails of cow dung all day."

I knelt beside her. "We shall finish this floor together."

She began to protest.

"Millicent! If Robert would toss me aside for smelling badly after a hard day's work in the scullery, he's not worthy of my love. Let's swill the floor together and be done with it."

She sighed. "As you wish-ish," and tossed a scrub brush my way.

We worked in tandem, down on our knees in pools of water, pushing the scrub brushes in a circular motion across the stone floor.

Soon, the head cook came into the room, a plump woman with wispy gray hair inching out of her cap. "You sisters work well together," she commented as she inspected the work tables, pots, and pans already dried on the rack. "Perhaps Isabella can come back tomorrow, Millicent. I received word that Cecily is still unwell."

Millicent and I exchanged a secretive glance. "Nay, miss. My sister can't return tomorrow. She must tend to our younger brothers and sisters whilst our mother is away," Millicent said.

The head cook shook her head, disappointed, and then smiled, revealing a charming set of dimples at the corners of her mouth. "You're welcome to fill in anytime, Isabella," and picked up two sauce pots as she left the room.

"Did you hear that, Isabella? If all else fails, you have a job here," Millicent teased.

"Nay. I wouldn't dream of giving you competition."

"No competition at all," she retorted. "No one can outperform me in cleaning."

I smiled. "Aye, you do a fine job, Millicent."

She wiped a bit of sweat from her brow and looked at her hands. "What will Robert say when he sees your hands made red from washing and your fingers purple, like mine?"

"He better welcome me with open arms," I said indignantly.

We laughed and managed to maintain a steady pace as we made our way on our hands and knees to the end of the stone floor.

12

Triumph of the Pagan Goddesses

My time in the scullery with Millicent ended at the hour of five, and I arrived with Thomas at Monk's Inn bearing sore hands and pain in my knees and lower back. Robert met us beneath the inn's gatehouse arch and rushed to embrace me.

"As promised, my friend, I have brought you your dear Isabella made weary from her afternoon spent in the scullery," Thomas said.

Robert's embrace was a balm to my aching body, his strong arms providing a much-needed comfort that went beyond the physical.

"As always, Thomas, you have kept your word, and I'm most grateful," said Robert.

"And I, too, Thomas, give you my wholehearted thanks," I said as I leaned into Robert. "And please express my gratitude to Millicent," I quickly added.

Thomas tipped his hat and bid us farewell. "May God grant you both a gentle repose tonight."

Robert called my attention to two large windows above the overhanging gallery. "There's our room. I picked it out especially with you in mind. It's quieter and brighter than those found on the first floor," Robert explained. "Come, my love." We stepped carefully on the cobblestone path to the inn's entrance.

Upon entering our room, my face was awash in the warm glow of candlelight. It was an ample open space, with the ceiling open to the rafters. After spending nearly three hours in the scullery with its low ceiling, this room lifted my spirits. A fire was blazing in the hearth, and three leather folding screens were fully open, concealing something near the fireplace. Just as I was about to take a peek, Robert placed his arms around my waist and pulled me close. He lifted my hair from my neck and bestowed a series of kisses.

"Well, Izzy, didn't I choose the perfect room for us?" he murmured.

"The queen herself would be satisfied to stay here."

"And now, my hard-working girl, I have a surprise, for you," he announced. He led me to the screens by the fireplace, pushing them back to reveal a wooden tub. Robert dipped his hand in the water. "Come, feel how warm it is."

I dipped my fingers into the water. It was indeed warm, and there was a sweet scent of lilac, a fragrance that always reminded me of spring. Sponges, soft and inviting, rested at the bottom to protect my feet from wood splinters, and a bar of castile soap, its smooth surface glistening in the candlelight, floated on the water. Lady Bramwell only used castile soap, imported from Spain, saying it was better for the skin since 'tis made from olive oil and not animal fat.

"I feel as if I stumbled upon a diamond – what joy it'll be to soothe my weary bones in this tub."

"Izzy, I have found my diamond in you. And now, I shall leave you to your soaking." He pointed to a chair next to the fireplace. "There's a linen smock for you there on the chair. I'll return in an hour, and then we'll sup."

I took hold of his hand, pulling him close to me. "Much consideration went into your planning, and I'm grateful." I kissed him deeply, inching my tongue into his mouth, savoring the taste of him.

He nudged me gently toward the tub and grinned, "Take your bath now."

When I heard the key turn in the door, I undressed, flinging my clothes on the floor, and eased myself into the tub. The sponges hugged my feet, and I sighed with relief as the warmth of the scented water rippled across my skin. The castile soap slipped out of my grasp a few times, and when I managed to grab hold of it, it felt like a brush with silk bristles gliding along my skin. I pondered what other delightful surprises Robert was planning next – perhaps supper in the room accompanied by music.

As promised, Robert returned to the room within the hour. The only concealment for my naked body was the white linen smock he left for me to wear. I felt uncomfortably exposed with Robert fully dressed in all his layers of clothing. I sat at the round table near the fireplace and wrapped the folds of cloth from the billowing smock around me.

"I thank you again for choosing this lovely room and the opportunity to soak in a warm tub. I imagine it must have cost you a small fortune."

He squeezed my hand gently as he joined me at the table. "No need to worry about that. It was the least I could do for the time you spent toiling away in the scullery for nearly four hours. And Millicent - did she drive you mad with her silly chatter and endless giggles?"

"A little in the beginning, but I have discovered she's caring and generous. I hope Thomas knows that. I fear it would be easy for him to take advantage of her."

Before Robert could respond, there came a knock at the door. "Supper," Robert announced with an eager smile. Before approaching the door, he tossed me a blanket with which I covered my smock.

A male servant who looked no older than fourteen, dressed in a bright blue vest with a black sash, entered the room carrying a tray of delectable dishes. "A good evening to you both," he said with a courteous bow, placing the dishes in a circular pattern on the table.

Every dish made my mouth salivate. There was ham and pea pottage, salted beef with mustard, bread, and butter. To sweeten our tongues, there was custard and sweet-tasting Portuguese oranges—the latest delectable sensation enjoyed by those who can afford them.

The flickering flames of the candles and the cracking fire in the fireplace made the room glow like an orange sunset in autumn. And I felt we were meant to be together in that golden ambiance of warmth. The words flowed between us effortlessly, and we exchanged tender glances in the intermittent silence.

"Have you had the chance to read *Heroides*?" Robert asked as he peeled an orange.

"I've read some of it and was taken by the women's searingly honest sentiments in their letters. As I told your cousin the other night, I wish all women could read *Heroides*, and for those who can't read, it should be read aloud to them."

"And why is that?" Robert asked, popping a slice of orange into his mouth.

Holding up two fingers, I began my reasons, "First, I can think of no other book that has expressed women's discontent with men's deception in love with such accuracy. Second, it challenges the notion that men have a more moral character than women. Thus far, all the men I read about used effective ways to win a woman's trust and love, only to abandon them."

Robert pondered my reasoning. "Indeed, Izzy. Together, we shall prove Ovid wrong. I shall look forward to the poem you will write about me, praising my constancy in love."

I smiled. "I wouldn't be here if I doubted that was true."

Robert began pulling at the collar of his shirt. "It has grown warm, don't you think? Would you mind if I made myself a bit more comfortable by removing some of my outer garments?"

"You may do as you wish, Robert. I'm comfortable in my smock. Shouldn't you be as well?"

He blew me a kiss and bowed low. "I applaud your sense of fair play, my lady."

My breathing quickened as he began removing his clothes, for never have I been in the presence of a man who disrobed. He started with his red jeweled belt and pleated jacket with black fur trim, letting it drop to the floor in a heap. I was careful not to let my jaw slack when I beheld Robert's colorful padded codpiece, displaying gold, brown, and pewter stripes. He struggled to undo the laces of his doublet quickly. And once he did, down came his silk hose, and he stood in his linen shirt, his bare legs exposed. Now we were on equal footing, nothing but loose linen garments covering our naked bodies – he in his shirt and I in my smock.

"Ah, there now! I feel much better," he exclaimed, swinging his arms as he walked around the room. "Still suffering from aches and pains, Izzy?"

"Just a slight pain in my right leg."

"I know just the remedy for that. Something I learned in France."

He knelt beside me and grabbed hold of my foot. Then he moved his thumb in a circular motion up and down my calf. My heart leaped when he began inching his hand up my thigh. He paused, "Shall I go higher, Izzy?"

I breathed, undid the last two buttons on his shirt, and slid my hand around his neck, pulling him forward. And it was then that Venus and Aphrodite, the pagan goddesses of love, triumphed over scripture. I touched his hand and whispered, "Aye, higher."

13

Surprise Visitor

Joy reigned supreme as I awoke beside Robert the following day after we had exchanged our betrothal vows. Robins were perched on the low-hanging bough outside our window and chirped sweetly, announcing to all who passed below that Robert and I were now joined as one. Robert's head lay in sweet repose on my breast, and I ran my fingers through his hair and glimpsed a wisp of a smile. Gently, I lifted one of his eyelids and whispered, "Good morrow, my love."

Robert rolled his head onto the pillow, stretched his arms, and yawned. "Good morrow, my wife-to-be."

I laid my hand on his cheek. "'Tis a monumental day for us, isn't it, Robert? We laid together last night, sealing our future fate as husband and wife."

"One half of my heart was yours before last night, and now blissfully, I proclaim, you have all of it," he said, pulling me closer.

He bestowed a series of soft kisses on my hand. "Do you know you have the same hands as the queen?"

"Do I?" I marveled as I brought my hand closer to observe it.

"Aye, such long and slender fingers like hers." His hands reached for my waist. "And also, like her, you have a tiny waist."

I sighed. "Oh, I wish I had her golden-red hair."

"Your honey-colored hair is gentler on the eyes," he replied, burying his face in my hair, which lay fanlike on the pillow.

"What else do you know about her?"

"Who?" he muttered absentmindedly.

I nudged him with my elbow. "The queen, silly."

He rolled slowly onto his side, facing me. "She has a fondness for monkeys."

"Go to! You're bluffing, Robert." I laughed.

" I vouchsafe, 'tis so. My brother told me. She keeps one on a long chain at Whitehall Palace."

"Tell me something else about her."

"She's a poor loser at card games. In that regard, she's much like my father. And here's something you'll enjoy hearing. She writes poetry."

I sat up in bed, astonished. "No?"

Robert nodded. "I hear she's quite good."

He attempted to pull me down beside him, and I playfully resisted. "Speaking of poems, Robert, have you read the poem I gave you?"

"I have, but first, I need to taste more of you before discussing that." Touching my nipple with his finger, he murmured, "I wish to see this pink bud stand erect." He cupped one breast, and his glorious tongue drew circles around my nipple. His tongue worked wonders, for my nipple hardened quickly, and he brought it deep into his mouth. Instantly, I felt a swelling and moistness between my legs.

Our euphoric coupling gave way to a light slumber. When we awoke, Robert was ready to begin anew. I giggled at how the heat rose so quickly in him and held his eager hands down.

"Nay. You promised to tell me your thoughts about my poem. Depending on what you say, you may or may not taste me again," I teased.

Grumbling, he got up out of bed. "You drive a hard bargain, Izzy."

"But where are you going?" I cried.

"To fetch your poem."

"You mean, you brought it with you?"

He turned to me. "Didn't you know? I carry it with me always."

He fumbled through his leather sack and pulled out my poem, waving it proudly like he was carrying the queen's banner. I fluffed up the pillows, piling them high so we could sit against them. Robert hopped onto the bed, adjusting his side of the cushions as he leaned into them.

He handed me my poem. "Take note, Izzy, of how I labored for you."

I couldn't imagine his meaning until I saw his comments in the margins. He really did care about helping me become a better writer. I laid my hand atop his. "I'm truly moved by your devoted attention to my poem."

"You show great promise, Izzy. Although I found your language unadorned, its simplicity is still very appealing. You have an ear for rhyme. You show it here. Listen:"

> *He that is void of any friend,*
>   *him company to keep,*
> *Walks in a world of wilderness,*
>   *full fraught with dangerous deep.*

"I have marked every line you wrote with fourteen syllables and those that don't to help you master the ballad form."

I examined every word of Robert's detailed notations, and the deep love I bore him plunged into a depth I thought was impossible. I leaped out of bed to get the lute that Robert had brought with him. "Play me a tune. For I feel merry, my love, and wish to dance."

Robert readily obliged, and I danced about the room in all my nakedness with no blush of modesty. So drunk in love with Robert was I. He, naked also, followed me about the room, playing his lute, his eyes flashing with merriment. We were in our own Garden of Eden, free and unashamed to bask in the beauty of our youthful nakedness, our movements unencumbered by layers of clothing. Suddenly, a furious knocking came at the door, bringing our revelry to a halt.

"Robert, you, saucy boy, opened this door at once!" bellowed a man's voice.

That commanding voice shouting for Robert could only belong to one person. "Your father?" I whispered in a panic.

"Damn him," he muttered.

I ran to the chair where I had placed my clothes the night before and dressed quickly.

The knocking grew louder, the tone more menacing. "Robert! I am not your serving boy to be kept waiting."

"Coming, father. Allow me to get dressed." Robert hastened to put on his shirt and breeches.

I feared meeting his father when he was in such a foul mood. And worse to meet him in the room where we had spent hours coupling under the sheets. I scurried to Robert with my kirtle half on and whispered, "Is it prudent for me to face your father now? Can't I just hide in the armoire until you make haste in getting him to leave?"

He grabbed my shoulders. "What's the point? He knows you're here."

"But how —Thomas?"

"Undoubtedly, he bullied Thomas relentlessly into telling him the truth of my whereabouts. Go lace up behind the screen whilst I answer the door."

My unsteady hands were slow to lace the strings of my kirtle. Just as I was about to ask Robert for help, he opened the door, and his father bounded into the room.

"Where's the girl? Don't tell me you have her hidden somewhere?" he barked.

I emerged from behind the screen, all laced up. "Nay, sir, I'm here." My heart was running wild, but I didn't avert my eyes from his disapproving glare.

Robert moved beside me and held my hand firmly in his. "Father, allow me to introduce Isabella Whitney, daughter of Geoffrey Whitney, a country gentleman of a small estate in Cheshire."

"I know very well who she is," he responded flatly. His stare was just as cold as his sister's when she first laid eyes on me. "She's the daughter of a country gentleman, Robert, 'tis true, but she's not suitable enough for our family's prosperity."

How dare he belittle my father's worth, I fumed.

"I say she's suitable," snapped Robert. I gave his hand, which had grown moist, a gentle squeeze.

His father's cheeks turned crimson red, and he made a feeble attempt to discredit Robert's feelings for me. "Don't think, Isabella, that you're the first pretty face to turn my son's head. There have been numerous others before you. Shall I tell her, Robert, of your declaration of love for our chambermaid?"

My hand went limp in Robert's grasp.

"That's an unfair comparison, father. I was only fifteen."

"And did I not pay a hefty fine at the beginning of this school year because you had a girl in your room."

I glanced at Robert.

"That wasn't me, father, but Thomas."

Millicent, I concluded.

Robert's father pounded his fist against the table, and I trembled. "Nevertheless, you broke the rule by helping Thomas sneak a girl into your room. You have a history of improper behavior driven by your impetuous nature. A lamentable trait fostered by your mother, who still indulges your every whim to this day. 'Tis time to grow up and accept your responsibility."

"Responsibility to fulfill your dreams, you mean," Robert retorted, his voice filled with defiance. "I've never pledged my troth to any woman. But, yesterday we pledged our troths to each other and consummated that promise last night. We're bound to each other, and you can't break it."

His father addressed me through a clenched jaw. "I would like to speak to my son alone, Isabella."

Robert held fast to my arm. "She shall stay."

I touched Robert's arm gently, my fingers trembling. "Nay, Robert. I'll go." With an icy stare at Robert's father, I turned and left the room. I didn't close the door fully, leaving it ajar, and moved into a dark corner near the door where I could still hear their conversation.

"Were there any witnesses to this folly of yours, Robert?"

"Only one witness that matters, God above."

Robert's father chuckled, and his tone was less severe. "You have relished in your manhood with plenty of maids. What you feel for this girl is merely a passion that will soon cool."

"'Tis love, Father. I'll not marry Rose Clavell merely for your personal gain."

I covered my mouth to silence my joy at Robert's affirmation of his love for me.

"Pish, boy! Think well on what you do before you squander the possibilities that lie before you."

"You have planned everything per your desires, not mine. You insist I stay the course at Gray's Inn, hoping it'll lead to a barrister position at Westminster."

"Aye, a fine plan," his father interrupted, his voice filled with impatience.

"And your desire to see me married to Rose Clavell, whose father is a distant relation to the queen, will help me ascend to a position in the queen's council."

"And how is that bad for you?" His father's voice rose in frustration.

"'Tis not what I want," Robert responded in exasperation. "You seek prosperity through your sons. Didn't my older brother help you secure a substantial land grant from the queen? Does your well of greed never run dry?"

A chair scraped loudly against the floor, and Robert's father cried, "By God, I will strike you for your insolence?"

I pressed my hands against the cold wall to steady my nerves. Please don't let him strike Robert, I prayed.

"By the duty you owe me as your father, do not pursue this fool-hearted act with Isabella. The very thought is abhorrent to me."

Robert held firm. "I'm bound to her. You can't break it."

Bravo! I silently clapped my hands in delight.

And then Robert's father delivered the fatal blow. "Pursue this, and you'll lose all the privileges you enjoy. I will cut off your allowance, and you shall not cross my doorstep, no matter how strongly your mother objects. Then we'll see how hot your love for Isabella burns when you're left groping for money to keep you in the lifestyle you have long enjoyed."

Robert's father flung open the door, and I winced as it hit the wall. I retreated further into the dark corner of the hallway. Robert followed and leaned over the railing as his father descended the stairs.

"Isabella will rob me of nothing, father," he shouted after him. "She'll mend and nourish my soul, for you have long neglected it."

I darted out of the dark corner to join Robert when all was silent. His fingers clung to the railing, and the vein in his neck was twitching.

I caressed his neck. "Oh, Robert. I fear your love for me has cost you dearly."

Robert closed his eyes and drew in a long, steady breath. "Cost me dearly, you say? Nay, my love. My life has just begun to have meaning. My father has long denied my desires because they threatened his ambition." He pulled me into him for a tight embrace. "'Tis you who makes me feel whole."

Arm in arm, we returned to the room. Robert poured himself a glass of wine and offered me one.

"Don't allow my father's words to trouble you," he said as he sat with his drink. "I'm not on my way to fiscal ruin. My three years at Gray's Inn have not been for naught, for I have acquired valuable contacts for getting work as a balladeer and musician."

"Really, Robert? It surprises me that law school can advance a music career."

Unfazed by my doubt, Robert retrieved his lute from the side of the bed and returned to the table.

"Did you know that Queen Elizabeth is the patron lady of Gray's Inn?"

"Nay, I didn't."

"'Tis her patronage that has helped the school rise in prominence. And because of that, it attracts the most notable and talented men to attend every major event at the school. The students benefit as we can dine and chat with them."

"What valuable contacts have you made?"

He smiled and began strumming the lute. "George Gascoigne, for one."

I shrugged my shoulders, for I had not heard of him.

"George Gascoigne is a rising poet and playwright," Robert explained. "A fellow of much wit. You would like him, Izzy. This past year, two of his plays were mounted at Gray's Inn, the queen being present for both. Naturally, I made a point to converse with him, and whilst we were talking, I discovered that he and I have much in common, for he, too, dropped out of law school to pursue writing."

"I had no idea that plays were performed at Gray's Inn with the queen in attendance."

"Only Gray's Inn holds that distinction," he bragged. "I have the name of another contact that will truly make your head spin."

The back of my neck began to tingle. "Pray tell, who?"

Robert walked to the bed, playing the lively tune, *Get Up and Bar the Door*. I followed him and sat on the bed.

"Well, who is it?"

"I have had the privilege of forming a close acquaintance with none other than Robert Dudley, the Earl of Leicester," he revealed with a smile.

"The queen's sweetheart?" I fell back onto the pillow, mightily impressed. "That is a noteworthy person, indeed. Did you two speak about the queen?"

Robert laughed. "Only of her interest in drama and music. He has formed his own troupe of players called Leicester's Men. This past Christmas, they entertained at court. He has proposed that I join them on their next tour of the north. I'll sing my ballads during the interludes."

I couldn't contain my excitement, sitting up straight and clapping my hands. "This is a golden opportunity, Robert! Your connection with Robert Dudley, the Earl of Leicester, could open doors for us. And surely this will please your father since Robert Dudley is close to the queen. You might even become a court musician." That possibility made my pulse race. "And as your wife, I would meet the queen and perhaps discuss poetry with her. And isn't Nicholas Bacon a member of her council?"

Robert nodded that he was.

"Then, finally, I could meet his wife, Anne," I squealed with delight.

"Aye, all that is true except for the bit about pleasing my father," he said, sitting on the bed. "He detests Robert Dudley, describes him as fiercely ambitious and arrogant, which I find ironic, for he shares those traits with Dudley — though he lacks Dudley's charm."

Amid such exciting news, a dark cloud descended over me. Robert would be leaving soon to tour with Leicester's Men. I placed my hand on the lute's strings to stop him from playing.

"What's wrong?"

"When do you leave to tour with Leicester's Men?"

He hesitated. "In two days hence."

"So soon! For how long?"

"One month," he replied with a sheepish grin. "I was initially unsure about Robert Dudley's offer, which meant leaving school. But now my situation has changed, hasn't it?" He laid down his lute and took my hands in his. "I have defied my father because I have sworn myself to you. We'll need money. Hence, I must begin making my mark as a balladeer. Today, I will confirm with Dudley that I will take the position."

"Your aunt will unleash a torrent of fury upon my head when I return. With your father's strong disapproval of our betrothal, she'll not allow me to finish my contract but throw me out on the street. What are we to do, Robert?"

He embraced me. "All will be well, Izzy. You forget one fact, my love. She dotes on me, for I'm her favorite nephew. No harm will come to you when she sees what lies between us, is true love and no dalliance. We'll go together to see her today."

"I hope your happy prediction proves true." I began to feel anxious. "We must make haste at once to see her."

He slowly caressed my thigh. "We have time, Izzy. 'Tis but

a short ride to my aunt's house."

I surrendered to Robert's strong embrace, suspending, for the moment, all thoughts of a doomed encounter with his aunt.

14

Facing Lady Bramwell

When we arrived at Lady Bramwell's house in the late afternoon, the sun had not yet descended behind the bell tower of Saint Paul's Church. Robert held my hand as I stepped out of the carriage. I strolled toward the back of the house whilst Robert instructed the driver to wait for us.

"Where are you going, Izzy?" Robert shouted. He strode over to me and took my arm. "We shall enter the house through the main door, not the kitchen."

I laughed at my foolishness. I was now betrothed to Lady Bramwell's nephew. Robert expected me to enter the house as he always did as a family member. In the whirlwind of just a few days, our lives had changed. Robert confidently mounted the stairs to the main door whilst I stepped with trepidation. The unease of not knowing Lady Bramwell's reaction to our news set my mind whirring with apprehension, so much so that I missed a step and nearly toppled down on my head.

Standing at the door, Robert held my hand. "Have faith. Remember, I'm her favorite nephew," he reassured me.

I was delighted to see Mistress Walden open the door, although her sober expression did not invite me to embrace her and deliver my joyful news. She spoke our names without enthusiasm and quickly ushered us in.

"Robert, your aunt wishes to speak with Isabella first. You are to wait in the library until she sends for you."

"What absurdity is this?" Robert's voice rose in protest. "Nay, we shall face her together." His defiance echoed through the hall, a clear sign of the tension that had been building between us and the formidable Lady Bramwell.

Her tone softened, recapturing the warmth I had grown accustomed to. "Cousin, your father was here early this afternoon. The news that you two have plighted your troths has deeply disturbed your aunt. You should abide by her wish to wait in the library."

Thus, I was to be the primary recipient of her fury, whilst Robert, her favorite nephew, would be reprimanded with a few choice words of disappointment. She couldn't have chosen a better room for Robert to wait in than the library; that forbidden room, which she had kept locked, was where our relationship took flight.

"Very well," Robert reluctantly agreed. "But I'll mark the time very carefully. If I'm not sent for in a timely manner, I'll seek out my aunt."

I smiled weakly as Robert kissed my forehead and entered the library, his footsteps echoing in the quiet room. Turning to Mistress Walden, I anxiously followed her, the hem of my kirtle swishing softly against the floor, to meet with Lady Bramwell.

"The house is like a tomb," I whispered. "Where is everyone?"

Mistress Walden took me by the arm and slowed our pace. "Lady Bramwell has sent many out on errands whilst others are busy with chores in the more remote parts of the house. Her daughters have remained at their uncle's house with their governess. Look to, Isabella, Lady Bramwell intends to reverse this recent turn of events as quickly as possible and, more importantly, as privately as possible."

"She'll not succeed," I said with absolute conviction.

Mistress Walden fell silent, shaking her head. "I pray for your sake that all goes well."

I followed her to Lady Bramwell's favorite sitting room and found her sitting on a high back chair with gold-laced spindles that resembled a queen's throne. She observed me with a grim expression. Her dark mood cast a shadow over the bright and airy room, with walls the color of a robin's egg and rosy-cheeked cherubs painted on the ceiling.

"Isabella, have you returned to collect your possessions?" Lady Bramwell asked. Her brisk and authoritarian tone was reminiscent of the first time I met her. Whatever strides I had made in forging warmer relations with her had cooled. My attentiveness to her daughter during her illness was forgotten. We had returned to our tenuous beginning, and I knew I would have to fight to save my contract.

"Nay, my lady. I hope to resume my duties until my contract terminates in five months." My voice, though calm, carried a firm resolve that I hoped would reach Lady Bramwell's ears.

She sported a vacuous expression as she picked up a book on the adjacent table with the clawed feet of a bull. I spied a green ribbon inching out of the middle of the book.

"You know this book, *The Education of a Christian Woman,* do you not?"

Heaven and Earth! She was going to read aloud a passage by that dour Spaniard, Juan Vives. I forced myself to smile, masking my disdain for Vives' thoughts.

" I know the book, my lady. My mother often refers to it for guidance on raising her daughters."

"Indeed. Perhaps she needs to read it to you again." She opened the book to where the ribbon marked the page. "There is one passage in particular that I would like to read to you, which I think is appropriate for the matter we are faced with." Lady Bramwell began to read.

"There are certain little fires within us which are, as it were, the seeds of virtue implanted by nature. If they were permitted to grow it would lead us to great virtue but depraved judgments and opinions can cause these little fires to glow and burst into flames."

She closed the book and placed her hand reverently on its cover as if it were the sacred Bible. "Do you see the connection between what I have just read and the situation we find ourselves in, Isabella? You are now a blazing fire in my house that I must extinguish. As a mother of two young daughters, I must employ women of virtuous behavior. You showed poor judgment in your hot pursuit of my nephew. Indeed, you spent the night with him and were discovered together by my brother this morning."

She desperately needed to be reminded of one fundamental truth. "Lady Bramwell, we are betrothed and fully intend to officially marry in the church."

A derisive laugh escaped her lips. "Your vows mean nothing, for it was made without witnesses or parental approval. No church will post banns of your forthcoming marriage whilst my brother is adamantly opposed to it. No priest will sanction your vows."

I faith! She may have been correct, but still, I stood firm. "We're committed to each other, my lady. God alone has heard our vows, and that's sufficient for us."

She rose agitatedly from her chair and walked to the window, gazing at the dry water fountain. Then she turned to hurl her next verbal attack accompanied by a sardonic smile. "Perhaps you were hoping to follow in the footsteps of Bess of Hardwick. Like you, she was of the middling classes and, through well-connected marriages, rose to the highest level of English nobility. But her marriages were sanctioned by the church whilst you have given yourself to whoredom."

I wanted to rush her and wring her delicate neck. "I did no such thing," my voice rising in protest.

She came within an inch of me. "Good God, girl," she hissed. "You knew how much I abhor behavior from any household member that incites gossip, thus casting doubt on my good reputation as the mistress of this house."

Returning to her chair, she sighed in disgust, "You should have tempered the heat you felt for my nephew by repeatedly cooling your thighs in cold water."

Like Robert's father, her mind was closed to reason. I racked my brain to find the right words that would convince her the love Robert and I had for each other was deep and binding, not sprung from the pleasures of the flesh.

Suddenly, Robert burst into the room exclaiming, "Prithee aunt, enough of this fray."

"I have not yet sent for you, Robert," she barked.

"But I'm here. There's no need to see us separately, for we are one."

With Robert by my side, my confidence to challenge Lady Bramwell's negative view of us regained strength. "My lady, it saddens me you believe our union was spurred only by sensual pleasure. I assure you it wasn't. Our mutual love of books and writing forged our relationship. Together, we seek to broaden our horizons."

Lady Bramwell sighed impatiently. "Isabella, what Juan Vives said thirty years ago is still true today, although you and I may wish it were not. A man requires many things to make his mark in the world: wisdom, eloquence, knowledge of political affairs, and talent. But this is not required of a woman. All that is required of us is to guard our virtue. Without it, we are nothing."

Robert, with a determined stride, approached his aunt. "I don't share that view. Richard Mulcaster says that God would not have given women the ability to learn if he had wished them to remain to small purpose."

Lady Bramwell raised her hand. "Enough. The views of Mister Mulcaster have yet to supplant prevalent thought. Now, let us turn our attention to the situation before us. You have played a pivotal role, Robert, in this folly. I fear your father is right. You are swayed too much by passion and pleasure. You would have done well to look to your older brother, for his behavior is worthy of imitation."

Robert's cheeks grew flushed. "It grieves me, aunt, that you firmly stand with my father."

"And why would I not? He has always proven to be a man of common sense and has always looked after the interests of his family. As a widow with young daughters, I have found his counsel invaluable. In time, you will see the worthiness of your father."

"I'll not argue with you about the failings of my father. Let's speak of another matter. As you no longer wish to have Isabella remain in your employ, will you, at the very least, provide her with a reference to seek similar employment elsewhere?"

"Would you have me recommend a young woman I now consider an eye-servant? Be sensible, boy!" Lady Bramwell's voice was sharp, her words cutting through the air.

Robert's silence was heavy with disappointment, his face a canvas of unspoken hurt at his aunt's resolute rejection.

"Then, there's nothing more for us to say. I bid God give you a good day, aunt."

"May God grant you the wisdom to rein in your passion and see reason. I pray you will return to your father, Robert, and abide by his will. As for you, Isabella, return home into the comfort of your family's bosom. I am sure they will forgive your lapse in judgment."

Robert took my arm, and we hastily left the room. As the door closed behind us, the sharp sound of the hulking wood punctuated our shattered hopes of a favorable outcome with his aunt. Lady Bramwell's words cut deep into my conscience. The day I left home, my father's words of counsel echoed in my head, 'One's good name is all one has, Isabella. Guard it well.'

"Oh, Robert, I have failed miserably in fulfilling my family's hope," I cried once we stepped outside. "My mother assured my younger sisters that they would one day follow in my footsteps and work in the home of a grand lady. It was my duty to abide by all your aunt's rules. My sisters' futures rested on my good name, which is now gone. I have let them all down." I buried my face in my hands and wept.

"Hush, Izzy, hush," he said softly, embracing me. "A pox on all who try to make us play the puritan. Don't worry. All will be made right."

I broke away from him. "How will it be made right? I refuse to go back home and tell my parents I have been dismissed with no reference and bearing the shameful appellation of an eye-servant." I grew desperate. "I'll go with you when you travel with Leicester's troupe of players, disguised as a boy if I must."

Robert remained calm. "That won't be necessary, for I have a plan."

15

Richard Jones was Heaven Sent

Once we settled into the carriage, I turned to Robert. "Tell me, what's your plan for us?"

"We'll go see Richard Jones. He'll help us," he replied confidently.

"Your printer friend, the one with the bookstall in St. Paul's churchyard?" I had a faint recollection of his visage but mostly remembered his unruly mass of red hair. "How can he help us?"

As Robert began to think aloud, his mood grew more optimistic. "Surely, he could make use of someone with your skills. You can assist him in keeping inventory of his books. In exchange, he can offer you a room and meals whilst I tour with Dudley's troupe of players."

It was a blissful prospect, but it seemed too good to be true. "I'm not so sure, Robert, about your plan. It's only possible for women to assist in a business like a print shop if they are the daughter or wife of the owner. Well, I'm not kin to Richard Jones."

"Izzy," Robert said impatiently. "Don't doubt my plan. He has no children, nor does his wife assist him in his shop. Not because he wouldn't allow it but because she doesn't wish to. He'll be receptive to the idea. I'm certain of it. He doesn't allow his thinking to be mired in old world views."

I relented, understanding that it was our best — really our only option. "Well, then, let's make haste to see him."

Robert touched my lap with a reassuring pat. "Don't worry. All will be well."

Fortunately, it was a short ride from the Bramwell House to Ludgate and, from there, a short walk to the neighborhood of St. Paul's Church. When we disembarked from the coach, we hurried to Paternoster Row, where printing shops abounded. At the sign of the raven, we stepped into Richard's shop. It was a spacious room that easily accommodated two large presses, rows of tables with type cases, and sticks of letters on flat trays. As it was the end of the workday, just a few workmen remained, cleaning their stations and preparing their tools for the next day. Our timing was perfect, for Richard could readily attend to us. He greeted Robert with a warm embrace.

"Have you come to peddle another romance ballad for me to sell, Robert?" He then shifted his attention to me. "I remember this pretty face. Your lady friend, Isabella, is she not?"

"I'm flattered you remember my name, Richard," I said, taking note of the deep-set eyes in his weathered fisherman face. But oh, how his eyes sparkled with the zest of life.

"Faith, I remember. 'Tis not every day that a student from Gray's Inn stops by my bookstall to buy a book by Ovid for a pretty young maid."

"She's now my betrothed, Richard," Robert quickly added.

Richard arched his brow, "Is she now?" He quickly offered his heartfelt congratulations, flashing his charming, crooked smile. "I wish your union prosperity and happiness. Isabella, I have known Robert for quite some time and have seen him in the company of many ladies," he said with a wink to Robert. "But when I saw you, I thought there was a clever and pretty girl who would be a good match for my friend. And Jove! I was right. For here, you both are before me, bound by love." His joyous laughter filled the room, a testament to the warmth of their friendship.

Richard's amiable manner lifted my somber mood inflicted by our failed meeting with Lady Bramwell. It starkly contrasted the cold reception we received earlier today in the Bramwell House.

Robert leaned into Richard and said in a low voice, "May we speak in private?"

"Aye, of course. Let's proceed into my office."

As we walked past the presses, Richard stopped to give instructions to a young man about Robert's age. "Make sure you hold the plate down long enough to get a good ink impression on the paper, John."

The young man obliged with a knowing nod and skillfully moved the press's heavy handle. His arm muscles contracted with every pull and push of the handle. I averted my eyes to the floor when he smiled at me and took hold of Robert's hand as we mounted the few steps into Richard's office.

Robert refused to sit but paced about the small office, pleading our cause.

"Here's the crux of the dilemma we find ourselves in, Richard. Isabella has lost her job with my aunt because of our involvement and subsequent betrothal. My aunt disapproves of our match, as does my father. Isabella has been dismissed and has nowhere to live whilst I tour the north with Robert Dudley's troupe of players for a month."

The mention of Robert Dudley's name instantly piqued Richard's interest. "Robert Dudley – the Earl of Leicester's acting troupe, you say? In what capacity?"

"As a musician providing entertainment during the interludes. I'll also be performing my ballads," Robert said proudly. "Hence, whilst I'm gone, I need a safe place for Isabella to stay."

There was a brief pause as Richard sat observing me. "And you thought to leave her with me?"

"That was my thinking," Robert said, sitting beside me.

Richard rested his chin on his folded hands, mulling Robert's request. Despite the uncomfortable silence, I managed to maintain a serene expression, my hands bound up tightly within the folds of my cloak.

Robert continued with his appeal. "She would be of enormous help, assisting your wife with housewifery tasks, and she could prove valuable to you."

"To me?" he asked, bemused.

"Aye, I could assist with any task that demands reading or writing," I suggested.

Robert took hold of my hand. "A truer word was never spoken. She can read as well as any young man starting his first year in college. I recently reviewed a poem she wrote, which I thought showed great promise."

Richard turned his head askance in my direction; his eyes gleamed with interest.

Robert pressed on. "Didn't you just lease the building adjacent to this one to use as a warehouse for your books?"

"Aye. That's correct," Richard said and leaned back in his chair.

"Well then, don't you see how valuable Isabella will be to you? She can keep an inventory of all your book titles. And being trained in my aunt's house will be of assistance to your wife."

Richard laughed and raised his hands to silence Robert. "Say no more. I don't doubt your word about Isabella. We have known each other for three years, and you have always proven true to your word."

"How many of my ballads have I given you thus far to sell in three years? Ten?" Robert enthused.

"Five, Robert. I am waiting for more," he scolded affectionately. He tapped his quill on the table and predicted in a tone of absolute certainty. "I wager my wife will be most obliging in allowing Isabella to stay with us whilst you are gone, especially with her experience working in your aunt's house. And I may be in luck too, for I expect to receive a large shipment of books that must be inventoried."

Now, Robert leaped forward with a wide grin, his arms outstretched to pull Richard into a warm embrace. "A thousand thanks. I am indebted to you." Robert turned to me, his arm slung around Richard's shoulder. "Didn't I tell you, Isabella, this man is forward-thinking?"

"Indeed, we are most fortunate to have you as our friend, Richard."

"No doubt your knowledge of reading and writing will prove useful to me, Isabella, but tell me, do you have much strength in your arms?" Richard asked as he led the way out of his office back to the workroom.

Perplexed by his meaning, I repeated his question. "Strength in my arms, you say?"

"Aye," he said, pointing to the young man who had smiled at me earlier. He didn't look at me this time, for he was focused on removing a sheet under the press plate.

"He jests, Izzy," Robert said. And then he added his own. "Don't consider putting her to work the press. I don't wish to return to an Amazon bride."

I playfully flexed what little muscle I had in my arms. "I think I could use more brawn."

Robert pulled me into him. "Possibly, but your soft touch is more to my liking."

Richard gathered his belongings. "John," he said to the young man working the press, "you'll close the shop tonight."

"Aye. God grant you a good evening, Master Jones."

"And to you as well, John." Richard turned to us and said with a cheerful smile, "Come now, you two, we will tell my wife our news. I know she'll take delight in attending to your hungry stomachs."

Once outside, Robert made a stunning request. "I must ask yet another favor of you, Richard."

Richard shook his fists in mock irritation. "How now, Robert, another favor? You'll wear my patience. Well — out with it then."

Robert's smile alerted me that Richard was merely jesting. He placed his hand on Richard's shoulder. "Will you and your lovely wife, Maria, bear witness as Isabella and I pledge our troth to each other? The first time, it was in the presence of God, but that meant little to my father and aunt."

Robert's earnest wish to pledge our troths again filled my heart with profound tenderness.

Richard beamed, "There's no other couple I would be prouder to be a witness for," he said, casting a warm gaze upon the two of us. "Now, to my wife. We have much to tell her."

When first told, Maria, although willing to host a betrothal ceremony in her home, expressed dismay at being ill-prepared. "Go to! So little time," she scolded both Robert and Richard. "I must lay out my best linen and dishes for the table. You don't leave me much time to prepare a special meal for the occasion."

"Forgive me, Maria," Robert said, his voice filled with regret. "But I leave the day after tomorrow. And it would greatly comfort me to leave Isabella blissfully content that we have repeated our vows with good friends as our witnesses."

"Aye, we can't ask for more than a simple celebration," I added. "More importantly, as Robert said, we will say our vows in the company of dear friends, who proved so generous in helping us."

She threw up her hands in resignation. "Very well. We must be satisfied with what I can do and be merry."

Robert kissed Maria's rosy cheek, and I quickly followed.

I was relieved that the day's tumultuous events had a peaceful outcome. The vows we exchanged in Robert's room at Gray's Inn were not mere words but a sacred promise sanctioned by God alone. I believe His Providence led Robert to seek Richard's help, a testament to His understanding of the true nature of love, far surpassing that of Robert's father and aunt.

Richard and Maria will now provide the missing piece that marred our first betrothal vows. Serving as witnesses, they would attest that our intention to marry was sincere, making it acceptable for Robert and me to live together as though we were man and wife.

CRSO

The day after we settled in at Richard's house, we exchanged betrothal vows again. At the hour of six, we all gathered in the parlor, a comfortable room whose canary-colored yellow walls evoked the sun's cheerful warmth of springtime. Shadows resembling long-stemmed flowers from the flickering flames of the candles danced on the walls. Despite wearing the same blue kirtle I wore when I sought Robert at Gray's Inn, I felt like a queen dressed in the most splendid finery, for I basked in the heartfelt love of all present. Maria placed a tiny wooden box on the table and bade me open it.

I gasped. Inside was a pair of shiny brass rings.

"It wouldn't be a proper betrothal ceremony without rings, would it?" said Maria.

Robert picked up the rings. "I promise they will be returned when I purchase gold rings for the church ceremony."

She waved her hand and said, "Nonsense. You'll keep them as a remembrance of this day. And let's not forget the breaking of silver," she added, retrieving a silver shilling from the pot in the fireplace with a spoon and placing it on the stone hearth. "I believe it's hot enough now to cut into two halves."

With her benevolent heart, dear Maria had thought of everything, and I felt an instant kinship with her.

"We have all the customs in place now," Richard said, wrapping his arms around his wife's shoulders and kissing her forehead

With one swift blow from his rapier, Robert quickly divided the silver coin into two pieces, one half for me and the other half for him, signifying that we would be joined as one.

"Shall we?" Robert said, holding out his hand for me to take it.

Looking into Robert's dark, soulful eyes, their depth accentuated by the flickering candlelight, I anxiously awaited his solemn pledge.

"Isabella, I take you for my only betrothed wife and therefore give you my troth that you will one day be my wedded wife. In the name of the Father, the Son, and the Holy Ghost. So be it," he vowed, guiding the ring on my finger.

I stared lovingly at the simple brass ring on my finger, a symbol of our commitment and repeated the same vow.

"Robert, I take you for my only betrothed husband and therefore give you my troth that you will one day be my wedded husband. In the name of the Father, the Son, and the Holy Ghost—"

Robert mouthed the final words with me, "So be it," which nearly made me laugh. I squeezed his hand and whispered, "Waggish schoolboy," before guiding the ring on his finger.

Richard gave each of us a piece of the cut silver coin and said, "Now you are joined as one, Amen."

We hugged each other, and Maria and I shed a few tears.

"Into the dining room, now," Richard cheerfully commanded. "We shall eat, drink, and be merry before retreating to our beds."

I was eager to sample Maria's fine cooking. Earlier in the day, I enjoyed smelling the aroma of her roasting and baking. I wasn't disappointed with the array of dishes waiting to be eaten. On her white linen cloth were assorted stewed meats, a lamb and fennel pie, freshly baked bread, and apple tart. She bade her helpers prepare scraped cheese with bits of sage and sugar. I wonder if she knew it was Robert's and my favorite cheese.

"What a delicious small feast you have prepared, Maria, and on such short notice, too," I said, putting my arms around her. "I heartily thank you."

"As do I," Robert beamed.

"With help from my kitchen maids, I hastily put together this celebratory supper. And without further delay, let's sit and enjoy. For I must say, everything looks delicious."

"Indeed," Richard said and filled our glasses with canary wine. We gathered 'round the table and helped ourselves to the good food before us.

"Now, Richard," Maria said, "what advice should we give these two who intend to marry soon?"

He took a sip of his wine and pondered the question. Looking directly at Robert and me, he said, "Look to each other for comfort and companionship in your union."

Maria nodded. "Aye, that's sound advice. And remember

that charity is a joint duty between husband and wife."

"I can attest to that," I said as I thought about my mother and father. "My father considers my mother wise, often seeks her counsel, and is much comforted afterward. When my mother finishes her housewifery tasks and has put my sisters and brother to bed, she relishes time spent in my father's company. I have often heard them laughing softly together. It never fails to bring a smile to my face."

"And I'm sure they perform charitable deeds together, too?" said Maria.

"Indeed, just this past Christmastide, they packed the cart with food from our Christmas dinner and delivered it to those in need in our parish."

Robert silently ate his meal, sparing a few smiles as I spoke of my mother and father. He must have been chagrined at having nothing relevant to say about his parents. I reached for his hand and gave it a gentle squeeze. He, in turn, bestowed an affectionate kiss on my cheek.

After dinner, when Robert and I took our leave of Richard and Maria, I began writing a letter to Mistress Walden, informing her that Robert and I had exchanged vows a second time in the presence of witnesses.

As he lay in bed, Robert cried, "Fie, Izzy! Why is it taking you so long to write a simple note to my cousin.".

"Be patient, my love. I'm nearly finished."

I didn't tell Robert I was writing the words with swirls and flourishes to resemble the style of writing seen in romantic ballads. The news of our second betrothal vows deserved to be encased in romantic lettering, but getting the lettering right took time.

"My loins ache for your touch," Robert implored.

"Just a little more time, and I will be done."

"What do you hope will happen when my cousin reads your note?" he sighed with impatience.

I was amazed that he couldn't see the significance of my efforts. I turned 'round to face him. "I believe Mistress Walden will tell your aunt what transpired here tonight, and she, in turn, will pass the news on to your father. And then hopefully, they will take our love seriously and begin to support us, however begrudgingly."

"We shall see," Robert muttered, turning on his side.

When I finished, I proudly showed him my beautiful handwritten letter. "Doesn't it have the mark of a letter bearing a grand announcement?"

Glancing at it, he said, "Aye, very nice. Before I leave, I'll tell Richard to have one of his apprentices dispatch it to my aunt's house." He pounded the bed with his fist. "Now, Izzy, to bed."

I smiled coyly and removed my shift. "I come most ardently, my love. For every inch of me yearns for your touch."

Robert pulled back the blanket on my side of the bed, "Come and let's satisfy our appetites till I take my leave tomorrow."

16

Bad and Good Tidings

A week had passed since Robert's departure, and I was still adjusting to his absence when I received a pleasant surprise. I had just started polishing pewter dishes, beakers, and pear-shaped flagons when Maria entered the kitchen in a flurry, waving a letter. I carefully tore its triangular blue seal and eagerly began reading its contents. Glancing over my shoulder, Maria said in admiration, "'Tis the handwriting of a well-bred lady, for the lettering is of the Italian style."

"'Tis from a well-bred lady indeed, none other than Robert's cousin, Mistress Walden." The first line of the second paragraph was particularly striking. "Marry! She's to be wed."

"That's good tidings indeed," Maria said.

"She's to marry the gentleman who accompanied her to Lady Bramwell's Twelfth Night celebration." I paused my reading and turned to Maria. "Faith, I remember him well, particularly the perfumed leather gloves dangling from his belt."

"Perfumed gloves, you say? He's a gallant, for sure."

"And such a pleasant one, too, kind and considerate, according to Mistress Walden. She wouldn't settle for someone with lesser qualities." I returned to the letter and grew enthused by her closing lines. "She says that she'll be staying at the London home of her future sister-in-law for the next few days and suggests I visit her there."

Maria clasped her hands. "My dear, you must go. Perhaps Mistress Walden has important news concerning Lady Bramwell that she wishes to tell you in person. Hopefully, a change of feelings about your betrothal to Robert."

"That's the outcome I prayed for when I sent Mistress Walden my letter. I could see her this Sunday?"

"That's a fine day for a visit," Maria concurred, pushing the cleaning cloth aside. "You'll finish your polishing after you respond to Mistress Walden. We'll see that Richard dispatches your letter this very day, and we shall tell the lad to wait for Mistress Walden's response. Go now, for Sunday is just four days away."

I dashed to my room and wrote Mistress Walden a short note accepting her invitation to visit.

My good Mistress Walden,
I send you my very hearty regards. 'Tis with great joy that I accept your invitation to visit you whilst you stay at the home of your future sister-in-law. I pray this Sunday is a favorable day for us to meet. The lad who delivered this letter to you will await your answer. I commit you to God's good protection. From Paternoster Row, the nineteenth of March 1568. Isabella.

∞

When Sunday arrived, I found myself at the exquisite home of Mistress Walden's future sister-in-law, who was conveniently away; very like that's why she readily accepted Sunday as our day to meet. Mistress Walden greeted me with her radiant smile, which set her face aglow with the look of a luminous bride-to-be. It was a welcomed change to the grim countenance she bore when I saw her last at the Bramwell House with Robert.

She led me up a central staircase as splendid as the one in Lady Bramwell's house and into an ornate private sitting room where she bade me sit on a long bench with a scallop-shaped back made comfortable by thick, crimson-colored cushions.

I initiated our eagerly anticipated conversation with the announcement of her impending nuptials. "Mistress Walden, I was filled with delight to learn of your union with that distinguished gentleman who graced your side at the Twelfth

Night revelry. Pray, when is the joyous occasion?"

Beaming, she spoke dreamily of that day to come. "On the fifteenth of May, Lord Anthony Chilton and I will be married. The ceremony will be in a lovely stone church on his father's estate in Yorkshire. After we are married, we will reside there as well."

Like Lady Bramwell, Mistress Walden was marrying into the ranks of the aristocracy and would live in a house grander than her cousin. She would soon acquire the title of countess, a higher status than baroness.

"I visited Yorkshire once in springtime with my mother. The valleys will be dotted with purple harebells, and the streams that cut across the rolling hills will glisten in the afternoon sun. What a beautiful setting to marry and reside in. No more London living for you." I laughed.

She waved her hand in mock farewell, "I happily say adieu to treading London's narrow cobblestone and muddy streets after the rains. Nor will I miss the foul odors whenever I had to walk by pissing alley lanes."

"Indeed, those are loathsome reasons against living in London. Still, I fear I would miss it terribly if I were to return home to Cheshire."

She touched my arm. "Of course, you would. You are a lively girl, and London best serves your literary interests. Your current accommodation in Paternoster Row suits you, for the area is home to many booksellers and printers."

I nodded happily. "Master Jones is a remarkable master tradesman. He runs two businesses, one for printing and the other for selling books. Although Robert and I are comfortable there, Robert is keen for us to find new accommodations when he returns from his tour."

She rose to ring a bell, and a pleased smile crossed her lips when a young maidservant, not much older than my sister, Mary, entered the room carrying a tray of sweet buns and mead, my favorite honey wine. She awkwardly set the tray down on the adjoining table where we sat and, with an uncertain glance at Mistress Walden, waited to be dismissed.

Mistress Walden gave an encouraging nod, eliciting the maidservant's grateful smile as she left the room. Unlike Lady Bramwell, she would prove a mild-mannered and benevolent mistress. I prayed my sisters would one day work for such a lady.

"And when does my wandering balladeer cousin return to you?" Mistress Walden said as she offered me a sweet bun with a hint of a sardonic smile.

"In three weeks."

"It appears Robert is resolute in giving up his law studies. Still, he should consider a possible return to the law since he's now responsible for you. He could always secure a law clerk position, his schooling thus far qualifies him for that."

My spine tingled, for I sensed the conversation might veer toward a topic that could lead to an altercation. I rose to examine a porcelain jar decorated with pictures of carp resting on a nearby table. "The potter who made this has extraordinary skill. Such rich colors of reds, yellows, and greens, the likes I've not seen. Very pleasing to the eye."

"Aye, 'tis a style uncommon for English potters," she noted, her voice carrying a hint of tension as she quickly returned to Robert and the law. "As I was saying about Robert, he —"

"Robert has no stomach for the law," I interrupted with a forced smile. "He no longer wishes to fulfill his father's dream but his own. The opportunity to perform with Lord Leicester's troupe of players was fortuitous. We hope the troupe will perform for the queen at her next Twelfth Night celebration at White Hall, where she will hear Robert perform his ballads."

I returned to sit beside her. "You did tell Lady Bramwell that we plighted our troths again with witnesses. Robert is resolute for her and his father to take our love seriously."

She placed her hands atop mine. "Alas, your news has not softened Lady Bramwell's nor his father's stance. It only helped to reinforce his father's conviction that Robert too readily succumbs to his passions."

I gently pulled my hands out from under hers. "'Tis indeed unfortunate that he has such a low opinion of his son."

Mistress Walden leaned into the lush cushions of the bench. "You can hardly blame his aunt and father for their thinking. It has been Robert's habit to discard his passions in the face of adversity and return to the comfort of his father's home." She observed me, and her tone became complimentary. "I must say that Robert has never so boldly defied his father. He's quite determined to plight his troth to a girl of his choosing." She slowly nodded, "Aye, I believe Robert loves you."

"Which means Robert will stay the course," I asserted.

She moved closer to me. "Dear Isabella, I hope with all my heart that Robert's love for you and his newfound interest in music will remain steadfast." She brushed aside a strand of hair that fell across my eyebrow. "Perhaps 'tis you alone who truly knows Robert better than I or his family."

Despite her meager words of encouragement, I knew she stood with Lady Bramwell and Robert's father. She was their blood kin, after all. I had no wish to stay longer. "I thank you for your invitation to come and visit you today. And now, I fear, 'tis time to bid you goodbye."

Mistress Walden smiled as she rose and saw me to the door. "I hope we see each other again."

"Aye. I hope so," I responded cheerfully but doubted we would. How could I see her again when she harbored such a poor opinion about Robert? The only truth was when she said, 'I believe Robert loves you.' But then spoiled it by expressing doubt—'I hope his love for you remains steadfast.' All in Robert's family who oppose us can hang. In due time, they will see their folly in judging us harshly.

About a fortnight after my disappointing visit with Mistress Walden, I was alone in the kitchen, kneading dough for meat pies. Maria had left to call upon her midwife friend for advice on a womanly problem and instructed me not to tell Richard of her whereabouts. Luckily, he didn't inquire about her when he entered the kitchen.

"Isabella, how would you like a reprieve from your domestic chores starting tomorrow?"

I stopped my kneading and waited with anticipation for him to continue.

"I just received a large shipment of books that must be inventoried. Are you much interested in performing that task?" he asked with a knowing smile.

I felt as if, at any moment, happy tears would stream down my face. "Richard, I can think of nothing that would give me greater pleasure."

He clapped his hands as if he had closed an important deal. "Very well. Be prepared to spend tomorrow and perhaps the next few days in my book's storage room. And mind you, Isabella, the work requires hours of meticulously recording book entries into the ledger."

"I have no fear of that, Richard. You'll see. I'll do a fine job for you."

After he left whistling a merry tune, I returned to my kneading, my hands moved with a renewed energy. The anticipation of the task that awaited me the next day filled me with a sense of contentment and purpose. When the dough was ready, I stuffed it with sweet pork whilst humming the ballad Robert sang for me at Bell Savage Inn.

When Maria returned, much to her surprise, she stared at twenty-five tiny meat pies ready to be taken to the communal ovens. "I' faith, Isabella, have you received word that Robert is returning this very day? I can think of no other news that would have made you perform your chores with such vigor." She examined the pies with admiration. "You have crimped the crests and pricked the tops to perfection."

"I wish Robert were returning, Maria, but the reason for my high spirits comes close to that happy prospect. Starting tomorrow, I shall work in Richard's bookroom, recording book titles in his ledger."

She laughed. "Is that it? You're a funny one to be so taken with books. When I was your age, I was content with my needlework, learning about music, and mastering the latest country dances."

I shrugged. "Pish - none of that suits me. And happily,

Robert fully accepts that. Do you not take great pleasure in reading, Maria?"

"Upon occasion, I do enjoy reading some of the romances Richard brings home."

"How fortunate you are to be married to someone in the book business who can provide you with stories of romance whenever you wish, and that Richard rejects the idea that such stories are unsuitable for women."

"Fortunate I am, but for a more important reason. We've been married for ten years now, and God has not blessed us with a child. You do know, Isabella, for many men, that would be grounds for a dissolution of marriage, but not so for my Richard."

"Are you still trying for a baby, Maria?"

"We are, and despite being thirty-five, God willing, I will conceive."

I offered an encouraging smile. "I can't believe that God, in all his wisdom, would deny such good people as you and Richard a baby. I'm sure it will happen – and soon."

She placed her hands in a prayer position before lifting the tray of meat pies. "Enough of this talk. Accompany me to the oven now."

I followed her, thinking how fortunate I was to stay with her whilst Robert was touring. It was like being in my mother's loving company, which gave me the patience to wait for his safe return.

17

A New Kind of Education

I arrived in earnest at Richard's bookroom, adjacent to his print shop, to begin the first assignment I've had not related to housewifery. My task for the morning was to unpack books from five crates and sort them into piles by subject. When I scooped the last armful of books and pamphlets from the first crate, one slipped from my grasp and, by chance, fell face-up to the title page. I gazed upon its extraordinary picture, the likes of which I had never seen. It showed a man down on his knees with a horse's bit in his mouth. A woman was sitting on his back, with a whip held high, as if riding him like a horse. I read the title aloud with wonder, *"The Pride and Abuse of Women."* What a loathsome title. I couldn't imagine my father uttering proud and abusive to describe my mother, nor Robert using those words for me.

Richard strode into the room as I was about to explore more of the book's contents. "How goes it, Isabella?" he asked, full of good mirth.

"All's well. Unpacking these crates of books is a thousand times more pleasant than housewifery chores."

"I knew you'd find the work agreeable," he said, glancing at the books spread out on the table."

"Aye, very agreeable. And full of new learning about the kinds of books people here in London read." I held up the page of the book with the loathsome picture. "For instance, never have I seen a woman depicted like this in a book, and with such a derisive title too."

"Doesn't it please you, Isabella, to see a woman exerting

151

control over a man," Richard teased.

"Nay. It doesn't please me to see someone humiliating another, regardless of the sex."

"I agree with your sentiment, but I'll tell you something that might surprise you," he said, pointing to the book in my hand. "Books like this attract multitudes of readers and turn a good profit."

I stared at him, my mouth slightly agape. "You mean books with unflattering content about women, like this one, appeal to your readers?"

He pulled a stool out from under the table to sit. "That book and others like it all contribute to the *querelle des femmes* literature.

I instantly recalled that French phrase uttered by Robert when we first met. "You mean *the woman question*."

With an approving nod, he said, "Writers and readers enjoy answering the central question - what is a woman's essential nature?"

"Do women possess Mary's virtues or Eve's vices?" I added, echoing Robert's words.

"Has Robert never mentioned the popularity of *the woman question* with students at Gray's Inn? 'Tis a lively topic for informal debates, and many students frequent my bookstalls looking for materials. That's how I met Robert three years ago."

"His father's affinity for the topic has turned him against it. He considers it a silly and worthless diversion."

Richard laughed. "Does he now? Well, he may be correct, but the topic sells well, and 'tis my business to give the public what it wants to read."

I began to remove books from the second crate. "Still, 'tis disheartening those books disparaging women appeal to your many readers. Are there none that praise us in *the woman question*?"

"Take heart, Isabella. Some authors argue that whilst women are not superior to men, they are at least worthy of praise."

"I'd like to read those books."

"I can easily arrange that." He stood and pushed the stool back under the table. "I'll take my leave of you now, for you seem to be getting on well here by yourself."

It didn't bother me to spend the day with no one else in the room to keep me company except for my thoughts. With Richard gone, I turned my attention to the new pile of books I had placed on the table. As I sorted them, I hoped to find a book that lauded women. Pish! I glared at many more titles similar to the first: *The Praise and Dispraise of Women, The Deceit of Women to the Instruction and Example of all Men, The Arraignment of Lewd, Idle, Forward, and Inconstant Women.* As I read each title aloud with disdain, I tossed them unto the pile designated, *the woman question.* God's Blood, I fumed as I read a few selected pages from the last title. What nonsense - it says women are vain and proud, gossip mongers, and, worst of all, possess insatiable carnal appetites that may lead to infidelity once married.

I pushed the pile away and lunged my hand into the third crate of books, bringing forth customary titles on cookery, falconry, historical tales, herbalism, needlework, and LO — a gem with the most pleasing title, *Defense of Women* by Edward More. Surely, this book must be different from the others. And to my blissful satisfaction, I was proven right! Mister More asserts that women do, in fact, possess a strong, virtuous character. He even advocates the establishment of special schools for women, arguing that women shouldn't be disparaged, for they are one-half of all mankind. Bravo, Mister More. I couldn't agree more with your wise sentiment. Hence, I placed his book above all the others concerning *the woman question.*

By day's end, I had sorted and recorded the titles from all five crates. Richard entered the room with a pamphlet tucked under his arm, whistling the popular tune, *Greensleeves.*

"All work completed, Isabella?"

I sat upright in the chair. "All books have been sorted and recorded."

"Good." He placed the pamphlet on the table before me. "I believe this will be of interest to you."

I read the title aloud, "*A letter sent by Maids of London to the Virtuous Matrons and Mistresses of the Same, in Defense of their Lawful Liberty. Answering the Merry Meeting by us,* Rose, Jane, Rachell, Sara, Philumias, and Dorothie." The names of the authors, women who dared to speak out, stared back at me. "The authors are women!" I exclaimed, my voice filled with a mix of surprise and admiration.

"Let me provide the context for the publication of this pamphlet," he explained. "A few months ago, a book appeared in print titled *The Merry Meeting of Maids*. In it, maidservants were criticized for their laziness and weak morals. The author, Edward Hack, describes how the maidservants he observed in and about London shirk their duties whilst out on errands, preferring to gossip and draw the attention of men. He goes as far as to say that he has seen this despicable behavior in church. This pamphlet serves as the maidservants' defense."

I placed my hand on the pamphlet with a sense of reverence. "Thus, this is a rare example of a defense of women by women."

Sitting at the opposite end of the table, he reviewed the titles I recorded in his ledger. "I caution you not to get too carried away, for many believe it wasn't written by the maidservants but by a man who took pity on how badly Hack disparaged them."

"And why is it so incredulous women wrote it?" I objected.

"Well, for one thing, naysayers say the maidservants possess too much knowledge of business law. But there's a contrary belief that a wealthy mistress who took pity on the beleaguered maidservants wrote it in their defense."

"Took pity, you say? More like she saw it as an attack on all women and was thus moved to write a defensive retort," I countered.

"Or maybe it was written by a man, an enlightened gentleman who came to the young women's defense," he said with a smile, returning his attention to the ledger.

Before I came across Edward More's book, I wouldn't have believed that was possible. Still, I cherished the belief that the maidservants were the authors.

"Don't concern yourself too much with who the true authors are. As long as the pamphlet remains in print, the names of the maidservants will forever stand as the authors. And the public will continue to pay a penny to read it."

I searched for a penny in my pouch and placed it on the table. "Here's a penny for my copy. One day, you may collect pennies from readers who want to read what I have to say in defense of my sex."

He didn't take my penny but, with an arched brow, asked, "I didn't know you aspire to be a printed author on *the woman question*?"

There was a look of solemn contemplation resting on his face. I feared I overstepped the bounds of proper female decorum in my ease with him. It wasn't appropriate that I, a woman, could conceive to share my writing in defense of my sex with the public – with my name boldly visible for everyone to see. Even Queen Elizabeth, in her exalted position, remains humble with all her subjects. She once said, 'I am, but a simple woman who only by birthright and by God's command to rule in a man's place can speak out for all to hear.' I had no such privilege to raise my voice for all of London to hear my thoughts on *the woman question*. Hence, I rephrased my comment with more humility.

"I wouldn't mind if you printed something I wrote concerning *the woman question,* but only if you deemed it worthy and could present it in a way that safeguarded my modesty and didn't cause offense to men."

Curiously, he said, "Let's see what kind of writer you can be. I propose a challenge. You compose your own letter rejecting Hack's attack on maidservants." He quickly retrieved a book from a low bookcase near the door. "Here is Hack's book. Read it, and then show me how adroitly you can wield your pen to defend your fellow maidservants."

I didn't hesitate to accept his challenge, even though I had never done that kind of writing before, having only tried to write verses about friendship and the beauty of nature. Indeed, I was flattered that he thought me capable. "Richard, I believe you have just initiated me into the debate of *the woman question*," I said.

Bringing his hands together, he chaffed, "Pray, I hope Robert forgives me."

I laughed. "Leave Robert to me."

಩ಠ

Alone in my bedchamber, I wished Robert was there to offer support. Although he disdained *the woman question*, I'm sure he would have indulged me on crafting a rebuttal to Edward Hack. I had pored over Hack's book, noting his criticism that I found unjust. Yet, how to shape my response eluded me. The clock struck ten, and I grew restless as the blank page mocked me. Richard's writing challenge should take little effort. After all, I was a former maidservant and, thus, qualified to counter Hack's accusations that London's maidservants were lazy, and possessed loose morals.

I recalled those lively maidservants I met the day I sought directions to Gray's Inn. I remembered their high-spirited remarks about their work and their mistresses. Like them, I decided to be forthright and inject humor into my response. Hence, negations of Hack's criticism tumbled out of my mind at lightning speed, spilling onto the page, and my letter took shape.

As the clock neared midnight, my three-page letter was finally complete. I sought the solace of my bed, my weary back yearning for rest after a day spent mostly in a chair. As sleep claimed my tired eyes, a smile played on my lips at the thought of Robert and his reaction to my efforts.

The following morning, I ascended the steps to Richard's office in the print shop at a quickened pace, brimming with anticipation of sharing my letter—my rebuttal—with him.

I found Richard sitting at his desk, thumbing through a pile of paperwork. He quickly diverted his attention to me. "Isabella, 'tis you! Good morrow."

"Good morrow, Richard." I smiled and anxiously placed my letter before him.

"What's this?" He glanced at it. "Your letter to Edward Hack? So soon? Not even Robert is as quick getting his ballads to me for printing."

"I spent the evening rereading Hack's book and then composing my arguments till midnight."

"Well then, let's see what you have done."

He gestured for me to sit opposite him. I obliged and frantically searched his office for something to focus on—anything to divert my gaze from Richard's critical reading. My eyes settled on an hourglass. With its flow of blue sand slowly funneling to the bottom, a sense of calm embraced me.

Richard's sudden burst of laughter pierced the silence, startling me. "You compare Hack to old King Henry's fool, Will Somers—oh, that's good." And then he proceeded to read my words aloud gleefully: "*Master Hack is a mere fool, another Will Somers, who engages in nothing more than babbling on about himself, wherein he seems to delight to hear himself talk.*"

The room fell silent again as he continued reading, marked by enthusiastic nods, a raised eyebrow here and there, and a quick series of chuckles. I watched his eyes dart across the page, reading with sharp precision like a hawk stalking its prey. Successful years in the book trade have taught him to recognize if a writer was worthy of his attention instantly. I prayed that he found evidence of it in my writing. He leaned forward in his chair and, to my delight, read my words aloud again: "*He is a mad merry man to dwell on this merry meeting of maids. He madly measures his word in merry meter.*"

"There's a clever girl, Isabella," he winked. "You steal his technique of alliteration to mock him. And I must say, your ear for rhyme is quite good."

Aye, I thought. That's precisely what Robert had told me. He silently read the last page, his gaze resting on my closing paragraph, wherein I addressed Hack's claim to know what young maidservants think whilst in church. I began to mouth the words, for they were firmly committed to my memory: *Were he as cunning as the Devil? He could not know since God alone has that privilege, above all others, to know the thoughts of men, women, children, and every living creature. Herein, it is more likely that he lies.*

Upon reading my final words, he uttered with conviction, "I see promise in your writing. Your letter is filled with harsh truths and expressed with much wit. Robert was right. You are very bright and have the makings of a good writer."

I smiled broadly. "Your words mean more to me than you can imagine."

With a mischievous grin, he said, "I bet you could do just as well defending your sex from the male detractors who warn men to woo women with caution, for as they say, women are inconstant in love."

Heavens above — that thought never entered my mind. But the idea intrigued me.

Although my experience as a maidservant equipped me with sufficient knowledge to craft a defense against Hack's unfair accusations, defending my sex on the topic of love was something else entirely.

"Perhaps, if I become more familiar with what men say about it, I'd feel better prepared to join in the debate," I said.

He gave a supportive nod. "I will recommend a few books to get you started."

John, Richard's pressman, appeared at the door and signaled for him to leave his office.

"Coming, John," he said. "And now, Isabella, off to work you go. There are more crates of books that need sorting and categorizing. I must attend to an issue with the new press brought into the shop yesterday."

I paused in the doorway, my thoughts racing with the prospects of Richard's idea. "Do you really believe a defense of women in love written by a woman would sell?"

"Reading a perspective on love penned by a woman would be new and generate much interest if presented correctly."

I couldn't wait for Robert's return. What would he say about my being drawn into *the woman question*? Would he become riled by Richard's idea? I hoped he would reconsider his rigid stance against it to support me.

In the remaining weeks before Robert's return, I read everything Richard recommended on the perils of men surrendering their hearts too quickly to women. *With painted mocks and inward hidden hooks, women trap you by trust,* was the common assumption. In short, women embody the duplicitous Eve. But the same can be said of men. Let's consider the women in *Heroides* who fell in love with those much-lauded Greek and Roman heroes. These men ensnared them into webs of deception for their own gains. If the besotted women were given similar advice as men - *to try before you trust*, their sorrowful ends could have been averted.

If Oenone had waited until she affirmed Paris's true character, she wouldn't have been so quickly beguiled by his sweet words. And what of Phyllis and Demophon - he deceitfully made extravagant promises to stay loyal to her but didn't. Would not the simple trusting Phyllis have been spared heartbreak if she had waited longer to try his true character before trusting him? They and many others would have been spared the heartache of their lovers' falsehoods.

For centuries, men have bestowed perpetual fame on the deeds of Greek and Roman heroes, all achieved at the expense of their wooing and betrayal of the women who loved them. Men call it fame, but by my pen, I would call it shame.

18

Robert's Return

The end of Robert's tour with Leicester's Men was drawing near, but the anticipation of his return was a constant presence. At night, in bed, I closed my eyes and imagined his warm breath on my ear, whispering, 'Soon, my Izzy, soon I will be by your side again.' My eagerness for his return was apparent to all who crossed my path, but none more so than Maria.

"Your cheeks burn brightly, Isabella," Maria observed with a knowing smile as I helped her clear the table. "The colour of ripe berries in summertide they are."

"Sparked no doubt by Robert's return on Sunday, eh Isabella?" Richard chimed from his chair in the parlor.

I sighed. "And yet, Sunday seems so far away."

"Oh, my girl, 'tis just a mere three days away." Maria laughed, placing the bowl of fruit on the table.

"But wouldn't you wait with unbridled eagerness for Richard if he was away for four weeks?"

She gazed at Richard, sitting by the hearth with a broadside ballad on his lap and some gathered about his feet. "Faith. 'Tis true. For a man with such a kind heart as his, I can't deny that I would be longing for his return."

"Do you hear Richard?" I called out. "Suppose women were allowed to pen their own words on how we feel about love. We would disprove the naysayers who say we are inconstant. Once a good man wins our love, we stay constant and true. 'Tis not true, Maria?"

"Truer words were never spoken," she replied, picking up

two apples. She bit into one and gave the other to Richard, where she joined him by the hearth.

Richard tapped his forehead. "Your astute observation has been noted, Isabella."

After putting the dishes away, I bade Richard and Maria a good night and retreated to my room. It had begun to rain, and the lovely lilting sound of the raindrops tapping against the windows provided a soothing musical accompaniment to the crackling fire in the hearth. I felt my eyelids grow heavy, and I lay down fully clothed on the bed to rest my eyes and soon fell into a sound slumber.

The serenity of my sleep was stolen by rapid, heavy footsteps mounting the stairs leading to my bedchamber. I rushed to the door. Perhaps Richard had urgent news about Robert. Just as I was about to open the door, it thrust open, and there, in dim light, stood Robert. I stood transfixed, stunned by his early return. Just as Penelope's love for the wandering Ulysses burned brightly with one look at his handsome visage, mine was set ablaze with one glance at Robert's face.

Closing the door with his foot, his arms tightly wound about my waist, he murmured, "Izzy, my love, have you grown as weary as I from being apart?"

And before I could respond, his mouth pressed down hard on mine. My fingers caressed his hair, and I felt something shiny in his left ear. Lo! A pearl earring. I touched his decorated lobe with an amused smile.

"Do you like it? 'Tis the fashion among musicians," Robert said, tossing his belongings on the bench and swiftly discarding his jerkin, feathered hat, and leather gloves.

"I must say it does make you look bewitching."

He settled on the bed with a piercing stare that made me grow hot. "Did Richard and Maria keep you busy to spare you the agony of thinking of me whilst I was away?" he teased.

Amused by his boyish conceit, I placed my hand over my heart. "I ached for you day and night, Robert, even though I was kept busy."

"So much so that you sleep in your clothes awaiting my return?"

I laughed and began to untie my bodice. In a flash, Robert was by my side, helping me undress.

"The books Richard gave me to read helped distract my longing for you at night. And when my eyes grew weary from reading, I drifted to sleep, and you always came to me in my dreams."

"Did I now, Izzy?" he grinned, lifting my smock to kiss my bare stomach. "I hope our dreams were similar, and what I did to you in my dreams happened in yours."

His kisses made my skin tingle with warmth. "Remove your boots, my sweet, so we can enact our dreams."

Robert buried his face in my neck and growled like a hungry lion. Laughing, I nudged him to sit by the hearth in the heavy oak chair.

"Help me remove these, Izzy," he sweetly commanded, holding up his leg, made heavy by the black leather boots that extended high beyond his knee.

After much pulling, both boots dropped to the floor in a heap. Robert leaned back into the chair and extended his hand to me, inviting me to sit on his lap.

"I will confess that holding you in my arms again was not all I looked forward to," I said tenderly as I unbuttoned his shirt. "There is much news I need to share with you, my love."

"Such as?" he asked, tilting his head toward the candle on the side table. Specks of gold twinkled in the brown of his eyes, making them sparkle like fairy dust. I wanted to crawl deep inside him. I kept all that I learned from Richard a secret till morning. Now was not the time for discussion but for remaining silent, allowing our bodies to rediscover the physical joys of being together again.

"There will be plenty of time for me to tell you about it in the morning. The hour is late." I moved to the bed. "Come to bed, my Leander."

"Leander?" he repeated with a knowing smile. "The Leander in your beloved tales of *Heroides*. The poor bereft soul who, when separated from the priestess Hero, his true love, braved the tempestuous wind and waves to swim to her only to meet his watery death."

I moved my hand to caress his bare chest. "The only true lover whose love was constant."

And between us, we enveloped the passion of Leander's undying love and succumbed to our erotic dreams.

The morning sunlight spilled across our faces, ushering in the busy morning that awaited us.

Robert had to seek new lodgings for us, and I had to finish the inventory for Richard's second shipment of books that arrived earlier in the week. I was about to ask Robert how he fared with Leicester's Men when he spied the latest book Richard gave me on the floor. It must have fallen off the table when we brushed against it in haste to get to bed last night.

He picked up the book and, in a tone of distaste, read the title aloud, "*Paradise of Dainty Devices*. Is this the kind of rubbish you've been reading whilst I was away? This collection of poems and epistles tell men to tread carefully with women for they will lead them to ruin." He tossed the book onto the table.

Despite his disdain, I remained calm. "That rubbish, as you call it, makes for popular reading. Richard seems to think there's room for a female response."

He let out a scornful laugh. "Go to! Don't tell me you harbor a desire to enter the fray of *the woman question*." He yanked the wet cloth in the washbasin and rubbed his eyes, mouth, and neck. "Where has your good sense strayed off to in my absence? I told you what I think about *the woman question*. 'Tis nothing but nonsense – worse, it's a literary game played for profit, aimed at the likes of my father."

"Richard is intrigued by the idea of a woman writing her view on the perils of women loving men," I countered as I struggled to put on my stockings.

He threw the washcloth in the basin. "Richard was just playing with you, Izzy."

"I think not," I snapped. "To be honest, I think my writing influenced his thinking."

He grabbed his hose and sat on the bench. "What writing?"

Lacing my bodice, I explained. "It all began when Richard put me to work in his bookroom. As I entered the titles in the ledger, I bemoaned that few books offered positive views of women. And then he showed me a book written by Edward Hack."

"That pompous moralist," Robert commented with a final pull of his hose up to his waist.

"Aye, the very same. Hack wrote scurrilous comments on maidservants. Having been a member of that group, I knew his views to be false. I expressed my dismay to Richard, and he became intrigued by what kind of rebuke I could write based on my experience."

"I see. Go on." Robert urged as he retrieved his boots from under the bed.

"He was much impressed by my rebuke. And not to boast, but it was quite good. Do you wish to see it?"

"Perhaps later."

"Richard praised my wit and my forthright way of expressing myself."

"Izzy, I was the first to tell you that you show great promise for writing. But I assure you, men wouldn't care to read what you say about their behavior in love."

I got off the bed and stood before him with my arms crossed. "Richard thinks it would attract much interest."

"Just write about what you know. You're a country lass. Stick to poems with pastoral themes. Richard shouldn't encourage false hopes. I shall speak to him on the matter," he said as he grabbed his doublet.

I pulled his arm with a fierce determination. "Don't you dare. He has shown us nothing but kindness. And I'll not have you tarnish the time that I have spent in his company."

He pulled away, his tone growing impatient. "As you wish,

Izzy. I will say nothing but enough of this talk on defending your sex in writing."

I followed him to the door, my voice steady. "I will cease talking about it today, Robert. But will not promise it won't come up again, perhaps tomorrow or the next day."

He gently nudged me towards the door and down the stairs. As we left the house, we went our separate ways. Robert to find new lodgings, and I to complete my final book inventory task, where I could contemplate in solitude the shape of my first poem in defense of women's constancy in love.

ೞ

Robert returned to our room in the early evening in high spirits and announced that he had found us suitable lodgings.

I put down my quill. "Pray tell, where?"

Rubbing his hands together in anticipation of making his grand announcement, he declared, "Brace yourself, Izzy. We shall move to Southwark."

Initially, I didn't share his zeal, for it would mean moving across the river, away from Richard and Maria. And more troubling was Southwark's reputation as the unruliest borough of Greater London. "Southwark? Are you sure 'tis the best place for us?"

He placed his hands on my shoulders. "Suspend all doubt, Izzy. 'Tis the ideal place for us. Actors, musicians, and writers are moving to Southwark. Think of the fun we shall have there as we join them and discuss the latest news. And every week, we can see plays performed in the courtyards of inns."

His response did little to assuage my uncertainty. "But I hear 'tis a wild place with all sorts of people out and about till all hours of night, for there's no curfew. The most dangerous sort on this side of the Thames cross over to the southside because the law cannot touch them there."

Robert nodded. "True. But our lodging is not near the river's edge." He took hold of his rapier. "You forget that I'm adept at using this. The only good sense my father had was to see to it that both his sons were trained in sword fighting." Putting it back in its scabbard, he added, "You are with me, my sweet. No harm shall come to you."

Despite my qualms, I understood Robert's attraction to Southwark. Aside from the entertainment to be found there, moving to the south side of the Thames would separate him from his aunt and father. And remove him, further away, from the grounds of Gray's Inn.

"We could give Southwark a try, Robert. And if 'tis not to our liking, we'll return to this side of the river."

He kneeled beside me and drew me close until our foreheads touched. "Of course, my love, we can always return if, as you say, 'tis not to our liking. But I think you'll be pleasantly surprised." His eyes darted to the paper with my writing. "What are you working on?"

"Shall I read it to you?"

Sitting on the edge of the bed, he signaled me to begin.

I sat up tall in my chair: *Beware of fair and painted talk, beware of flattering tongues, the mermaids pretend no good, for all their pleasant songs.*

"Ah, your contribution to *the woman question*, no doubt," he said with a wry smile.

"Aye," I replied, jutting my chin forward, ready to retort if he objected.

He fell silent as he began unbuttoning his jerkin, which didn't please me. I labored to find the right words to convey the inconstancy of men in love, and he offered no comment, no validation of my thoughts.

A moment passed, and finally, Robert said, "You paint an interesting image with your words, Izzy. 'Tis clever of you to compare men to mermaids with their siren songs. Those legendary creatures have long been associated with the wiles of women."

At last, a fair response. "I fancy that Ovid himself would have approved comparing men to mermaids. For all Greek heroes, except one, wooed their women with sweet words, only to prove false in the end."

He kissed me on the forehead. "'Tis a good start, my love. And now, let's attend to our stomachs – I'm famished. Shall we get ready to join Richard and his wife for dinner? It'll be a celebratory dinner, for by the end of the week, we shall embark on a new phase of our lives together in Southwark."

I repeated his words softly: 'In the next phase of our life together.' It was a sentiment that filled me with much hope.

19

Our Time in Southwark

It was late morning when we arrived in Bankside, the vibrant and infamous neighborhood of Southwark by the river's edge. In truth, this was the first time I had witnessed such a concentration of alehouses and taverns on a single street. The raucous voices of the rowdy patrons filled the air with their ceaseless clamor and bursts of laughter. And even at this early hour, I observed throngs of men, young and old, jostling at the doors of brothels, engaging in conversation with rouge and vermilion-lipped prostitutes.

I grabbed hold of Robert. "Let's make haste to a quieter part of town," I urged, knowing he would understand my unease in such a rowdy place.

The cacophony of Bankside gradually faded as we approached London Bridge. With the tide at its peak, the rush of water coursing through the bridge's arches was a much more soothing sound than the uproar of men reveling in their ale. I cast my gaze upwards as a flock of blackbirds soared northward above the rooftops of the imposing houses on the bridge. As we drew closer to the dreaded gateposts, I tightened my grip on Robert's hand and shut my eyes.

"Prithee," I begged, "check if traitors' heads are posted on the gateposts. I cannot bear to look."

"'Tis your lucky day, Izzy, for there are none, but brace yourself for soon there will be. Catholic rebellions are afoot in the north, now that Mary, Queen of Scotts, has sought refuge in England."

"Then, whilst we're here, I shall depend on you to be my

eyes every time we pass the bridge."

When we made our turn onto Borough High Street, I nearly lost Robert as a flock of braying sheep, spooked by a firing musket nearby, began pushing their heads against my knees and thighs. I shouted for Robert, and with quick strides, he took hold of my outstretched hand and pulled me away from the crazed sheep.

Robert laughed. "I nearly lost you there, Izzy. The damn sheep nearly carried you back down the hill to London Bridge."

I scowled at brushing away the loose dirt and bits of hay from the sheep's wool that clung to my skirt. Robert offered assistance as we continued our walk. Robert pointed to the grand inn on the corner where the road crossed the thoroughfare to Canterbury and Dover.

"That's the Tabard Inn – have you heard of it?"

I slowed as we passed the Tabard, viewing its stables, gardens, and a pleasant courtyard with upper galleries to watch performances. I envisioned Robert and me peering over the rail at the actors below. "I believe I have heard of it. Chaucer makes use of it in his *Canterbury Tales*."

Robert nodded. "Chaucer's pilgrims began their journey there to visit the shrine of St. Thomas Becket. And the one who was judged to tell the best tale was to win a dinner at the Tabard."

"But as I recall, there was no winner."

"Correct. Sadly, Chaucer died before completing the work. But in his honor, we'll dine there later today. What say you to that, Izzy?"

I pulled his arm into mine. "I'm all for that, Robert."

From the Tabard, Robert led me onto another street where the houses were set apart with patches of grass and trees between them. He stopped in front of a house with a gabled rooftop and windows projecting out to the street. A lantern hung over the door; next to it was a sign of interlocking vines.

"Welcome to our new abode, The Ivy Inn. Do you like it?" Robert asked.

"Marry, I do." I readily sat on a bench in the adjacent small garden, basking in the peacefulness of the inn. "We shall be ensconced here away from the noise of revelers in Bankside, enjoying peaceful nights."

Robert put his foot on the edge of the bench to stretch his leg. "Aye, away from the noise and the stench at low tide. Although I'm afraid we're not far away enough to discard our sweet-smelling posies," he added with a laugh and led the way inside.

The amiable, widowed innkeeper immediately accosted us, her enthusiasm palpable. Tall and plump, she spoke with the warmth and excitement of a child having encountered their favorite relative, making us feel instantly welcomed and valued.

"Ah, Mister Barrington, you've arrived right on time, and with your betrothed, Isabella, I presume?" The innkeeper's charcoal-colored eyes sparkled with curiosity and delight.

"Yes, Mistress," I said.

"Your room is all ready for your use. Mind you, Isabella, 'tis the best one in the house. Just last week, a courtier from the court of Queen Elizabeth graced that very room with his presence," she said with a proud nod, sharing this piece of noteworthy news.

She continued with her incessant praise of the room. "I had two available for lease, and Mister Barrington picked the grander of the two. I dare say, with his eye for impeccable accommodations, your betrothed will give you a grand home one day. Mark my words," she concluded with a wink.

Robert smiled patiently, "May we have the key, please, Mistress Orellana."

"Right away, my good man." She went to the hooks hanging on the wall behind an enormous desk and retrieved our key. "There you go now, you two, up to the top floor."

I caught the middle-aged Mistress Orellana observing Robert's well-shaped legs as we ascended the staircase. 'Tis true what they say. A man's shapely leg will draw the attention of many a female. I have grown accustomed to women of every age admiring Robert's legs.

Stepping into our room, I was captivated by its generous size and opulent furnishings. My gaze swept from the spacious bedframe adorned in blue velvet to the Oriental carpets gracing the floor, and finally to a pair of silver-plated candelabras adorning the mantel. But, best of all, the long oak table with intricate inlay could easily accommodate both of us writing simultaneously, with me at one end and Robert at the other. I sat at what would become my side of the table for writing.

"Robert, this is a room for the likes of your aunt or cousin who will soon be a countess. How could we afford such a room as this?"

Robert shrugged. "I managed to pay it with the balance of my allowance that I had not spent and the money made from my tour with Leicester's Men. Set your heart at rest, for the room is paid for at least two months."

"Robert Dudley, the Earl of Leicester, must be a very wealthy man to pay his players so handsomely."

"Aye. He has acquired good fortune from his association with the queen," Robert replied, expressing his admiration.

He quickly turned his attention to the trunk, a weathered oak with brass fittings, containing our possessions and his prized collection of bows and arrows, their polished wood gleaming in the sunlight, lying beside it. The previous day, Robert hauled the chest on a creaking cart over London Bridge with the help of Thomas and a few friends from Gray's Inn.

"With a stroke of luck, Thomas managed to retrieve most of my clothes just before my father arrived at school, ready to seize all my belongings," Robert said, his relief palpable as he pulled out doublets from the trunk.

He tried on a pale red doublet with slashed sleeves exposing the azure-colored cloth underneath. "What do you think, Izzy?" he asked as he strutted about the room.

"Very becoming. That style pulls in your waist, accentuating your chest."

"'Tis my favorite," Robert said, carefully removing it and

laying it atop the other doublets on the chair.

Inside the trunk was a treasure trove of Robert's cloaks with gold and silver threads and jerkins with silver and gold buttons. I spied a hat lined with silk and adorned with a snowy-white feather and placed it on my head. "Such finery, Robert. You have more fine clothes than I do."

He retrieved his hat from my head whilst uttering an impatient sigh. "Don't underestimate the value of fine garments, for they mark me as a gentleman."

How contrary of Robert. He despised his father's ways. Yet, he couldn't relinquish all the pleasures that came with his father's wealth and the upper-class distinction it brought him.

"Tomorrow, Izzy, we shall do some shopping to enhance your wardrobe," Robert said, lying on the bed, watching me pull my limited number of clothes from my travel bag. Then, smiling, he bade me lie beside him upon the green coverlet, its color resembling a lush meadow in summer, ripe for love-making.

∞

By the end of the month, living in Southwark, we had developed a leisure routine of day and evening activities, from our pick of favorite places, to which we returned repeatedly, creating a comforting and familiar rhythm to our days. After breakfast, we often sat on a grassy knoll overlooking the river with a direct view of The Tower of London, where Robert would tell spellbinding tales of men and women held captive within its stone-cold walls. One, in particular, stood out in my mind: a story of a long-ago rebellion. In his engaging manner, Robert began his tale.

"In the sweltering summer of 1450, the rebel Jack Cade led an army of men into London. He was determined to force the king to reform his government and rid it of corruptive officials whose policies were making the lives of ordinary citizens in the southeast of England a misery."

Pointing to the bridge, he continued. "But the citizens of

London drove them out, and in retaliation, the rebels set fire to London Bridge. Many people whose homes were on the bridge perished in the flames. Jack Cade fled but was soon captured. His severed head hung at the entrance to the bridge."

I shuddered. "All those innocent lives lost as the bridge burned. Promise me a more cheerful tale next time to begin our day."

A sudden wind rose from the river, and I inched closer to Robert, resting my head on his arm. I gazed upon the Thames, crowded with boats of every size moving like pieces on a chessboard. In the quiet that followed, I couldn't help but imagine my brother, Brooke, joining us, his infectious laughter filling the air as he acted out the stories Robert told. I tenderly touched Robert's face, aching for the day he would be introduced to my family. Soon, I promised myself – soon.

Every Wednesday afternoon, Robert was in Paris Garden practicing archery, and I willingly accompanied him. One breezy afternoon, I picked up one of the lighter bows to shoot the arrow at the target, but it kept hitting the dirt mound.

Robert feigned grave disappointment. "Oh, come now, Izzy. This is the fourth Wednesday you have accompanied me here as I practice. Yet it seems you have learned nothing from observing my expertise with the bow."

"I have not had the benefit of your long experience," I called out as I ran to fetch my third fallen arrow. "You have been doing this since you were a boy."

"My father insisted that his sons become skilled archers. In my grandfather's day, it was an essential skill if one wanted to serve the king. Although, not anymore. An educated man is the requirement today."

"I'm grateful to him, for the sport has given you these herculean arms," I said, kissing his upper arm.

He grinned. "Stand back, my love, and behold my mighty arm."

I waited in anticipation for the arrow to be released.

He narrowed his eyes. "Tell me, Izzy, are my feet pointing

in a straight line toward the center of the target?"

He was teasing, for he knew they were.

"And the placement of the first three fingers of my right hand on the bow seems right to you?"

"They are just as they should be. I remember well, Robert, what you taught me. 'Tis the Mediterranean draw. Now enough of this foolery, and let the arrow fly to its mark."

"As you command, my lady." The arrow cut through the air and hit Robert's target with a decisive thud.

I clapped my hands and cheered, "Bravo, master archer." Robert then swiftly unleashed a series of arrows, one after the other. Observing his arm muscles contract with every pull of the bow's string never ceased to arouse me. And afterward, we stole away into one of the windmills that stood nearby, blissfully spending the rest of the afternoon hours there.

Our evenings were reserved for writing. One evening in late March, when the full moon shone like a golden orb in the night sky, Robert was sitting at his end of the writing table, nearing the end of writing a ballad, whilst I was at my end working on my poem. Robert had begun a new romantic ballad of Sibylla, a Jerusalem queen who reigned during the Crusades. He had high hopes Richard would print it, and Robert Dudley would stage it at Whitehall for the queen's entertainment this summer.

I rapped on the table to get Robert's attention. "Tell me what you think of these new lines of verse for my poem, Robert."

He paused his quill and nodded for me to begin.

"Some use the tears of crocodiles, contrary to their heart. And if they cannot always weep, they wet their cheeks by art."

As I paused to read the next lines, Robert asked, "And that follows the stanza that begins with *Beware of fair and painted talk*?"

I marveled at Robert's memory for he heard the opening lines of my poem nearly five weeks ago.

"And do I hear an ode to Ovid in that last line?" he added.

With a vigorous nod, I confirmed his guess. "I pay tribute to him in the next verse. Listen. *Ovid, within his Art of Love, doth teach them this same knack, to wet their hand and touch their eyes: so oft as tears they lack.*"

"Although I disagree with the intent of your poem, to show that men, and not women, lack truth in love, you have done well with it thus far," he replied and promptly returned to his writing.

"By God, Robert, you are stubborn. You continue to criticize the popularity of *the woman question* in literature but fail to see that there's money to be made there - according to Richard."

He raised his hand to quell an argument. "Just keep writing, Izzy. It doesn't matter if it gets printed. Just write for the pure love of it. I'll always encourage you to share what you write with me and whoever calls upon us for a visit."

I observed Robert as he moved his pen at a furious pace, all the while thinking that if Richard printed my poem, Robert would have to accept the validity of *the woman question* as a viable topic in the literary market. I prayed he would. For if not, there would be contentious talks between us.

We both worked late into the night. I fell asleep at the table but awoke fully clothed in bed the following morning. Robert was sitting in the chair by the window, clutching his ballad.

"'Tis finished, Izzy. After I carried you off to bed, I continued working."

"You must have worked through the night as if the devil was holding a pitchfork to your arse!"

He laughed. "Money is what drove me, Izzy, for we shall need it soon. I'm hoping that Richard will print and sell this ballad. He should be drawn to it for 'tis a tale filled with love, deception, and betrayal."

"And Robert Dudley is another source of money for us. Perhaps he has another job for you, with performances in London this time."

He averted my gaze. "I'll pay a visit to Richard today."

I got out of bed and stretched my limbs. Between yawns, I

said, "I'm most eager to see him again. Why don't we invite him to sup with us at George Inn? There are many tasty dishes to be had there."

We had become well acquainted with dining at the George Inn, stopping there to sup at least once a week after taking in performances at the Tabard Inn.

Robert gave an approving nod. "A most excellent idea. I'll mention it to him. He can choose the day."

In the late afternoon, Robert returned with the happy news that Richard had accepted our invitation to sup in three days. This news was made less joyful when Robert informed me that Maria had just left for Kent to care for her sister, who had fallen ill after her pregnancy.

"Perhaps we should postpone our invitation until she returns," I suggested.

Robert removed his gloves and flung them on the bed. "I don't think that's necessary. Richard was enthused to meet us at George Inn. Besides, I'm anxious to hear his thoughts. What could be a more perfect setting for discussing my ballad than with wine and good food? I promise we'll extend another invitation as soon as Maria returns."

I picked up his gloves made of Spanish leather and returned them to their proper place. Robert was forever misplacing things. "When will she be returning home?"

Robert shrugged. "I didn't ask."

"I hope the next time I see Maria, she'll tell me she's with child."

Robert drew his brows together. "I didn't know she and Richard were trying for a child."

"She did mention once she had been trying for quite some time but to no avail."

Robert opened the shutters, and a gentle breeze ruffled his hair. "Richard would make a fine father and Maria a most caring mother. I pray God will make it so if she yearns to be a mother."

"I told her as much."

It struck me that Robert and I had not discussed the

particulars of having a family of our own one day. Most certainly, when the happy day comes when we exchange vows in my parish church, my parents will expect to be made grandparents.

"Do you long for children, Robert?"

With a shrug, he responded, "I haven't given it much thought." And then his eyes grew wide. "You're not?"

I laughed and crossed my hands to indicate no. "But soon, we should discuss what our future will hold. What kind of house will we live in and where? How many children do we desire? I feel two are sufficient, do you?"

"We have much to do before we have that talk, eh, Izzy?" he said, pouring himself a glass of wine.

"Do you remember your sweet declaration to me the night we walked back to your aunt's house from the inn?" I asked, but Robert stared blankly at me.

Before he picked up his glass, I placed my arms around his neck. "Let me jog your memory, my love. I will be your Nicholas Bacon, you said. And if we marry, we will have a household of servants and governesses. You made that sweet promise to assure me I would have time to write as a wife and mother." I sealed my remembrance with a kiss on his lips. He picked up his glass. As I observed him, I added. "I thank God you're blessed with an excellent mind, but 'tis important to tread a steady path with your eyes open to opportunities of all sorts, not just in music but other endeavors. Even possibly returning to the law if all else fails. Right, my love?"

He stared at me, his lips set in a straight line. "Let's wait and see what comes, Izzy."

20

Happy Reunion

We made arrangements to meet Richard on the first Friday in April. At the hour of six, I begged Robert to make haste, for I knew that, unlike Richard, a punctual man, Robert was not.

"Your beard is perfectly trimmed. Stop fussing."

No longer a student at Gray's Inn, Robert was now at liberty to grow a beard and was most meticulous in keeping its shape short and well-rounded.

"Richard is no babe or a doddering old man. He'll not lose his wits if we're not there to greet him right on the hour."

He gave a final inspection of his bearded face and nodded his approval at his reflection in the mirror. "Ready," he said, smiling.

I helped him secure his gold-tipped ruff around his neck. Finally, after many prolonged minutes of Robert's primping, we set off to meet our dear friend at the foot of London Bridge. Despite the onset of spring, a lingering chill in the air allowed me to wear the moss-green velvet cloak that Robert had purchased for me.

"Such a delight to behold the two of you together again," Richard beamed when he greeted us. "Isabella, you're looking well. Southwark has proved to be a happy place for you." His voice was warm and filled with genuine affection.

I smiled. "My eyes are glad to see you again, dear Richard."

Robert took command. "Let's away. Supper awaits us at the George."

We walked briskly to the inn, myself positioned happily

between Richard and Robert.

When we stepped into the crowded dining room of George Inn, the attending serving boy, who walked with a slight limp, ushered us to our table. Robert acknowledged a man wearing a silver and red striped hat topped with a reed-thin feather, sipping his ale as he looked out the window facing the street below.

"Who did you wave to?" I asked as we took our seats at a round table at the room's far end.

"That's George Gascoigne seated by the window, alone."

"A rising courtier poet," Richard added. "I haven't seen him since his last play was staged at Gray's Inn in November last year."

Robert leaned in with his elbows on the table. "Did you hear that he recently married the widow of a prosperous merchant? A move no doubt intended to repair his fortunes," Robert added with a grin.

Their comments piqued my curiosity, and I stretched my neck to look in the direction of where he was sitting. Much to my surprise, he was advancing toward our table.

Robert offered a half smile but welcomed him with a polite handshake. His hair was dark like Robert's, but besides a short-rounded beard, he had a mustache that added volume to his thin lips. I thought he was handsome enough to catch the eye of a wealthy widow.

"George," Robert said, "you know, Richard Jones."

Richard greeted him with a vigorous handshake. "I congratulate you, George. I heard the queen was much impressed with your translation of Ariosto's *Suppositi* at Gray's Inn, calling it witty. It has won you her favor."

He smiled and tapped his chest. "She did prefer that one to the tragedy presented months earlier."

Robert drew George Gascoigne's attention to me. "And this lovely maid is my betrothed, Isabella Whitney."

He gave a gallant bow and kissed my hand. "A pleasure, Miss Whitney." And then, without waiting for an invitation to join us, he nonchalantly claimed a nearby stool. "Do you mind if I join you? My carriage is not yet ready to take me home."

"By all means, sit," Robert said with modicum enthusiasm.

Sporting a wide grin, George nudged Robert. "Tell me, Robert, is what I heard true about the recent tour of Dudley's troupe of players?"

Robert shifted his attention from George to Richard and me and then back to George. "What have you heard?"

"That one of his actors, Mark"— he stopped short, struggling to remember the actor's surname.

"Well, if you can't remember his name, let's talk of something else," Robert said eagerly.

"Tarleton," George exclaimed, pounding the table once. "Aye, Mark Tarleton. He got into a bit of a fray with an audience member who hurled an insult at him. In turn, Tarleton broke character and drew his rapier to silence the offender."

"A minor incident, George, not of much interest," Robert said dismissively.

"Minor?" George disagreed with a loud laugh. "A brawl broke out between the actors and the friends of the ruffian who uttered the offensive remarks. I heard the sheriff's lord-lieutenant was summoned. And that brought the tour to its untimely end."

Richard and I exchanged a glance of surprise. I crossed my arms and looked at Robert. The vein in his neck began to twitch. What jolting news, I silently fumed. Robert said nothing to me about the tour being cut short. God's Blood, Robert! You could have returned to me sooner than when you did. Where did you go? And more vexing, whose company did you keep?

George pressed on. "How long did it take Dudley to wrest himself away from the queen's side to bail his actors out of jail?" he chuckled.

"I don't know, for I left after the show was shuttered," Robert snapped. "I have no doubt that Dudley quickly made arrangements to release his players from jail when he was informed of the mishap. And now, George, shouldn't you check to see if your carriage is ready?" Robert said, urging him to leave.

"I'll accompany you to your carriage, George," Richard readily offered. "There's a question that has perplexed me since I saw your first play, *Jocasta*, at Gray's Inn. Come, let's proceed and perhaps you can shed light on it." He put his hand on George's shoulder and led him away from the table.

What a true friend Richard proved to be. I was sure he sensed my growing ire over the revelation that Robert's tour lasted less than four weeks. I was grateful he had the good sense to allow us some private time together.

I turned to Robert as soon as they left our table. "Go to, Robert!" I hissed. "What noteworthy news George Gascoigne imparted just now. Your tour was cut short. Evidently, you saw fit not to return to me but went elsewhere?"

Robert cleared his throat. "Aye, I did go elsewhere. I paid a visit to my cousin in Yorkshire."

"Mistress Walden?"

He nodded. "She was at the home of her future father-in-law making preparations for her wedding."

"How strange that you kept that a secret. Especially when you know of the close bond I once had with her."

"My mother was there. Visiting my cousin allowed me to see her, for as you are well aware, my father has forbidden me to enter our family home. Imagine how difficult that was for me. We fell into a heated argument about family loyalty and honor. I didn't wish to speak of that with you."

I wrung the napkin incessantly until it fell into a wrinkled heap on the table. "And imagine how difficult it was for me to discover that you concealed the truth about the tour and your whereabouts afterward."

"Let it rest for now, Izzy. For look – Richard returns."

Robert threw back his shoulders when he took his seat. "All this talk has delayed our meal," he signaled for the attendant servant to come to our table.

For Richard's sake, I remained quiet. But my anger over Robert's dissembling made it impossible for me to engage with him. Thus, I directed all my attention to our guest and allowed him to dominate the talk as he responded to my rapid-fire questions. I didn't give poor Richard time to breathe. As soon as one question was answered, I followed up with another: Tell me about all the books you have received since my last inventory. Any notable books on *the woman question*? Any written in praise of women? How are you managing with your new press? Tell me all about dear Maria's trip to care for her sister.

As I listened to Richard's detailed responses, questions concerning Robert swirled in my mind. When he saw his mother, did she disparage me like his father did? Was it just his mother there, or did his sister accompany her? And what did she have to say about me? Throughout the meal, Robert sat stoically with his fist clenched on his lap.

Whilst we ate sweet dishes of rose pudding, each with a sugared rose in the center, Richard broached the subject of Robert's ballad.

"Robert, your mastery of the ballad meter is beyond doubt. But I do have a caveat."

"Go on," Robert replied, his tone a tad defensive.

"People who buy romantic ballads enjoy mulling over the author's words of wisdom at the story's conclusion. But curiously, that's missing from your work."

"Are you recommending I conclude my ballad with an explicit moral message, like in *Aesop's Fables*?" Robert asked impatiently.

"Aye, I am," Richard said, enjoying the last spoonful of his pudding.

Robert dropped his spoon in the bowl. "I have grown weary of moralizers. Do you have any other caveats?"

I prayed there was no other. Robert had labored to write the ballad and was optimistic that Richard would readily print it. To make one change should prove no hardship for Robert, but he might not take kindly to other recommended changes.

"The popular characters found in romance ballads are absent from yours," Richard continued. "There's no Cupid, not even his mother, Venus."

I could hear the impatient tapping of Robert's foot. "I saw no need to add those hackneyed characters," he said.

"Hackneyed they may be, but readers are enchanted by them and clamor to read romance ballads wherein they appear," Richard asserted.

"I was aiming for something more original. I'll not contrive the storyline so that I could include Cupid or Venus."

Richard leaned in toward Robert, his hands folded in front of him. "Originality is admirable, but if you wish to appeal to the buying public, Robert, you must bend to popular taste."

Robert seemed stunned into silence but then quickly rebounded. "You're not the only printer in the whole of London. I'm sure I can find another that deems my ballad worthy— without the moralizing message and inclusion of popular mythic characters."

I winced. For shame! Robert grew too hot. Had he forgotten Richard's generous help when we were turned away from his aunt and father?

Richard bit into a slice of candied pear. "You are free to try another printer. I cannot begrudge you that."

The vein in Robert's neck began to twitch again as it did when George Gascoigne revealed the news about the failed tour. "You've grown accustomed to the comforts of profiting off popular literary taste," Robert said, reaching for his cape. "We bid you good night, Richard."

We'll talk again when you are calmer," Richard responded with a patient smile.

Not wishing to call the attention of others to our altercation by insisting we stay, I quickly readied myself to leave, casting a sorrowful glance at Richard.

"Be of good cheer, Isabella," he said affectionately. "All will be well between Robert and me." He pointed his finger at me, saying, "You keep reading and writing, my girl. Think well about what we discussed when you assisted me in my shop."

Robert tugged at my arm, "Come, Isabella."

"Go now and give me a smile," Richard said.

I could barely manage a weak smile. "God give you good night," I said, reluctantly following Robert out of the dining room.

My head was filled with one word – shame, for Robert's rudeness. As we walked away, he uttered something to me, but his words were lost in the din of a group of men assembled around a large table, shouting and cursing whilst playing cards. I stepped out into the cool night air as Robert settled our bill. A lustrous full moon met my gaze. Are you responsible for Robert's foul mood tonight? I whispered. Within minutes, Robert emerged carrying a lantern. The moonlight alone was not enough to safely guide us back to our inn. As we crossed Borough High Street, a long line of young men, linking arms, some staggering, crossed our path. Robert held me back, allowing them to pass.

We were halfway to our inn when I could no longer bear the uncomfortable silence that had fallen between us since leaving Richard.

"Why couldn't you at least consider Richard's suggestions? He's willing to print your ballad if you make the necessary changes. Didn't you say we are in need of money?"

"I'll seek another printer. I think Richard's wrong. My telling of Sibylla's story is perfect as written."

I breathed in deeply as I tried to tolerate Robert's obstinance. His lofty idea of altering the form of the standard romance ballad would cost him dearly.

"Perhaps public taste will change to appreciate the kinds of ballads you want to write, but your main concern now should be making money. I need not tell you that my mother and father expect me to marry a man with a sufficient income to support a wife and children."

He took hold of my arm. "Be patient, my love. Although Robert Dudley has fallen out of favor with the queen, she'll speedily recall him back to court. She always does. I'm certain he'll see my ballad's worthiness once he hears it."

Our discussion continued as we entered our inn and ascended three flights to our room.

"If anyone would delight in hearing a ballad about the tribulations of a woman ruler, it will be Queen Elizabeth," I said. "Let's hope Robert Dudley reconciles with her soon. If not, you'll have to think hard on what you'll do next."

"I'm not worried. The queen cannot bear having him out of sight for too long."

Once inside our room, we settled down for the night. As I undressed to my smock, Robert stoked the fire, poured himself a glass of wine, and sat by the hearth.

"Izzy," he said, full of good cheer, "come join me."

I sat opposite him whilst he poured wine into my goblet. He gazed at me and raised his drink to make a toast. "If I were a painter, I would paint you just as you are now, with your breasts visible beneath your smock and your hair falling about your shoulders. I would call you Beauty – Helen of Troy."

He was in a buoyant mood and now was the opportune time to interrogate him.

"Since your tour with Leicester's Men was interrupted, were you fully paid?"

He shrugged. "Not yet. But not to fret, for Robert Dudley is known for making late payments to his actors."

"Where did you get the money to pay for such a fine accommodation as this one?"

"My mother." The truth brought a warm flush to his face.

At that moment, I recalled Robert's father's words the day he discovered us together, 'Your mother has fostered your impetuous nature. For she indulges your every whim.' Evidently, she continues to want the best for her boy. Will she imperil our relationship or help it?

Robert poured himself more wine. "I tell you truly, my mother is clever in getting money from my father. He denies her nothing, for deep in his heart, he knows he's much indebted to her."

"How so?"

"My mother, an only child, was born into a family of enormous wealth, which by comparison made my father's possessions appear meager. His land holdings were greatly enhanced when he married her."

"And even though your father denies your mother nothing when it comes to money, she cannot sway him to take your side concerning us?"

"Nay," he said bitterly and finished the remains of his drink in one swallow.

I stretched my arms over my head. The sheerness of my smock redirected Robert's attention to my breasts. "Tell me, my love, did your mother travel alone to see your cousin?"

"Must we continue talking about my visit to my cousin, Izzy?"

"Now that we are in the private confines of our room, why can't you speak of it?"

His eyes darted away from me. Clutching his goblet, he rose to stoke the fire once again. Whilst gazing at the flames, he drank. I grew suspicious. He requires much drink to bolster his nerve to tell me of his visit. "I'm waiting."

He turned to me. "You must be willing to bear news that may be unpleasant to your ears."

I folded my hands tightly on my lap. "Pray, go on."

"Rose Clavell accompanied my mother."

The very mention of her name pricked my ears. I had prayed that I would never hear her name uttered again.

"The daughter of the viscount that your father wanted you to marry?" My voice rose to a crescendo.

He put his finger on my lips. "Calm yourself. I knew you would be troubled by this news, the very reason I didn't tell you."

"Heaven and Earth, Robert, why did you stay?"

With a weary sigh, he dropped into the chair. "My mother felt, and rightly so, that I owed Rose an apology. For the embarrassment she suffered when I didn't present myself at the dinner my parents had arranged for her family the day you sought me out at school."

"I didn't keep you away by force. I hope you told her it was your decision not to go home."

He reached for my hand. "I couldn't resist you, my

delicious Izzy."

"Did you tell her that?"

"Nay. Not in those very words."

"And how did she respond to your apology?"

I caught a hint of a smile. "I must say she took it all very well. She's very sweet and gentle-mannered."

I stood up and brought my empty glass down hard on the table. "Robert! You appear to have enjoyed Rose Clavell's company a little too much."

He wrapped his arms around me, but I turned away, my back facing him. Undeterred, he grabbed me about the waist, pulling me into him. "Mistress Clavell is nothing to me. She doesn't equal your wit or looks." He gently kissed me about the neck. "She could never possess your skill in satisfying me."

I marched from him to the fireplace, where I needlessly stoked the fire.

"Let's to bed, Izzy, and entwine our limbs for warmth and satisfaction."

I wanted to order him to sleep like a dog by the hearth. "I want only to sleep, Robert, nothing more. This night has been marred by revelations that have made my mind and body weary."

Robert sat on the bed, looking contrite. "I would not dream of forcing myself upon you if 'tis not your desire."

I grabbed the handle of the bed warmer and warmed the bed's sheets with vigor.

"You will feel better tomorrow, my love," Robert said.

I put my hand up to silence him. "To bed now, Robert, each on our own side."

21

Another Tour

The black cloud of jealousy hovered over me for days after Robert confessed that he had spent time with Rose Clavell. It played havoc with my mind. I envisioned them together, taking long walks in the garden at the future home of Mistress Walden. With trepid steps, Rose made her way through the intricate garden maze with Robert gently guiding her. At dinner, Robert sat beside her, whispering words sweeter than honey that made her blush. My mind became plagued with such visions that it became difficult to write until, one day, I finally ousted all thoughts that spurred my jealousy. Henceforth, I relented to believe Robert's impassioned words that I was the only one for him. 'Banish thoughts of Rose Clavell. You are the one I crave, not her,' Robert repeatedly said with hugs and kisses, which I welcomed. In time, harmony was once again restored between us. So much so that one early morning in April, I picked up the dreaded needle to satisfy Robert's request.

"The embroidery on my shirt has come undone," he complained.

I took the shirt in my hands to examine the unraveling black thread. "The thread most likely snagged around the jagged edge of one of your doublet's buttons. You must handle your clothes with greater care," I advised, returning the shirt to him.

"Can you mend it?" he said, a doubtful expression crossing his face.

"Robert Barrington, do you think I lack the skill to do it?" I responded with a look of indignation.

Robert laughed. "Since I've been with you, I've never seen you pick up the needle."

"I prefer the pen to the needle."

He feigned dismay. "Oh, woe is me to have fallen for such a maid."

"Go to, Robert, enough of your teasing." I took the shirt from him with a playful slap to his arm.

Robert put on his jerkin. "I'm off to seek leads on potential jobs, Izzy."

I settled into the chair with my needle and thread ready. "God willing, you'll return with good tidings."

"I feel good fortune will visit me today," he said with a smile, bestowing a sweet kiss on my cheek before he left.

I decided to impress Robert by embroidering matching designs on the shirt's cuffs. I soon regretted it, for the shirt was made of delicate linen, requiring more patience and time than I was willing to give. But I remained steadfast in completing the task.

When Robert returned three hours later, he found me, as he had left me, in the chair with the needle in my hand. He kneeled beside me. "Izzy – good news. We no longer need to draw from my mother's money. For I have found employment."

"That's welcoming news indeed. Tell me more."

"Robert Dudley's brother, Ambrose Dudley, Earl of Warwick, has offered me work with his troupe of players."

With a rush of anticipation, I paused my needlework and squeezed his hand. "Pray you'll stay put in London this time?"

Robert nodded no. I fell silent and solemn, for it meant I would be left alone again.

"Smile, Izzy, 'tis good news," he urged.

"Is it? I would rather you had told me you found a job here."

"What do you suggest? I work as a waterman, singing my ballads whilst plying the oars. Would that satisfy you?" he jibed, pouring himself a glass of wine.

I continued my needlework on the cuffs of Robert's shirt. "Didn't you once tell me that your education at Gray's Inn provided you with enough knowledge to find a job in the law?"

Robert's jubilant mood turned pensive. "Aye. I did say something like that. I meant that when all possibilities in music have failed, and we desperately need money, I would consider returning to the law."

He removed his jerkin and doublet, placing them on the back of the chair. "I'm surprised that you fail to see the importance of this opportunity with the Earl of Warwick's acting troupe."

Carelessly, I stabbed my finger with the needle, so distressed that Robert would be off touring again. "Pray, inform me. Then perhaps I will share in your joy."

"Don't you see, Izzy," he began in earnest. "I will be kept in the bosom of two courtiers very close to the queen. Ambrose Dudley is always in the queen's good favor. She calls him the good Earl of Warwick." He laughed and leaned forward in his chair, using his hands to elevate the importance of his news. "I've been told by various sources that both Dudley brothers are vying to have their acting troupes entertain the queen at Whitehall this Christmas."

I pushed the thread through the fabric, making several stitches at once on the second cuff. "And 'tis your belief that you'll perform your ballad about Sybilla at Whitehall?"

Robert nodded with unwavering confidence. "I'm certain the queen and her court will lavish praise on my ballad. And once Richard hears of it, you'll witness how swiftly he'll rush to print it." He reclined in his chair, serenely savoring his wine with a smile that radiated assurance.

"And where will you be off to this time? Pray, not to the north again."

"To the county of Kent."

"And for how long?"

"Just a little over a fortnight. And here's something you'll like. The Earl of Warwick pays his actors on time."

"Once the tour ends, you must return to me. 'Tis not as

before when you left me in the safe hands of Richard and Maria whilst you toured with Leicester's Men. I'm uneasy being in Southwark alone. The laws are lax here. I worry about what villain might cross my path."

"I'll have Thomas look in on you. 'Tis but a short ride across the river to get here."

Always looking to Thomas for a quick remedy, I thought bitterly. "Robert, 'tis not the same as having you here every day."

I laid his shirt on the table with the sleeves extended, showing my handiwork at its best. "How soon do you leave?"

He inspected the mended embroidery at the collar. "I must leave in two days."

"I swear, Robert, you'll wear out my patience one day." I snatched the shirt and threw it on the chair where I had labored over it since the morning.

Robert quickly retrieved it. "I just found out late this morning that the Earl of Warwick was looking to replace a musician who had suddenly departed." Touching my embroidered design on the cuffs, he smiled. "'Tis exquisite work, Izzy."

His compliment did little to appease me. The sudden demands of his touring began to cause me much displeasure. "Robert, these sudden departures must cease."

He hung his head low like a contrite child. "Sometimes it can't be helped, but aye, I promise to choose with greater care next time." He laid the shirt carefully in his trunk. "I saw Thomas today, and after I told him my news, he suggested we all meet before I leave. Are you agreeable to that?"

I retreated to my side of the writing table to begin work on my poem, rather proud that I had completed fifteen stanzas without Robert's help.

Robert tapped the end of the table. "Izzy, are you agreeable to meeting Thomas?"

"I shall think upon it," I said without looking up from my writing.

"I believe Millicent will come with Thomas," Robert added.

I oft thought of Millicent and the kindness she showed me. For her unsolicited help in gaining entry onto the grounds of Gray's Inn, she asked for nothing in return. Her main concern was to see me happily settled with Robert. She proved to be a good friend.

"In that case, I will agree to go," I said without looking up from my writing.

We passed the night away engaged in our distinct endeavors, I in my writing and Robert sitting by the hearth, reading Dante's *Divine Comedy* in its original Latin. Every now and then, I caught Robert casting a glimpse my way, but he knew better than to interrupt me and merely smiled when our eyes met.

૭૪୫૭

Shortly before sunset, the day after Robert announced his new tour, we made our way down High Borough Street to Bankside to meet Thomas and Millicent.

"How long has Thomas kept company with Millicent?"

"Close to a year, I believe."

"That's an unusual amount of time, isn't it?"

"What do you mean?"

"You once said that student liaisons with women who work in service at Gray's Inn were short-lived. A year is a considerable amount of time to be with someone."

He draped his arm around me. "Aye, but Millicent delights Thomas. Her bawdy humor provides much-needed relief after hours spent studying the law."

"Mind you, Robert, Millicent might harbor hope that she's more than just Thomas's playfellow in bed after having been with him for nearly a year."

"She appears to be content." He pulled me in closer. "Don't concern yourself with their affair."

"'Tis hard not to when I consider her a true friend. She's helpful and honest, like the country maids I know at home."

As we neared the foot of London Bridge, dusk had settled,

and the tide had receded, carrying with it a pungent mix of odors from the floating debris. Yet, the air was alive with the energy of the throngs of visitors disembarking from the boats, eager to immerse themselves in the evening's revelries.

Robert wandered over to a white-painted wall opposite the Paris Garden steps, where we would meet Millicent and Thomas. He pressed his hand against the wall, his head held high.

"Whilst my grandfather served the queen's father, King Henry, it fell to him to close down the alehouses behind this wall. For you see, they were nothing more than brothels," Robert chuckled.

"I didn't know your grandfather was in royal service," I said, astonished more by that revelation than brothels fronting as alehouses.

He recounted his family's history as if it were a minor detail. "When my father was ten, my grandfather was knighted for steadfast service to the king and country. And thus began the ascent of the Barrington name into the ranks of the upper class."

He stepped back from the wall and made a sweeping gesture across it with his arm. "On this wall were painted signs of the alehouses in brilliant colors, large and bright enough to lure men from the other side of the Thames to visit."

He slapped the wall as he walked away, laughing. "I confess, my grandfather was a bit of a rascal. He oft made visits to a Flemish woman who ran a brothel. It went by the innocuous name of The Antelope. He granted her a special favor and set her up elsewhere, a short distance from his home. You can be sure my grandfather took advantage of that," he said with an impish smile.

My parents would be impressed that Robert's grandfather was knighted. Still, their ears would turn red by his association with brothels in Southwark.

We crossed the street to the landing stairs when we heard the boatman's familiar cry of 'Land Ho.' People disembarked eagerly from the boat. Robert waved his arms when he saw

Thomas and Millicent emerge from the small crowd of passengers.

"Ho! Thomas!" Robert shouted as he raced to meet him.

Millicent scurried away from Thomas and embraced me. "How now, Isabella?" She took me aside and said, "All's gone according to plan since I saw you last." She punctuated her remark with her customary silly giggle – a sound I once found irksome. But now it rendered a soft smile from me. Yellow ribbons shimmered in her black hair, and she wore a matching-colored scarf around her neck. A gift from Thomas, I hoped.

"Yes, Millicent. I'm content to have Robert's love."

"Fair, Isabella," Thomas said, kissing me on both cheeks. "There's a glow about your countenance, which only means you are happy with my dear friend."

"Of course! Why wouldn't she be?" Robert said, taking my hand. "Now, let's all away to Horseshoe Alehouse."

Linking arms for safety, we passed streets with grim-sounding names such as Ax Yard, Deadman's Place, and Foul Lane. My heart raced to be in the neighborhood, Liberty of the Clink, where criminals seek asylum from London's enforcers of the law.

"Are you afraid, Isabella?" Millicent said with a low giggle.

"With the good sense God gave me, 'tis fitting that I should feel anxious walking these streets."

Robert, who was at the end of our line, gripped the hilt of his rapier. "I tell her that only a simple-minded criminal would pry upon an innocent. For it would mean jeopardizing the pardon they gained for keeping out of trouble for one year whilst living here," Robert said.

"Still, I can't help fearing the worst," I said with a shudder.

Just as we were about to pass an alley, a young woman dashed out of it, her sudden appearance startling us. She was ill-kept, with her knotted hair absurdly piled high upon her head, and she flashed a sly smile as she kept pace with us. "Why don't you two gallants and your companions follow me to the Bell Tavern? 'Tis just a short walk from here. I'll make it worth your time for a sixpence."

"Sorry, not tonight," said Thomas, tossing her a coin.

"Ah, you're a soft-hearted one," said Millicent, leaning into him.

The whore took the coin with a smirk and tossed it high before clutching it. She exposed an ample breast, "See what you missed," she cackled and ran ahead with lightning speed, disappearing as she turned the corner.

When we reached Horseshoe Alehouse, several beggars loitered nearby. Neither Robert nor Thomas was generous this time around. As we approached the door, we heard hearty laughter from inside. In amusement, Robert and Thomas looked at each other and said in unison, "Let's make haste."

Thomas thrust the door open, revealing a spirited gathering mostly of men listening to a pair of balladeers singing bawdy songs.

"Quite good, are they not?" Robert observed.

I looked around the unadorned room with its long tables, benches, and ale barrels on wooden stands. A large black and white dog on the dirt floor awoke with a start and lumbered over to us, pressing its heavy head against my knee.

"Never mind him miss. Just give 'em a soft tug on the ears, and he'll leave you be," advised a woman carrying ale pots, her mouth painted an unflattering shade of purple. Looking into the dog's brown droopy eyes, I gently tugged on both ears, which sent his tail wagging. Satisfied with his treat, he returned to his resting place.

We waited until the balladeers finished their song to find a table. The room buzzed with laughter and shouting. Men sat with their legs splayed across the benches, taking swigs from their ale pots. Millicent giggled and pointed to a man in a dark corner groping a woman with her bodice partially unlaced.

We settled down at the less crowded table. Everyone kindly moved in unison down the bench to allow us ample room to sit at the end. Straight away, Robert and Thomas grabbed ale pots and walked to the nearest ale barrel to fill them up. I noticed some men with their sleeves rolled up and the laces on their wrinkled shirts untied. They nudged each other and pointed to Robert and Thomas, whose silk doublets and cloaks conspicuously set them apart from all the others. And the gold chains Robert wore further marked him as a gentleman.

When Robert and Thomas left the table, Millicent anxiously turned to me.

"Tell me, in which tavern do you lodge? When I asked Thomas, he refused to say."

"We lodge at the sign of the vine in Roper Lane. 'Tis but a short walk from the foot of London Bridge." How curious, I thought as I glanced at Thomas and wondered why he would keep it from Millicent.

I gave her hand a gentle squeeze. "It'll please me to keep company with you again, Millicent, whilst Robert is away."

She observed Robert and Thomas engaged in a boisterous conversation with other young men waiting to fill their ale pots. "Look at the pair of them. They're like blood brothers, those two. Always looking out for each other and guarding secrets," she said with a hint of resentment.

"Secrets, you say – of what nature?"

"Aye, secrets. This past Monday, whilst bringing clean bedlinen to the room next to Thomas, I overheard Thomas and Robert talking, for Thomas's door was not fully closed. I heard Robert say, 'Keep this letter with the others, and mind you, guard them well.'

I desperately wanted to dismiss my suspicion that the letters might have come from Rose Clavell. "Robert must have been referring to letters from his mother, I'm sure of it."

Millicent raised an eyebrow. "Perhaps, and then perhaps not."

As Robert and Thomas approached our table, Millicent whispered, "Not a word about this to Robert, do you hear?"

"Nay, not a word."

No sooner had we begun to enjoy our drinks than two men from the table who were eyeing Robert and Thomas when they first entered the room approached our table. One was slender and tall like a maypole and moved with an unsteady gait. The other was portly with a stubbly brown beard.

"Roaring boys are about to pay us a visit," Millicent warned us.

"What do you mean?" I asked.

"Alehouse bullies." She turned her attention to Robert and Thomas. "Let's just drink our ale and pay them no mind."

"If they address us, we'll hear what they have to say," said Robert.

"Agreed," Thomas added. "We have our rapiers ready."

I didn't like the sound of that. "Rapiers at the ready, you say? I pray you'll not engage these men in an altercation."

"We shall see how it plays out," Robert said calmly, not averting his eyes from their hard stares. "Perhaps they'll return to their table, and your worrying would have been all for naught."

The devil take those fellows — for come to us they did!

The shorter one pressed his knuckles on the table. "What have we here? By their fine garments, I say they are gallants," he sneered. His voice was low and rough, unpolished compared to the mellow tones of Robert and Thomas.

"Aye, of delicate rearing," the other one added. "And look, they brought along a gentlewoman into our midst."

I flinched as he fingered the lacy cuffs of my sleeve.

Robert stood and swiftly slapped the offender's hand away. "Stand back, knave. You're not fit to gaze upon her beauty, much less touch her."

"In your teeth," he bellowed and threw a punch at Robert despite being unsteady on his feet. But Robert's reflex was quick, sending the long-limbed bully tumbling over one of the ale barrels. The sleeping dog awoke, barked loudly, and, within seconds, was nipping at the fallen man's ankles.

I grabbed Robert's hand. "Let's away now!"

Not to be outdone by Robert, Thomas seized the other roaring boy by his beard and yanked him to the floor, causing a stool to crash down in their midst. A cacophony of enraged shouts erupted as the fallen men's comrades surged to their feet. Robert and Thomas were backed by the young men they conversed with earlier. All I could discern was a chaotic blur of motion as fists flew and blades were unsheathed. In the midst of this maelstrom, I lost sight of Robert and Thomas, swallowed by the tempest of violence. Zounds! My mother was right. Alehouses are not fit for gentle, decent folk.

Millicent snatched a lantern from the table and, grabbing my arm, shouted, "Let's away."

She pulled me toward the door. Once outside, I trailed behind her as she took quick steps away from the alehouse.

"How can we just leave?" I objected. "Shouldn't we have waited, at least by the door?"

She stopped short and turned to face me. "There'd be no constable in this part of town to break up that fray," she said, pointing back at the alehouse. "If Robert and Thomas lose the fight, we wouldn't be safe waiting for them. More than half of the men were friends of those two knaves who caused us trouble."

She locked arms with me and pushed me forward. "We'll return to the Paris Garden steps and wait for Robert and Thomas. Don't worry about those two. They'd escaped brawls before."

She pulled the hood of her cloak down, partially obscuring her face, and motioned for me to do the same. I complied, my hands trembling, my mind filled with the unknown dangers lurking in the shadows. Fie upon both Robert and Thomas for their reckless decision to bring us to this alehouse in such a perilous part of town. I could only hope that they had the wits and the luck to escape unscathed.

"Calm yourself, Isabella. I've one of Thomas's penknives hidden on my person, and I know how to use it to ward off an attack."

I prayed that she spoke the truth and was not just offering false words of comfort. "Do you, truly?"

"Aye. Once, whilst walking home alone, a ruffian came upon me, demanding that I lift my skirt. I stabbed him inside his upper arm, and then as he bent forward, I jabbed his neck," she said, lunging her arm upward.

"You'll have to teach me how to wield a penknife in self-defense," I said, pulling myself closer to her.

Shortly after we reached the Paris Garden steps, we heard men shouting our names. Millicent held the lantern high, but at once, I knew it was Thomas and Robert. They raced toward us.

"Are you badly injured?" I asked, lightly touching the few bloody cuts on Robert's face.

"We are but slightly bruised," Robert assured me with a triumphant smile. "Isn't that right, Thomas?"

"We were nipped a few times as we fought our way to the door," Thomas added, wincing as he touched his cuts, which appeared deeper than Robert's.

"You showed good thinking in leaving the alehouse amid that fray," Robert said, aiming a kiss at my cheek.

I quickly turned away from him. "And you showed poor judgment in bringing us to that alehouse. It was Millicent's idea to leave when the fray began. Had I been alone, I wouldn't have ventured out into the dark."

Robert draped his arm over Millicent's shoulders. "You're a quick, thinking fox, Millicent."

Thomas pointed to the river. "Look, the wherry approaches," he said, grabbing Millicent's hand. "Let's make haste." Before Thomas crossed the street, he turned to Robert.

"Godspeed on your tour with Ambrose Dudley. Let's hope you can stay till the end with no mishap from the actors this time."

Robert chuckled. "Unlike his brother, Ambrose maintains a firm control over his actors. Our audiences in Kent should prove to be less unruly."

Thomas took my hand and before bestowing a kiss, said, "Isabella, I'll call upon you to ensure that you're safe and lack for nothing whilst Robert is gone."

"God grant you a good night and see you both safely home," I said.

Millicent and I exchanged a knowing glance. I expected a visit from her whilst Robert was away.

When we returned to our room, Robert made the final preparations for his departure the following morning. Whilst singing a few lines from his ballad about Sybilla, he tossed a pair of leather gloves and assorted colored caps into his travel bag. I observed him from the bed.

Content he may have been, but for sure, I was not. The evening was a disaster.

"I must say, Robert, this was not the special evening you promised me before your departure."

With an expression of contrition, he sat beside me on the bed. "Put the blame on those two knaves. I'll make it up to you when I return. With the money I earn from this tour, we'll dine at the finest inn with no other guests. Say you forgive me, Izzy, for tonight's mishap."

"I'm tired," I said with a yawn and lay down, obscuring my face with the blanket.

For a few minutes, all was quiet until I heard Robert strumming his lute.

"Listen, Izzy," he entreated. "I composed this for you."

I pulled the blanket away from my face as I listened to Robert's melodic tune. "Are there no words for that enchanting music?"

"Not yet. Whilst you were still asleep the other morning, I gazed upon you as the first rays of sunlight streamed into the room. Right then, I picked up my lute and composed this melody."

"Indeed, Robert, as quick as that?" I found myself doubting his moment of inspiration.

He drew his face near mine and whispered, "Forgive me, Izzy, forgive me."

22

The Letter

I oft retreated to the inn's garden for days after Robert left. There is no greater solace for the soul, my father would say, than flowers in bloom. I had bundled a small bunch of cowslips from the garden with a ribbon. My mother had told me that if you wash your face in milk infused with the petals of cowslip, your beloved would never leave. She promised to sprinkle the steps of our parish church with the sweet-smelling petals of cowslips on my wedding day. Whilst dreaming about that eventful day, I heard Millicent's unmistakable giggle. I rushed to the garden's gate to greet her. I didn't expect to see her so soon after our time together at the alehouse. Still, my eyes were glad of her.

"Millicent!" I said, beaming.

She hurried into the garden. "At last, Isabella, just us two – alone."

Her eyes twinkled as she spotted a small patch of daisies, and she bent to touch their milky-white petals. "My favorite flower," she giggled as she picked one and placed it in her woolen hat.

"Come here, Isabella," Millicent said, patting the bench. "I've something for you." She removed from her pouch a letter with a torn seal. "Here's the letter Robert gave Thomas for safekeeping."

I stared at the missive, filling her hand like an ominous shadow. "How did you come by it?"

"I bedded Thomas last night," she announced with no hint of shame. "This morning, whilst he slept, I went to his lock box where he keeps important letters. I found the key, and would you believe — this one was lying on top, ready to be taken." She pointed to the letters of Robert's first and last name. "I don't know many letters, but I know the letters 'R' and 'B'. 'Tis Robert's initials, isn't it?"

I nodded that the letter was indeed addressed to him. "If Thomas looks for it, he'll know you took it."

She grew impatient. "Thomas won't look for it now that Robert's gone. And even if he did, what can he do?" She smirked. "Report me for theft? He won't, for he knows I'll say I have spent many nights in his room. If I spill that information to the right people, he'll be fined or, worse, dismissed."

"He'll deny it, and Robert will too."

Millicent stood and rested her hand on her bum. "If he denies it, I'll describe his birthmark just above his arse to prove it was so." She sat and held out the letter to me. "Come on, read it! See if it's from Robert's mother."

I prayed it was, but deep down to my core, I knew who the sender was. My fingers felt numb, for I dreaded lifting the broken seal and looking at the letter's contents. And when I did, my worst fears were realized. Rose Clavell expressed her adoration for Robert in beautifully scripted lettering. Had she only declared her affection for him, I would have dismissed the letter as the longing of a maid unrequited in love. But she referenced Robert's feelings for her as well.

It pierced my heart to read: *You say my desire to be with you, Robert, 'tis not entirely hopeless. Thus, I will cling to my dearest hope that your words are true.*

I felt as if the earth had cracked open, and I plummeted into its crevice, looking up as I fell, with Millicent's face and the garden whirling above me in a blur.

Millicent grabbed my shoulder. "The letter isn't from his mother? Is it?"

I forced the truth out of my mouth. "Nay. 'Tis from Rose Clavell, the viscount's daughter, the very maid Robert's father had set his ambition for Robert to marry."

"I knew it! Why else would Robert boast about the letter if

it wasn't from a maid who's so sweet on him? I knew Thomas wasn't talking about Robert's mother when he asked Robert if it was wise to keep up a correspondence with her."

"And what was Robert's response?"

She closed her eyes, trying to remember. "Harmless?" She pondered the word aloud. "Aye, that's what he said. 'Tis harmless." She crossed her arms, her face contorted with anger. "Harmless for Robert, but harmful for you!" she huffed.

My gaze drifted to the cowslips on my lap. Wedding flowers — indeed! I threw them to the ground and crushed them with my foot in a fit of rage. Robert's betrayal was like a knife plunged into my heart, leaving me utterly broken. The tears came, uncontrollable and hot, streaming down my face. Millicent, her face etched with worry, was beside herself.

"How now, Isabella? Let's go inside," she nudged my shoulder repeatedly until I stood, then walked me inside, up three flights to my room. Fortunately, Mistress Orellana didn't see us, and I was spared having to explain my pitiful state. But then again, quick-thinking Millicent would have given her a plausible reason to satisfy her curiosity. Once inside my room, I collapsed into the bed, my tears unrelenting as they fell. Millicent remained beside me, stroking my hair and uttering curses about Robert that would usually, under different circumstances, have caused me to blush.

⚜

For several days after Millicent's visit, I found myself in a state of deep contemplation, grappling with my own uncertain fate. I fervently hoped that I hadn't unwittingly stepped into the role of one of Ovid's tragic heroines, those who, blinded by love, had fallen for unworthy men. The thought of being as easily swayed by Robert's flattery as Medea was by Jason or as Dido was by Aeneas, filled me with anger and self-doubt. These conflicting emotions found their way onto the page as I penned my thoughts:

Constance Briones

As by Aeneas first of all,
who did poor Dido leave,
Causing the queen by his untruth,
with sword her heart to cleave.
Jason that came of noble race,
two ladies did beguile:
I muse how he durst show his face,
to them that knew his wile.

My pen went silent when Mistress Orellana knocked at my door. "There's a young gentleman named Thomas Cox who wishes to see you," she said.

After discovering that he was complicit in Robert's correspondence with Rose Clavell, I didn't wish to see Thomas and uttered no sound.

Mistress Orellana knocked again with impatience, "Miss Whitney? Do you hear? A young gentleman wishes to see you!"

I sat very still, with my eyes fixed upon my words, until her footsteps faded, and then I moved my pen again. But alas, my solitude was brief, for Mistress Orellana returned and knocked with greater urgency.

"Miss Whitney, the young gentleman begged me to knock at your door again. He says he must see you."

I knew Thomas wouldn't let the matter rest. He would insist that Mistress Orellana unlock the door to ensure, as only he would say: 'I had not fallen victim to an unfortunate mishap.' I tousled my hair before I opened the door.

"Forgive me, Mistress Orellana," I said with a feigned yawn. "I arose early this morning after a restless night and then fell into a late morning slumber."

"I shall tell Mister Cox that you will come down," she said, looking irritated, no doubt, at having to climb the stairs to the third floor twice.

Rushing to the washbasin, I placed a cold, wet cloth on my eyes to soften and brighten the surrounding skin. Indeed, I have endured many sleepless nights since Millicent's visit. I quickly combed my hair and straightened the deep folds in my skirt, which had formed whilst I sat cross-legged, writing at the table. Before I left, I breathed thrice, my anger at Thomas's insistence that I see him threatening to spill over, and I fought to rein it in.

As soon as Thomas saw me, he flashed his customary wide smile and leaned in to kiss me on my cheek, but I pulled back. His eyes flashed surprise, but he adeptly recovered his composure and sat opposite me, studying my face for any hint of displeasure.

"My dear Isabella, I came willingly at Robert's bidding to see how well you fare. My eyes rarely deceive me, and I shall happily report to Robert that you look just as lovely as when I saw you the night before his departure."

I couldn't force the slightest hint of a smile. What I once viewed as Thomas's harmless, friendly chatter was now seen as shameless fawning.

"Let there be no hesitation on your part," Thomas continued, "to call upon me for whatever you need. For you are my dear friend's beloved."

I wanted to order Thomas to silence his foolish tongue and tell him what was in my heart: *You speak falsely of wishing to keep my union with Robert strong.* Unfortunately, the only way to prove I was correct was to fling Mistress Clavell's letter in his face. But I had to endure his hypocrisy in silence for Millicent's sake.

"I thank you, Thomas, for your concern. Go and happily report to Robert that all is well."

He fell silent, his eyes flickering with doubt. I smiled inwardly at his unease.

"Come, sup with me, Isabella," he commanded cheerfully. "It would please Robert and me to treat you to a good hearty mid-day meal."

"I thank you, Thomas, but nay. I'm not hungry."

He dismissed my rejection with a sunny smile. "Then I shall call upon you later to join me for dinner – at the hour of six."

"Don't trouble yourself to return."

He reached for my hand. "How oddly, you reply, Isabella. 'Tis no burden for me to call upon you but sheer delight."

His fawning began to grate on me. Raising, I said, "I must return to my room and continue with my writing. I bid you adieu, Thomas."

"Isabella, clearly something is amiss." His voice faltered as he rose from his chair, his ingratiating smile gone.

"Nay. Nothing is amiss. I simply wish to release you from your promise to Robert. I assure you I'll be fine here on my own till he returns," I said, now smiling effortlessly. His confusion gave me much pleasure.

"But, my dear Isabella," he protested with a nervous laugh. "I'm afraid only Robert can release me from my promise. I gave him my word as his most trustworthy friend."

"Oh, but I hear you are quite adept at playing the messenger. Write to Robert at once, telling him that I released you from your promise to him."

Before he could object, I swiftly made my way out of the room and up the staircase. He followed, pleading for me to return. It did me good to walk out on him. Let him experience how I felt, bewildered and agitated when I discovered his role in Robert's secret correspondence with Rose Clavell.

Once I returned to my bedchamber, I continued writing about that scoundrel Jason, whom all men praise for his pursuit of the Golden Fleece.

> *He took his ship and fled away*
> *regarding not the vows:*
> *That he did make so faithfully,*
> *unto his loving spouse.*
>
> *Have ye such deceit in store?*
> *have you such crafty wile?*
> *Less craft than this, God knows, would soon*
> *my simple soul beguile.*

I took a deep breath and I pondered whether Robert had become my Jason. Robert will answer that question upon his return. I'll confront him with Rose Clavell's letter. Hence, I expect him to say that he will cease all correspondence with her and that his allegiance is only to me. He will have to, for I gave my body and soul to him, sacrificing my virtue and my parents' will. I stood more to lose if he proved untrue. I cursed them both - Rose Clavell for her relentless desire to have Robert despite his betrothal to me and Robert for his self-conceit. His ego craved the adoration of two women. Mine alone was not enough for him. But upon his return, it would have to be.

23

Millicent's News

When Millicent came to call again, it was a glorious Sunday, the first since spring began, not made dreary by the rain. To get my mind off Robert and away from the confines of the Ivy Inn, I welcomed a day away from Southwark with her. As we strolled toward London Bridge, I broached the topic of Thomas's visit.

"Thomas came to see me as Robert bade him do, but I refused his invitations to supper and dinner."

She glanced at me with a knowing smile, "Aye, I know. When you told Thomas not to come 'round again, he grew troubled and suspicious. When he discovered the missing letter from Rose Clavell, he marched to the Inn's kitchen to see me. Oh, if only you could have seen his face," she jeered. "Red as the devil's it was when I confessed to taking the letter. He cursed me, called me a scheming whore, and said our relationship is no more."

I tenderly took hold of her arm.

"Pish! Don't you worry, Isabella. I'm no fragile damsel." She threw back her head in defiance. "I care not a fart for Thomas."

How true Robert's words were about Millicent. Her bawdy humor made for amusing company, and I found her resilience in the demise of her long affair with Thomas admirable. "'Tis good that falling out with Thomas has not caused you much distress."

She half-smiled. "I always knew I couldn't win Thomas's love, for my father is no gentleman. It was just a merry dream, that's all."

When we reached the bridge, I was glad to see there was but a small crowd assembled, mostly gentlefolk, dressed in unadorned brown and grey wool clothing, wishing to spend a day in central London. And being Sunday, the farmers who oft-delayed the crossing with their carts heavily laden with sacks of grain and peas and their flocks of sheep remained home. There would be more room to stroll freely and point with outstretched arms to the spike heads of criminals at the drawbridge tower, which Millicent did with much glee.

I fixed my eyes on the ground. "I cannot bear to look at those severed heads, with their expressions frozen, twisted with fear when the ax fell. 'Tis truly like looking into the pit of hell."

"What a silly you are," she laughed. "That one there – the old gent in the middle of the four with the grizzled beard looks quite peaceful."

I squeezed her arm as we passed under the gory sight. The bridge's walkway resembled more a city street than part of a bridge, with dwelling houses above shops. We pointed to the shops that attracted our interest with childlike enthusiasm, imagining ourselves as daughters of prosperous landowners like Robert's father, ready to spend our fathers' money on chains of gold and silver ruffs adorned with glass beads, white embroidered gloves, and silk scarves that would add a dash of style to our gowns.

Halfway across the bridge, the crowd suddenly stopped. Ahead of us was a group of onlookers staring with amazement at the palatial house that straddled the bridge.

"Do you hear them? They're strangers," Millicent whispered.

"Perchance, they are Dutch, admiring the work of their countrymen. Robert told me that the gilded house was partly built in Amsterdam and assembled here."

I couldn't help but join them in gawking at the massive house with its steep gables, gilded vanes, and enormous sundials. "They're right to stop and marvel. 'Tis magnificent."

"Let's hope whoever lives in that grand house doesn't come to the window to empty a chamber pot. I don't fancy getting a whiff or drizzle of a rich man's piss when the wind blows," Millicent cackled.

"Not much chance of that happening," I said, nudging her forward. "For look, they're done with their viewing and are moving on."

When we reached the other side of the bridge, we found ourselves on the bustling thoroughfare of Thames Street. "Where shall we go?" Millicent said.

I knew where I wanted to go but wondered if Millicent would feel the same about going to St. Paul's book market on the green.

"What fun's to be found there?" Millicent cried.

"Wouldn't you like to hear a scandalous tale?" I said, hoping that was enough to entice her to change her mind. "Plenty such stories can be found there for the price of a penny."

Millicent kicked at a few stones and muttered, "Hmm, maybe."

"And we can stop at the bakehouse on Pudding Lane to buy a seed cake to take with us. It'll be fun, Millicent, I promise you."

"Seed cake and a scandalous story?" she mused. "Why not! Lead the way, my merry friend."

We trotted off to Pudding Lane with the lively gait of two frolicking ponies. Within a short time, we found ourselves on the south side of St. Paul's church. We settled down with our treat and a riveting tale of murder under a tree with a smooth, silvery trunk. In between bites of our tasty seed cake, I read aloud the story of a cuckold Kentish gentleman mercilessly murdered by his wife and her lover. They were helped by the lover's sister and two servants of the victim's household.

Millicent stared in disbelief when she heard the wife's determination to carry out the murderous deed. "Zounds!" Millicent exclaimed, wrapping her arms around her knees and leaning forward to hear every lurid detail of the second murder attempt. "She tried murdering her husband not once, but twice? Read on."

I raised my voice for dramatic effect at pivotal moments in the story, wanting Millicent's nerves to tingle with each dastardly action described.

"And then the lover's sister, who took part in the murderous deed"— and here I brought my voice to a pitch, "struck the husband with a great pressing iron! And the wife's lover" — my voice sounding shrill, "lunged forward from behind the hapless husband and cut his throat!" I concluded the passage by sweeping my hand across my throat.

"What a moll she was," Millicent sneered. "And the husband, a fool not to know his wife was up to no good. For didn't she lay with her lover whilst her husband was in the house? Why did he allow it – I wonder?"

"The prologue says that his wife inherited her first husband's assets upon his death, making her quite the wealthy widow. Her second husband must have felt he had much to lose if she left him. Thus, to keep her content, he allowed her a lover."

Millicent scoffed. "I know no man from my lot who would make himself a cuckold just to keep his hands on his wife's money. Read on, Isabella. How did this bloody mess end?"

I moved my finger to the last paragraph. "The wife was hanged by the neck with a chain. Her lover and his sister met the same end. As for the two servants who helped them, the man was drawn and hung in chains, and the woman was burned alive."

Millicent smiled like a contented cat who snagged a mouse. "Nothing better than a good execution to set everything right." She clapped her hands. "What a sensational tale it was, and for the price of a penny, too!"

We laughed, having enjoyed a riveting tale that provided respite from our troubles with Robert and Thomas.

After I finished the final bites of my share of the seed cake, I stood up and stretched. "Are you up for a challenge, Millicent?"

I caught a glint of curiosity in her eye," I might be."

"I'll race you to the cathedral's roof."

Disinterest crossed her face. "You feel like mounting close to three hundred steps?"

"I heard the view is splendid, and isn't this the perfect day to be perched high above London?" I said, standing on my toes with my arms stretched toward the cloudless sky.

The corners of her mouth quickly turned up. "See you at the top of London!" she yelled, sprinting past me. I watched her scamper up the grassy path to the roof's entrance, her mustard-colored cape falling off her shoulders. She was one of the most spirited girls I've ever met. What wondrous adventures we would have had together if we had been born men.

As I mounted the stone steps that snaked their way up to the roof, I called out for Millicent, but she didn't respond. Marry! She took my challenge seriously and playfully wanted to keep me guessing how far up she had gone. I couldn't hurry to catch up with her, for an elderly couple gingerly mounted the steps ahead of me. About halfway up, they slowed even more, for the width of the steps shrank. I placed my hands against the narrow walls to maintain my balance. When I finally came to the flat, broad surface of the sun-drenched roof, I beheld Millicent waving her arms and smiling triumphantly. She rushed toward me.

"Close your eyes," she said and led me by the hand to the roof's edge, marked off by a low wall.

"Now open your eyes. Lucky for you, Isabella, I got here just minutes before you and found this spot with the best view."

The towering steeples of the cathedral cut into the sky and from this lofty height, I felt as if I had stepped into God's heavenly kingdom. Looking down at the view below, the Thames carried sailing vessels atop its fast-moving currents. My eye moved further up the river where London Bridge and the bulbous-shaped domes of the dreaded Tower of London stood. Directly below, were the streets I had come to know, each selling its distinct brand of goods. Watling Street had all kinds of woolen cloth to buy, Friday Street was where Lady Bramwell bought her dresses of imported silk, and Goldsmith's Row boasted shops of exquisite jewels and gold and silver plates. Tailors on Bow Street crafted the latest fashion to tempt young men like Robert and Thomas to spend their fathers' money. Saint Martin's Street was where shoemakers made boots and shoes with fancy buckles that I hoped to wear one day.

But the street that warmed my heart the most ran directly astride the church, Paternoster Row, with its printers and bookbinders. Their trade nourished my soul and brought Robert and me together. I felt that London was our city, Robert's and mine. The seeds of our passions were sown here, making us a part of it. It grieved me to think that I might have to depart from London. Unthinkable! There were no towns in England that could rival all that it had to offer.

"Are we not fortunate, Millicent, to live in this magnificent city?"

Millicent scoffed. "I leave London to you." And then added, "In a few days, I'm returning home to Cornwall."

"What's there for you in Cornwall that's better than this?" I said, making a sweeping gesture with my hand across the view before me.

"A man —a good man."

I stared at her, for I'd never heard her speak of a man other than Thomas.

"A widower much older than me wants me for his wife," she confessed, a surprisingly shy smile crossing her lips. "When my father first heard of it, he was ready to send me packing quickly. But being with someone my father's age didn't sit well with me. Before I left home, the widower told me, if you don't fare well in London, my girl, come back. For I will not withdraw my offer of marriage."

I fell silent, taking in this new information, and moved along the wall until the corn-grinding windmills on the river's south bank came into view. "A widower? Any children?"

She giggled as she held up five fingers.

"Zounds – five!"

"And all boys," she cackled.

My brother Brooke sprang to mind. He could be unruly, needing my mother's firm hand to end his waggish antics. A household with five young boys like him who needed a stepmother seemed daunting. Still, if anyone could handle the task, it was Millicent.

"And does he have a pleasing face?"

She shrugged. "He's not handsome like Thomas or Robert, but I like his face well enough."

"Do you love him?"

"Pish," she said, walking away from me. "I'm nearly twenty-five and have no time to wait for love. I'll go home to my widower."

"Even though you go to him, not a virgin?" I whispered.

"I was no virgin girl when he asked me," she blurted, making her way to the staircase that led to the street. We placed our hands on the stone wall to help guide us down the narrow, winding steps.

As we left the churchyard, we passed a young man reading verses aloud to a well-dressed gentleman with a bulbous nose. When the young man finished, the gent nodded his approval and gave him a slip of paper. The poet bowed gratefully and shook his hand.

"There goes a fortunate young man who found a patron," I uttered wistfully.

Millicent linked her arm to mine. "I'll wager your verses are better than his."

We had not walked far from the church when Millicent asked, "Do you still love Robert?"

Since the revelation of Rose Clavell's letter, my feelings for Robert should have grown cold. But my love for him burned fitfully with joy, desire, anger, hate, and the grace of forgiveness. I hoped that upon Robert's return, he would prove that he was deserving of the love I bore him.

"Call me a fool if you want, but I still love him. When he

returns, I will know my fate. To stay with him here in London or start anew."

Millicent, ever understanding, bit her lip and refrained from passing judgment. "I hope your love for Robert proves worthy, and you can remain here in your beloved London with him."

I embraced her for her kind words. To the devil with Thomas and Robert, to have thought ill of her. She's only lesser than them for her lack of money, not her character.

"I have no doubt that your widower will treat you well."

"If he doesn't, he'll feel the end of a broomstick on his head. You can be sure of that."

She laughed, and I did, too. For I knew she meant it.

Part Three

Becoming

Had I a husband, or a house, and all that longs thereto
Myself could frame about to rouse, as other women do:
But till some household cares me tie,
My books and pen I will apply.

Isabella Whitney

24

My Fate is Decided

When Robert and I were betrothed, I anticipated bringing Robert home to meet my family on May Day. I saw the scene unfold in my mind. My sisters, Mary and Dorothea, with garlands of bluebells and dandelions on their heads, and my brother Brooke happily pulled Robert into the house, asking him questions about himself and his family. Robert laughed heartily and responded to each question. My father stole Robert away to help him and his friends erect the towering maypole in the town's center. We all danced around the maypole, accompanied by Robert's singing. My mother's and father's broad smiles signaled that they were pleased to have Robert as my betrothed - their future son-in-law. But upon Robert's return to the Ivy Inn, all blissful images of May Day in my dream, which was just a week away, vanished.

When Robert entered our room, he didn't greet me with poetic utterances of his love for me, nor did he bestow his customary kisses on my forehead and cheek, saving his last deep kiss for my mouth. Instead, I received a brief kiss and a curt statement, "Izzy, we must speak on a very delicate matter." I surmised that his coldness was deliberate, a well-calculated move designed to help him break away as quickly and efficiently as possible, with no tears or drama. It broke my heart, but I steadied myself.

"Yes, Robert, there's much to discuss." I, too, could assume a lawyer's cold deportment as well.

He removed his cape and sat in the chair by the hearth. "Please, Izzy, come and sit," he said.

I joined him in that warm corner of the room where we oft sat and had lively discussions. Robert sat tall with one leg crossed over the other, and I pressed my back into the chair, my head held high, ready to begin our talk. Silence filled the air between us as we waited to see who would first express a grievance. I opened the argument.

"You weren't forthcoming, Robert, about your relationship with Rose Clavell. I read her last letter to you, which was full of sweet sentiments and longings – undoubtedly encouraged by your attentions to her."

"It was wrong of Millicent to take the letter from Thomas's lockbox and show it to you," he retorted, his voice tinged with anger. "I hear she has gone from London for good. We're well rid of her mischievous ways."

I leaned forward, my voice sharp with accusation, pointing my finger at him. "You mean Thomas, and you are well rid of her. Do not include me in your use of the word we. For she had proved truer than you or Thomas." The words hung in the air, leaving a bitter taste on my tongue.

He uncrossed his legs and crossed them again, which I took as a physical manifestation of his unease. "I admit, it was a cruel way for you to find out. But, I assure you, Izzy, I would have told you." His voice, usually so steady, wavered with the weight of his admission.

I laughed bitterly. "The letter I read wasn't Rose Clavell's first to you. You have been corresponding with her for quite some time, but now you must put an end to it."

He averted my stare. Gazing at the roaring fire in the fireplace, he quickly announced what I most dreaded to hear. "I think it best that you and I part."

The swift delivery of his words struck a hard blow. Still, I didn't wince or burst into tears. I had none left to shed, for they had already been spent the moment I read the letter from Rose Clavell and for days after. In its stead was a steely determination to hold him to his promise of marriage — indeed, had he not pledged his troth to me, I wouldn't be in this situation, fraught with uncertainty and loss of virtue.

"You forget we were betrothed, first with God as our witness, then Richard and Maria. You would leave me no choice, Robert, but to bring you to court for breach of a marriage contract."

My heart raced when I noticed the trace of a smug smile creep over his lips. "That wouldn't be wise," he said.

God's blood! How dare he utter such a thing. I rose from my chair and dug my nails into the chair's cloth. It was all I could do to prevent myself from slapping him hard across the face. Although I'm sure that would happen at any given moment.

"Not wise?" I hissed. "I sacrificed my good name because I truly believed you loved me. Or did you, Robert?" I took a deep breath, so rattled was I by his arrogance and, worse, his indifference. "I'm beginning to suspect you held out the promise of a church wedding to get yourself a bedmate."

He shook his head with a vigorous denial. "Not true!"

"Have no doubt, Robert, that I will bring you to court for breach of a marriage contract," I asserted, my voice rising.

Robert moved to the small table by the window and filled a goblet halfway with wine, which he downed before turning to me. His manner was gentler as he expressed his view. "Think well about your threat, Izzy. It would take years for you to obtain legal status for our betrothal in court. My father would openly declare that he never approved of our union. My aunt would also denounce you in court. Think of how your parents would react to my family's derision of your name?"

Oh, he knew his law very well, I seethed. How his words sickened me - uttered only to serve his purpose. The love that once sweetened the air around us had now turned stale and foul, making it easy for me to hurl hard truths.

"Leaving me for Rose Clavell suits your needs well enough. You need not worry about providing her a home — her father will see to that. And he, being kin to the queen, can bend her ear to consider you for a position as a court musician. It all seems like a cozy arrangement. You have no love for Rose Clavell. And well you know it."

Robert banged his fist on the table. "Hold your tongue, Izzy. Of late, you have become shrewish."

His calling me a shrew bothered me very little. I imagined Robert Dudley had described the queen as such whenever she reprimanded him for his countless indiscretions.

Robert continued, growing more agitated. "You have become overbearing with your nagging about my returning to the law. I will abide it no longer." He pointed to his trunk and said, "I'll send someone to fetch it in the morning. You may stay here until the end of the month when you depart for home."

I sat at my end of the writing table, where I oft wrote, and Robert joined me. But this time, there was no deep literary discussion. "I don't intend to go home but to stay in London."

"Remain in London?" he asked, astonished, and sat opposite me at the other end. "But how can you? Without a reference from my aunt, it would be impossible for you to secure a position in another house." He shook his head. "'Tis in your best interest to return home."

"No," I said so resolutely it aroused a sense of urgency in him.

"You're a pretty and clever girl who could easily find the love of another back home with whom you would get all the benefits of wifehood," he exhorted.

Again, I responded with a resounding no. "A different fate awaits me. I sense it in my very marrow. Robert, I'm not afraid to tread a different path than what's expected of my sex."

He stared at me in disbelief as he rose from the table. "What's it to be then, Izzy – a writer's life?" he said, his mocking tone making my blood boil.

With a swift motion, I retrieved the papers, which contained months of my writing, laying them out on the table until they covered half of it. I pressed my hands firmly on the papers, declaring my commitment to writing. "Aye, Robert. A writer's life is my calling. I'm certain my pen will be my ally. I will not depart London to appease your discomfort."

He moved closer to me and picked up one sheet, tossing it

to the table. "Be careful, Izzy. You don't want to live a spinster's life years from now because you were pursuing a foolish dream of becoming a writer."

I quickly retrieved it, placing it with the others. "You are hell-bent on seeing me gone from London. Are you afraid of Richard printing my poem that casts men as scoundrels in love, explicitly depicting your behavior? By God, I will, Robert. Try explaining that to your lovesick Rose Clavell."

He flinched as if my words were like darts hurled at his face.

"Check for my name in the bookstalls of St. Paul's on any given Sunday next month," I predicted with a confident smile.

He pivoted on his heels, snatching his cape. "Do as you wish, Izzy," he declared, his voice tinged with resignation as he approached the door.

I followed him and seized his arm, refusing to release it when he turned to face me.

"Shall I tell you, Robert, what doomed our relationship? I now see very clearly the difference between you and me. Words mean everything to me. I choose them carefully with much deliberation because they reveal the essence of who I am. But words mean nothing to you, there are mere trifles. Aye, they tumble gracefully from your tongue, but ultimately, they are worthless because they don't bare your soul. You're a hollow vessel, Robert Barrington."

A sorrowful expression etched across his face. "When I said I loved you, I meant it. I have loved you like no other woman I've known."

I believed him, but how he could bury his love for me to procure a more comfortable married life with Rose Clavell was unfathomable. I let go of his arm and opened the door. "Aye, you loved me, Robert. But not enough to weather the tribulations of love."

He strode past me and descended the stairs with purpose. When I heard the main door close, I sank to the floor. I could feel the fury of tears in my eyes, but I refused to let them fall. Like the women in *Heroides*, I, too, had fallen victim to my passion and was forsaken by a man I loved too fast and too soon. But unlike them, I would not break.

ଊଞଈ

Hours after Robert left, I went to Mistress Orellana to see if she would generously give me a cup of milk, a pinch of sugar, and nutmeg. I desired a warm glass of posset. It was a drink my mother recommended to calm one's nerves. As luck would have it, Mistress Orellana had the necessary ingredients and graciously gave me what I needed without question. Returning to my room, I set the milk to boil slowly over the fire. I added wine and stood watch to ensure it didn't burn. Once the posset was ready, I sipped it slowly and contemplated my options now that Robert had left me.

Returning home was out of the question. My mother's pain would only bring me more heartache. My failure in love and dismissal from Lady Bramwell's employ would elicit a sorrowful sigh and a swift rebuke from my mother. 'When you left for London to begin your service with Lady Bramwell, we expected you to be an exemplary model of modesty and diligence for your sisters, making us all proud. But instead, you gave yourself over to a passionate indulgence. You have failed us.'

'Perhaps we should have kept her at home,' my father would chime, observing me through heavy-lidded eyes laced with profound disappointment. Facing both my parents would be an additional layer of pain I could not forebear. Henceforth, I remained resolute in finding a job, returning home only when Richard published my poem. Then my mother would retract that I idled my time away, lost in romantic dreaming.

I made a list of potential jobs, foolishly writing maidservant first but quickly put a line through it. Without a reference from Lady Bramwell, finding a similar position in a grand home that offered room and meals would be impossible. I then jotted down cook but quickly put a line through that as well. That was a man's job for which they were paid decent wages to cook in large taverns and inns. I didn't strike a line through the dreaded job of scullery maid. I remembered well how hard Millicent and I labored that day in the kitchen at Gray's Inn. Still, for that job, a recommendation wasn't an absolute requirement.

I added other jobs to the list, which didn't need to be crossed off, such as washerwoman, seamstress, and spinning cloth. I wasn't at liberty to be selective. If my father had been a tradesman instead of a gentleman living off the income of a small estate, my choices would have been better. The trade guilds allow daughters to work in their father's shops and go as far as to enable widows to run their husband's businesses. Still, my mother would be livid to hear me say I wish my father worked as a tradesman.

The sound of distant laughter wafted into the room from the open window that faced the street. I saw a man and woman laughing and walking arm in arm toward the inn. It reminded me of all those times Robert and I returned to our room in equally high spirits after spending time at the tavern with his friends or seeing a play at the Tabard—a pox on you, Robert, for not staying true.

I returned to the list I had begun to compose, and my hand mindlessly wrote Mistress Walden's name. Indeed, I had momentarily lost my good sense and furiously drew lines through her name until it was no longer decipherable. I had fallen into disrepute for having had sexual relations with my mistress's nephew. Asking Mistress Walden for help would be considered an impertinence. In recommending me for a maidservant position to one of her friends, Mistress Walden would risk tarnishing her reputation and evoking the ire of that spiteful witch - Lady Bramwell.

With my next thought, the corners of my mouth turned upwards into a gentle smile. How foolish of me not to have considered my cousin William straight away. He was an excellent choice to turn to in my time of need. He never failed in providing sound counsel and in keeping my trust. I immediately wrote a letter informing him of my dire situation.

Dearest cousin,

I find myself in a most deplorable state. I lost my job with Lady Bramwell after entering into a relationship with her nephew, Robert. And now he has gone from me and into the arms of the daughter of a viscount. Imagine my horror at this outcome. For we were betrothed not once, William, but twice. The second bearing witnesses to our intention to marry in the church. Thus, you can imagine how seriously I took Robert's love and devotion to me. Robert's father, outraged over our betrothal, severed all financial ties. We settled in Southwark and lived contently together as husband and wife. He departed from me solely for his comfort in pursuing his musical aspirations. Rose Clavell, the object of Robert's current affections, will cater to his every need as his mother always had. I have come to somberly recognize the essence of Robert - born into privilege, handsome, charming, but arrogant, spoiled, and capricious. The only good to come from my relationship with Robert was my friendship with Richard Jones, a prominent printer and bookseller. He's most generous and supportive of my writing endeavors. Prithee, cousin, I implore you to leave your studies at Oxford and make haste to visit me here in Southwark. We could devise a plan to reverse my life's downtrodden path. From Vine Inn, in Roper Lane, in the borough of Southwark, the tenth day of May 1568.

Your devoted cousin, Izzy

Within a week of sending my letter to William, he responded with six short words:

I will arrive on Monday next.
William

25

A New Beginning

Sitting in the inn's garden waiting for William, I felt the stirrings of a poem. With graphite in hand, I commenced writing about the delights of flowers, which I consider the most delicate of God's creations.

> *And though good fortune hath denied*
> *to hoist me on her wheel:*
> *Yet now she stood me in some steed,*
> *and made me pleasure feel.*
> *For Fortune to this spot me brought,*
> *where fragrant flowers abound.*
> *And for my part, I may be bold,*
> *to come when as I will.*

I spied William crossing the road just as I finished the last line. I leaped to my feet and waved a nosegay of purple and gold flowers I had made for him.

"William over here!" I shouted.

He advanced quickly, and I rushed to the gate. His hair was shorter since I last saw him on Christmas day. And I laughed, thinking I could no longer tease him about his long locks, making him look like a French courtier.

"This is for you," I said, my face lighting up with memories. "A token of those blissful and carefree days when we would sit amidst the wildflowers of Nantwich castle, engrossed in books and conversation."

Taking the nosegay, William smiled. "I do remember with

fondness those days spent in the meadow listening to you read, but dear cousin much has happened since those idyllic days. We have much to discuss."

"Indeed. But not here." I took his arm and eagerly led him inside the inn.

As we passed the parlour, I saw the same man and woman whose laughter I had heard from the street below my window the day Robert left. They were clearly smitten with each other, uttering sweet words, clasping hands, and laughing softly. Perhaps they were recently married and awaiting the visit of family members. The devil take you, Robert! That's the scene William should have been privy to with you and me sitting there awaiting him instead of the awkward situation I find myself in with my dear cousin.

We mounted the steps, proceeding upward to the third floor. As we approached the second landing, I saw Mistress Orellana leaving one of the two rooms on that floor. Beside her stood a reed figure of a young chambermaid carrying folded linen bed sheets. Mistress Orellana eyed us curiously.

"How now, Isabella? And who's this fine young man who accompanies you?" she said, gazing at William with interest. She had grown accustomed to Robert's ostentatious manner of dress, who favored short doublets and silk hoses. In contrast, William sported modest knee-length breeches and plain shoes with no silver buckles. Nor did he wear a pearl earring in his lobe like Robert.

"Mistress Orellana, this is my cousin William, who has come to visit from Oxford University," I said proudly.

"Ah," she uttered approvingly, nodding to William, "a scholar from Oxford. I thought as much, for you have the look of a serious-minded young man. Do enjoy your visit here, William."

"It seems a fine establishment, Mistress, with a lovely garden. My cousin is most fortunate to be staying here."

Mistress Orellana smiled. "God give you a good day," she said as she descended the staircase with the chambermaid trailing behind her. With every line of instruction snapped by

Mistress Orellana, the chambermaid responded, "Aye, Mistress," and "I shall remember Mistress."

William leaned into me and whispered, "I hope the young chambermaid does remember, for Mistress Orellana strikes me as someone who doesn't take kindly to repeating instructions."

I nudged him to go up one more flight of stairs. I opened the door to my room and bade him enter. William couldn't help but notice first the commodious bed fitted with linen sheets and plush cushions. I felt naked and exposed as William gazed at the spot where Robert and I romped lustfully under the sheets.

I directed him to the round table by the fireplace where I had laid a modest meal of bread, cheese, and nuts. But he was more interested in looking around the room that Robert and I had shared during our time in Southwark. William examined the designs in the hexagonal medallion in the center of the oriental rug. Little did he know that Robert's naked body oft graced that very spot. His eyes rested on the pair of silver-plated candelabras on the fireplace mantel. He walked over to the oak table where Robert and I oft wrote together and traced the silver-color wood inlay with his finger. He turned to me with a wry smile. "There can be no doubt, Izzy, that Robert is a young man who thrives living in grand style."

William had ascertained Robert's core truth without ever having met him. In an instant, he deduced that Robert couldn't bear to forgo the comforts of his class and had thrown me over for someone with a far more enticing dowry that would put him back in his father's good favor. By marrying Rose Clavell, his father would forgive Robert's refusal to stay in law school since the Barrington name would advance to a higher level of the upper class.

Seated at the round table, William was ready to partake of the food. "Take heart, Izzy. Robert was nothing more than a mirage of dazzling light and sweet air. As you described him, he was a man of striking appearance and charming manner. But what worth is that when his nature is fickle, easily swayed by his whims?" He then cast a sidelong glance at me," I recall cautioning you last Christmas, when you first spoke of your interest in Robert, to tread carefully."

I stiffened as I sat opposite him. "Aye, William, but I believed Robert's love was constant and true, especially since he defied his father's wishes, who refused to recognize our betrothal vows. And so intent was he to make his father and aunt take our love seriously that he arranged for us to repeat our vows in front of witnesses." I shook my head. "I found no reason to doubt that he had every intention of taking the next step – to exchange vows in the church."

William said nothing but picked up a handful of hazelnuts to nibble on. An uncomfortable silence fell between us. He thinks me a ninny!

"I have grown weary discussing Robert. 'Tis done," I said resolutely. "It was a love that went horribly awry, and I'll no longer punish myself for Robert's betrayal."

I sat opposite him and poured wine into William's glass. "How fare my mother and father?"

William cut himself a piece of cheese. "They're well and most eager to see you four months hence, at which time your service contract with Lady Bramwell would have ended."

Nibbling on the cheese, he eyed me curiously. "I say, Izzy, just how long can you keep what happened with Lady Bramwell and Robert a secret?"

I felt my cheeks grow warm with shame. "I don't enjoy concealing the truth from my mother and father. Only I don't want to return home a failure. I've something in mind that I hope will make them proud."

"What is it you intend to do?"

"Unlike Robert, I'm willing to forego comfort to remain in London and write."

He stared at me. "I didn't know you felt so strongly about writing."

" I'll become a washerwoman if need be. And when I return to my room at the end of the workday, with my fingers swollen and raw from washing coarse linen, I'll place the pen between my fingers and write."

William remained silent, contemplating my response as he sipped his wine. He was either impressed by my fervor to write or thought me mad.

"But consider Izzy, is writing a sensible undertaking?" William pondered aloud. "It's hard enough for a man to earn his keep as a writer, let alone a woman. And what would you write about? You can't translate religious texts into English."

He thought I had gone mad to take up the pen. True, the path for female writers was narrow. But William didn't mention the topic that Richard suggested I write about. "I'll write of a woman's view of men in love."

With a bemused expression, William exclaimed, "And what makes you think men will pay to read about that?"

I playfully swiped a piece of cheese off William's plate with a smile. In between bites, I said, "Richard Jones, the master printer I mentioned in my letter, believes men will." I swallowed the remaining piece of my cheese with a gulp of wine before concluding my argument. "Good God, William! Why should a genuine female voice be absent from the popular debate on which sex is truer in love?"

William leaned back in his chair, sporting an amused expression. "Your printer friend may be right. If that's the subject, I would like to read what you say."

We both laughed and briefly felt as carefree as I did back home when William and I met for our reading lessons in the meadow.

William set aside his plate and cleared his throat. "I'm going to relay to you a sad tale I heard. The sister of a fellow I know at Oxford found herself in a similar situation to yours, with a minor difference. It was her parents who disapproved of her young man. Despite their objections, she followed her heart and was jilted by her betrothed as you have been. Sometime later, she was found begging for alms, pale and sick. Had they not found her when they did, she would have likely turned to prostitution to earn her keep."

"Merciful heaven, thank God she was found," I said, aware

of the unpleasant fate that would have befallen the poor wretch.

William rose from the table to stretch his legs. "'Tis a fate, whilst rare for young women from good families, does happen to some unlucky in love." He looked me squarely in the eyes.

"Let's keep our family safe from such scandal. I believe I have a temporary solution to your problem."

Clasping my hands above my head, I exclaimed. "God in heaven, William! Lady Fortune has deemed you my savior."

William smiled half-heartedly. "I'm glad you think of me as such, but hear my plan first. You might change your mind."

He returned to the table and finished the last morsels of the cheese and bread on his plate. I reigned in my enthusiasm, resting my hands on my lap. And I nodded for William to begin.

"I have a friend, Lawrence Fergus, whose father is a prosperous London merchant in the cloth trade. He mentioned that his mother is seeking a charwoman. Someone to come to the house daily to assist her staff with household chores. My recommendation would be enough to get you the job."

I breathed relief. "'Tis the perfect solution for my problem."

"Mind you, Izzy, as a charwoman, you'll have to perform some unpleasant duties, unlike those for Lady Bramwell, such as emptying chamber pots and cleaning and scouring pots and pans. I know you hate the needle, but you might have to do a bit of sewing."

I was overjoyed at the prospect of having a job. "I'll do whatever Mistress Fergus wants without complaint - I assure you."

Satisfied with my answer, William rose from the table and removed a slip of paper from the pouch on his belt. "The first thing we must do is find you somewhere to live. My friend gave me the names of lodging houses near his family's business in Lombard Street. I have enough money to cover three weeks, after which you'll pay for the lodgings from the wages you'll earn as a charwoman."

I thanked Lady Fortune for giving me such a generous cousin. I knew how hard William worked in between his studies to earn money. He was not above working alongside the field-hands who worked his father's land. Last August, during the sweltering hot days, William toiled in his father's fields without complaint. I knew his goodness would be rewarded. Lady Fortune would not forget him in his time of need as he had not forsaken me in mine.

"William, your sacrifice to pay for my room will not be for naught. Something grand will come of it."

"That's my hope. Now, let's make haste to visit the lodging houses my friend has recommended. The day is short, and I must return to Oxford tomorrow."

I felt a pang of regret that he would leave me so soon, for having him with me was a great comfort. I scampered to fetch my cloak. Of the two lying on the chair by the bed, I chose the pale yellow one not because Robert had given it to me but because it was William's favorite color. I quickly tied the strings into a tight knot, not wanting to fuss with it coming undone whilst we were out and about searching for new accommodations.

As I closed the door to my room, I vowed that day I would make William proud by performing my duties for Mistress Fergus with unwavering diligence and then return home a published author by the end of summertide. My mother should be impressed with the money I earned from selling my poem, no matter how meager the sum.

CR&SO

By late afternoon, we had seen rooms in three lodging houses in and around Lombard and Candlewick streets. All dismal — tiny rooms with no windows and reeds strewn on the floors. There was one more lodging house on the list to visit. I prayed this last one, in Abchurch Lane, at the very least, would have a window. As we turned the corner of Lombard and Abchurch, a pretty stone church perched on a patch of raised ground caught my eye.

"That's Saint Marie Abchurch, built in the twelfth century," William said with a nod toward the church.

"Does this street take its name from the church?"

William nodded. He oft enjoyed dispensing historical tidbits, and I never tired of hearing them. He continued, "Not long ago, the queen granted the church to Corpus Christi College in Cambridge."

"No one I know, not even Robert nor his law school friends, could match your knowledge of our country's religious history. I bet I can point to any church in London, and you would have something to say about it."

With a bashful smile, he remarked, "I think you're probably right."

I poked his arm. "More humility, I pray."

Abchurch Lane, like the other streets we had visited that afternoon, was a cramped maze of buildings, devoid of any greenery. The overhanging gables seemed to close in on us, and the pungent smell of urine hung in the air. As we made our way up the street, a young man with a ruddy complexion and a dirty white tunic dashed past us, his shoulder brushing against William's. Startled, William instinctively grabbed my hand, pulling me out of harm's way. A middle-aged gentleman, his leather glove raised high, shouted 'thief' as he chased after the young man, who was now far enough to escape his pursuer.

"Remember, Izzy, do not visibly keep your purse about your person but hide it well," William advised.

In my current circumstance, my weak purse would likely anger a thief for having little to offer him. He might prey upon my body as compensation if he was a depraved knave. I trembled at the thought I would have to continually guard myself against the threat of rape in these parts of the city. I kept this disturbing thought from William.

William stopped before a four-storied building bearing the sign of a red fox. He looked at me with a glint of hope in his eyes. "This is the final lodging house on the list. Prepare yourself to make a decision by the end of this visit."

I nodded, knowing full well I had to prove my mettle by forsaking the comforts of my family's home. I must face living humbly in one of the squalid neighborhoods we visited today to remain in London to write.

He lifted the latch and let it drop thrice against the door. When no one came to the door, I stepped in front of William and lifted the latch higher, repeatedly letting it fall with dull thuds against the weathered black door.

A young woman with a heart-shaped face and kind eyes answered the door. A hopeful sign, I thought.

"Good day, Miss. Are you the landlord?" William asked politely.

"Nay. That would be my mother," she said with a curious look as she eyed both of us.

"My cousin here is looking for a room to lease. Perchance you have one available that we can look at?"

She eyed us with a hint of skepticism, her lips pursed in a way that suggested she was used to men accompanied by women who were not their wives. "There is one, vacated early this morning," she finally conceded.

"May we see it?"

She nodded. "I see no harm in showing you both the room. This way."

We followed her up a creaky staircase to the third floor and stopped in front of a brilliant red door. She opened the door and bid us enter as she stood in the doorway. I breathed a sigh of relief, for there was a window in the room, albeit a small one. Like the other rooms we saw that day, the floor was covered with reeds, which didn't appear to be freshly laid, and the barest of furnishings – nothing more than a low stool and a tiny bed. I sat down on the bed, its uncomfortable mattress stuffed with flock, and laid my hand on the coarse, well-worn bed linen.

"How much is the room?" William said.

"It'll be one shilling, four pence per week."

William mulled over the sum, which made the young woman grow impatient.

"I must warn you this room will go quickly with the country folk pouring into London looking for jobs," she added.

William sat next to me on the bed. "What will it be, Izzy? You must decide now."

Sensing the urgency in the landlord's daughter's warning about the room's popularity, William answered, "My cousin will take the room." Turning to me, he muttered, "'Tis the best room we have seen thus far."

"My mother will return shortly. You may wait for her here until she arrives and make the necessary transaction with her," the young woman instructed before departing, leaving the door open.

William took hold of my hand. "Promise me, Izzy, you'll not tarry here too long. Do what you must do as quickly as possible and return home," he implored. "For the air here abounds with infections. And if you need to venture out after dark, hire a lamp boy to accompany you. Promise me that, or else I cannot leave you here."

I placed my hand on William's shoulder and promised him, "By day, I will work hard, and at night, I will forsake all except my writing."

I walked to the window and looked down on the busy street below. A group of children weaved their way around piss puddles that glistened under the light of the late afternoon sun. Their mothers chased after them, cursing them. I turned from the window and said to William with a reassuring smile, "By the end of summertide, I will row home in Lady Fortune's barge, a published writer."

26

Unsettling News

Fortunately, my lodging in Abchurch Lane was only a footfall away from my new job. Every morning, before I left for work, I scattered rosemary, with its scent of pine, amongst the reeds to mask the unpleasing smell my shoes carried into the room when I returned. After I finished my morning task, I would embark on a simple route to walk north up the hill in Abchurch to Lombard Street, the site of many drapery shops. The owners of Fergus Drapers were Mistress Fergus and her husband, who founded the business. In a short time, they had amassed a loyal customer base of wealthy families who understood that clothing made from the highest quality distinguished them from the rest of us.

Like Lady Bramwell, Mistress Fergus could be just as exacting with her expectations. Still, she was more forgiving of mistakes made on the job. At the end of the workday, she always bid me a hearty farewell and thanked me for the services I performed that day.

Mistress Fergus was a woman of a slight build. Her curly red hair and impish face reminded me of a woodland fairy as she flitted about with boundless energy. During my third week of work, Mistress Fergus scurried into the kitchen and took hold of my arm. "I hear you're good with numbers?" she asked anxiously.

I nodded quickly. "Aye, Mistress Fergus, I kept inventory for a master printer not too long ago."

"Quickly now! My daughter got her courses this morning. Hence, I'll need you to assist me in the shop today."

I followed her whilst the other servants who did not possess my skills with numbers stared enviously. For them, there was to be no respite from the doldrums of housewifery work.

As I crossed the threshold into the drapery shop, I was enveloped in a sea of rich, vivid colors. The shelves that spun 'round the room were filled with fabrics in shades of Tyrian purple, crimson, pale reds, gold, and silver — all meant to be worn by the upper class and not by the likes of me. Swaths of brocade and damask, like gossamer wings, were draped over tables. Great reams of satin, velvet, and taffeta fabrics were poised for transformation into garments adorned with jewels and embroidery by master tailors.

Mistress Fergus observed me with pride as I gazed about the room in wonder before thrusting a hastily scribbled piece of paper into my hand. "A young lady will be coming this morning. Here's a list of things she wishes to purchase. Gather up these items. Then, go to the back room, where you'll create a display for her private viewing. Now, make haste!"

I picked up a small basket and quickly attended to my treasure hunt for the items on the list. I began with delicate imported Belgian lace, followed by ribbons with a floral motif, needlepoint cuffs, and wide-stretched trims. Gold cords were next, and I took a few that were braided and others that were twisted. I gathered glass buttons and pearls that could easily be sewn onto silk or velvet cloth. Like me, the young lady preferred the fan-shaped ruff left open at the front. She was modest, for she requested enough gauze to cover her bosom. The final item to go into the basket was hanging tassels in shades of gold, silver, green, and blue.

I hurried into the back room and stopped short when I saw an exquisite gown on a long work table. I poked my head from behind the black curtain that separated the main room from the backroom.

"Mistress Fergus, there is a beautiful silk taffeta gown here. Is it also for the young lady?"

She raised her hand to silence me as she quickly jotted

information into a ledger. When finished, she lifted her chin. "Aye. My brother was commissioned to make the gown for the young lady." Her eyes gleamed with delight at the mention of her brother. "He recently moved here from Edinburgh and brought his magnificent tailoring skills. I introduced him to a few of my loyal clients who were impressed with his work."

"Will your brother be here when the lady tries on the gown?" I asked, hoping I could glimpse the lucky young woman wearing it.

"I have sufficient knowledge and skill in tailoring to make the necessary adjustments and relay the changes to my brother."

I have never met anyone like Mistress Fergus. She started as a young woman in trade, an expert seamstress working alongside her brother. Now, she was the wife and business partner of a prosperous merchant who had established an exemplary business importing expensive fabrics. 'Tis a truly impressive outcome.

I turned my attention to the silk taffeta gown once more. Mistress Fergus's brother did a masterful job of embroidering spring flowers in threads of silver and gold into the pleats. Along the hem was delicate lace. Very likely, it was a wedding gown meant for a May wedding.

Judging by its size, it was meant for someone with a tiny waist. I squeezed my hands 'round my waist and wistfully recalled Robert had once said my teeny waist rivaled our queen's. This gown could have been made for me as well.

I had finished placing the last item from the basket into a pleasing display when Mistress Fergus frantically called out my name from the other room. I rushed to see what was the matter. Shaking her head in dismay and heading for the door, she said, "I don't know where my mind has drifted off to this morning!"

"Is there a problem I can help you with, Mistress Fergus?"

"I'm returning to the house to fetch the gloves the young lady requested. My daughter finished embroidering them early this morning."

"Oh. Please allow me to fetch the gloves for you," I said, approaching her.

"Nay. I know where I placed them. I shall return promptly. If the young lady arrives, let her in and have her sit upon that chair and wait for my return."

"Very well, Mistress Fergus," I said serenely, hoping to appease her agitated state.

No sooner had she left than two well-dressed women wearing caps decorated with jewels and feathers approached the shop. I rushed to the door to welcome them. God's breath! I was confronted with a face I had never hoped to see again.

"L-Lady Bramwell," I stammered, horrified by the unexpected encounter.

The laughter she shared with her young companion as she entered the shop fell silent. Her icy glare still capable of sending a chill up my spine. I could almost feel the weight of her disapproval in the air, the tension thickening with each passing second. "How now, Isabella? You are in trade now?"

"Aye," I readily lied, thrusting my hands behind my back to conceal their trembling. I was satisfied to let Lady Bramwell believe I was an apprentice for a draper and not a charwoman. Merciful heaven, had she come to the shop yesterday, she could have caught me carrying a chamber pot or lugging a pail of water from the nearby conduit. She would have thought how low I had fallen. For such duties, I never had to perform whilst I was in her household.

My gaze fell upon the young maiden who stood by her side. In an instant, I knew who she was — Rose Clavell. Hence, the splendid gown I so admired was tailor-made for her. Peering at her face, I couldn't fathom how Robert found her attractive, for her countenance did not rival mine. Her face was shaped like a full moon, not classically oval like mine, and her dull shade of brown hair made her skin pallid.

"Rose, Isabella was in service at my house in London for a short time," said Lady Bramwell.

"Oh, I see. I am pleased to make your acquaintance, Isabella," she replied politely, her manner indifferent. There was no glint of recognition that she had heard my name uttered before.

All the passionate intimacy, the laughter, the learning, the exalted moments of joy Robert and I shared, and my heartache remained his secret. He had reduced me to a non-entity.

Mistress Fergus returned to the shop with quick, lively steps, clutching the gloves in her hands. Indeed, her daughter did a fine job with the needlework. A perfectly stitched crimson-coloured heart lined with golden thread adorned the middle of each glove.

"Miss Clavell and Lady Bramwell, what joy it is to have your presence grace my shop once more," Mistress Fergus said. "All is ready for your viewing. Please come this way."

"Shall we follow, Lady Bramwell?" Rose dutifully asked.

"You go, my sweet girl. I will come anon."

"As you wish," she replied, following Mistress Fergus into the backroom.

Lady Bramwell turned to me when the thick black curtain closed behind them. "I am pleased to say that Robert has regained his common sense, for he is to marry that sweet girl on the last day of this month. The banns were posted in both their parish churches last month," she said, with a gleam of satisfaction in her stare.

The information Lady Bramwell so proudly announced quickly seeped into my mind and made me painfully aware that if the banns were posted last month, Robert knew he would marry Rose Clavell the day we parted. He withheld that vital information, and his pernicious lie numbed me to the core of my being. Oh — may the devil take him!

"No doubt his quick return to his senses was spurred by monetary incentive, for Robert is not marrying for love. He told me as much," I said. And I didn't care that Robert said no such thing to me. Still, his silence when I told him he didn't love Rose Clavell was sufficient proof.

Unfazed by my remark, she continued. "Robert has come to embrace his family's values and no longer wishes to go against his father. I hope you come to your senses too, Isabella, and return home."

Robert wasn't the only one eager to see me gone from London. "That's my intention, Lady Bramwell. I'm here for a brief time until my poem is published. A master printer in London has assured me that he'll publish it" — another lie, but I strongly believed Richard would.

I turned away from her and began rearranging the display of damask and brocade swaths on the nearby table. She moved behind me.

"How unfortunate for your parents, Isabella, that you have not come to your senses."

My blood grew hot when she mentioned my parents. I swiftly turned to face her. "I remember well, Lady Bramwell, your brother's behavior at your Twelfth Night celebration, rousing your guests to join him in a sparring match on which sex is truer in love. My poem touches on that very subject, and I have answered his question using his son to exemplify all the ill traits of a man in love. Make sure you give him my poem to read once it's published. Perhaps you'll find it enlightening, as might Rose Clavell."

She observed me with a tight lip. "You were always forthright, Isabella, but tread with care. Despite a queen governing this country, women must not be too bold with their tongue."

Rose Clavell's voice ended our conversation as she exclaimed, "Lady Bramwell, come see the gown. Look how well it fits!"

"Oh, to be a young bride and so in love," Lady Bramwell said with a smug smile. She then turned from me and walked a few short paces to the black curtain, which she parted with a flourish. "Robert's eyes will sparkle as he watches you approach the altar dressed in such finery," she declared, loud enough for me to hear.

Within minutes, Mistress Fergus returned with a twinkle in her eye. "Did you hear, Isabella? My brother's gown is a success." She waved me toward the door. "You may return to your duties in the house. The washerwoman was quite disgruntled when I stole you from her," she laughed. "Now go. I can manage the rest of the day on my own. Many good thanks for your help," she added.

I was only too pleased to bolt from the shop. I had no desire to see Lady Bramwell leave the shop with her arm entwined with Robert's happily expectant bride. As I returned to Mistress Fergus's house, I could only think of Robert's bold-faced lie on the day we parted. And the audacity of Lady Bramwell to announce Robert's eminent marriage to my face and with such a gloating smile. Let Robert hang — along with the rest of his miserable family.

☙❧

That night, in my room, spurred by Robert's betrayal, I worked like a woman possessed to hone my poem to perfection, wherein I would proclaim men as scoundrels in love. First, I gathered all the fragments of verse I had written thus far about deceitful lovers and laid them on the floor. My knees sank into the reeds as I began reviewing my writing to select the most effective lines of verse and combine them into a coherent whole.

Just as I was about to start my review, a large fly hit my forehead, and another whizzed frantically over my head. I swatted at them. Be gone, I hissed, for I have important work to do. But they hovered near, and I saw more near the window. Fie! How I detested them. There was no reprieve from their constant intrusion, not with the pervasive smell of piss and excrement in the street below. I picked up the paper upon which I wrote the lines: *Beware of fair and painted talk. The mermaids do pretend no good for all their pleasant songs,* and decided it was the perfect beginning for my poem. How curious that Robert considered the lines clever when I read them aloud. Little did he know, or I knew I would later use those words to describe him.

It took me most of the night to select lines of verse and

collate them into ordered stanzas, but happily, my poem slowly began to take shape. As I read the emergence of my poem aloud, I paused, for something seemed amiss. I thought about everything I read concerning *the woman question.* What do all those poems have in common? And then it came to me. The common practice of male poets was to state the purpose of their writing in their poems' opening lines, aiming to protect men from female deception. I should follow their lead. Being a woman, I would state in my opening lines that women should beware of men who intend to woo them falsely.

I sat on the lumpy bed and maintained a steady position by placing my foot on the chair's spindle. Reaching for the pen on the seat and carefully dipping it in the inkwell, I addressed my poem to the much-maligned female readership.

The Admonition by the Author, to all young Gentle-women: And to all other Maids being in Love.

> *To you I speak: for you be they,*
> *   that good advice do lack:*
> *Oh, if I could good counsel give*
> *   my tongue should not be slack.*

> *But such as I could give, I will.*
> *   here in a few words express:*
> *Which if you do observe, it will*
> *   some of your care redress.*

I brushed the feather end of the goose quill across my lips as I read the first line aloud meant for my intended audience. Richard would surely agree that women of all classes were targets of derision and men's deceptions. Following the first stanza, I copied what I wrote just days after Robert left me for Rose Clavell. It was a fair warning my mother would agree with.

Trust not a man at the first sight,
  but try him well before.
I wish all Maids within their breasts
  to keep this thing in store.
For trail shall declare his truth,
  and show what he doth think:
Whether he be a Lover true,
  or do intend to shrink.

I put my pen down as the couple in the room above mine began their nightly sounds of groans and sighs, which would only grow louder within the ensuing minutes. I had grown accustomed to their nightly bedtime ritual. Their coupling, accompanied by bed thumping and the man's grunting, would end quickly. It struck me as unlikely that the gruff, burly man I oft passed on the stairs could wield his coxcomb to drive a woman into such euphoria. It had to be feigned, I concluded. I'll leave her a copy of my poem when 'tis finished, as it would do her much good to read what I have to say about men in love.

Satisfied with my introduction, I moved on to find examples of famed men who grossly misused their lovers' devotion. I had plenty of verses about the scheming heroes from *Heroides* and settled upon Paris, son of King Priam, and Demophon, son of Theseus and King of Athens and Phaedra. I wrote a new verse about Leander, the young commoner who fell devotedly in love with Hero, a priestess of Aphrodite. He would serve as a model of the ideal, faithful lover that young women should seek.

Hero did try Leander's truth,
  before that she did trust:
Therefore, she found him unto her
  both constant, true, and just.

Constance Briones

But like Leander there be few,
* therefore, in time take heed:*
And always try before you trust,
* so shall you better speed.*

I pressed on with my writing into the early hours of the morning. There was no relief from the heat; thus, I discarded my shift as I unabashedly did for Robert. The passion I carried for him that made me abandon my duty to my family had now moved to my pen. I wouldn't yield to slumber until the poem induced by Robert's deception was finished. I wiped away the sweat from my forehead with a rag and wished I was home, wading in the cool water of the River Weaver whilst my father and brother fished on the river bank. And then, a thought sprang to mind. Women are as easily beguiled as the fish who swim contentedly in their watery world until a hook, bearing attractive bait, lures them away. I began to write anew.

The little fish that careless is,
* within the water clear:*
How glad is he, when he doth see,
* a bait for to appear.*
O little fish what hap hast thou?
* to have such spiteful Fate:*
To come into one's cruel hands,
* out of so happy state?*

My eyes filled with tears, for the attractive bait was Robert and I, the fish.

And since the fish that reason lacks
* once warned doth beware:*
Why should not we take heed to that

that turn us to care.
And I who was deceived late,
by one's unfaithful tears:
Trust now for to beware, if that
I live these hundred years.

I put down my pen and sighed in quiet relief. My poem was finished. And now to Richard, tomorrow shall I go and pray he thinks my poem is worthy of publication.

27

A Matter of Waiting

I sped down Cheapside, eager to reach Richard's shop before the hour of seven. Even though it was the end of the work day, merchants were still keen to sell their wares to all who passed their stalls. I caught the attention of a woman about my mother's age, wearing a white apron and a wide-brim hat.

"Where you off to in such a rush? Come here, and I'll sell you one of my delicious meat pies at half price. Can't go wrong with that, 'eh?"

On any other day, I would have taken her offer. But today was the exception. Thankfully, Cheapside was one of the few paved streets in London, which enabled me to quicken my pace. Once I reached the end of Cheapside, where the road splits right to Newgate and left to Paternoster Row, I hurried into Paternoster Row, straight to Richard's door. Whilst no one was looking, I bent down and quickly slid my hand to my girdle pouch to retrieve my poem.

The door was unlocked, and I quietly let myself in. John, his journeyman, stood beside the larger press whilst Richard inspected a galley beside him. John poked his arm as I approached. Upon seeing me, Richard beamed and gave me a warm embrace.

"My dear girl, how my eyes are glad to see you. John, you remember Isabella Whitney, don't you?"

John nodded and stepped forward. "Aye. Good day, Mistress Whitney."

As I peered into his eyes, I noted they possessed a most enchanting shade of blue. It reminded me of the bluish hue

248

reflected in ice crystals when the sun hangs high in the winter sky. Strange that I had never noticed his striking eyes before. I was too enchanted with Robert to pay mind to anyone else. Fool-hearted me!

"Come and sit, Isabella," Richard said, pointing to a bench.

He laid his hand on John's shoulder. "All looks well, John. Before you give it to the boys to ink in the morning, level the metal type a bit more to get a smoother printing surface."

John nodded with a pleased smile and retrieved his cap from a hook. "May God grant you both a good evening," he said, tipping his hat as he took his leave.

"And the same to you, John," Richard said, his eyes following John as he closed the door and left.

"A fine young man," he said, his voice filled with genuine admiration. "A meticulous worker, every day I am grateful that I had the wisdom to bring him on board." He carefully placed the galley he had been inspecting on a sturdy wood and metal frame.

He turned to me with a disarming smile and said, "Why is Robert not with you? Pray he's not still miffed over our disagreement to improve his ballad."

Alas! My heart sank. Richard was unaware that Robert had left me, a fact I had hoped Robert would have informed Richard by now. But no, Robert's petulance always got the better of him when things didn't go his way. He still harbored resentment towards Richard for not publishing his ballad as is, without revision.

A small lump began to take form in my throat. "I'm no longer with Robert. He has thrown me over for another."

Richard took a moment to respond. "That's distressing news not only for me but will be for Maria, as well. I thought I knew Robert." He moved closer, sitting beside me on the bench. "Had I any hint that he was playing a game of deception with you, I would have stopped it. But how is it that you're still in London and not returned home to your family in Nantwich?"

"My cousin has made it possible for me to remain in

London. It seems fate has other plans for me. I've come to see you about your printing a poem I wrote. It would be my contribution to *the woman question*."

"You took my suggestion seriously?" he said with that funny, crooked smile I have long missed.

"I didn't forget what you told me, that a woman writing a poem showing that men are deceivers in love would be worthy to print."

"'Tis true. There's money to be made on that subject. Do you have it with you?"

With an enthusiastic nod, I placed my poem in his hand and felt like I was presenting Richard with a precious jewel.

He read the title aloud with interest, "*The Admonition by the Author, to all Young Gentlewomen: and to all other Maids being in Love.*"

He paused, raising an eyebrow. "Does this poem derive from your experience with Robert?" And I nodded that it had.

"Then your words should ring true, for it sprang from your pain and disillusionment with love," he said with growing curiosity and turned the page. I studied his face, hoping to catch a glimpse of approval.

"I see that you have borrowed some techniques from the works of George Turberville."

"Is that a bad thing?"

"Not at all," he said with an approving smile. "He has set the standard for this type of writing, and others must follow his lead. As he does, you tell your readers your intention for writing the poem. And you use famed classical characters as examples to prove your point."

"Just as Turberville used Helen of Troy to prove his point that women are deceivers in love," I added.

"You have become an astute learner of *the woman question* in literature," he commented with an appreciative smile.

"Does that mean you are willing to print it?"

He folded his arms across his chest, his hand clutching the pages of my poem. "I can't make any promises, but leave this with me, and I'll study it further. Come back Thursday next, and I'll have an answer for you then."

I was disappointed that he didn't readily say yes to publishing the first attack on men in love written by a woman. I was so confident that I had done an excellent job of it.

Richard carefully began to remove sheets of paper hung on the line to dry. I offered my help, and we assembled them neatly in a pile on one of the tables near the larger press. "Where are you staying, Isabella?"

"I found a room in Abchurch Lane."

"Abchurch Lane," he repeated with a hint of concern. He hastily reached for his satchel and to my dismay, shoved my poem inside between all the other papers, not placing it on top so he could readily retrieve it to read once he was home. "Come, I'll accompany you to your lodging house."

"The sun will not yet set for another hour. I'll make it back safely." I paused at the door before leaving. "I shall return Thursday next for your answer," I said decidedly.

Richard nodded. "May God see you safely home."

I closed the door behind me, a bit despondent that Richard didn't readily agree to print my poem as I had hoped. But he did say I had become an astute learner of *the woman question*. Surely, he will see that my poem suits his desire to publish something new and different on that topic. My confidence began to rise, and I walked with a bounce to my gait to Abchurch Lane.

ༀ

A week after meeting with Richard, I had my first captive audience ready to listen to snippets of my poem. I couldn't have asked for better listeners than the two maidservants I worked with in Mistress Fergus's house.

I began reciting my best lines of verse whilst we sat at the kitchen table, making deep cuts into long pieces of stale bread and smearing them with glue for flea traps. Their comments bolstered my confidence that Richard would find my poem worthy of publication.

Frances, twenty years of age, with a patch of freckles on her nose, said, "You say in your poem, *Try not a man at first sight, but try him well before.* By God, Isabella, that's good advice I could have used with my Martin. He spoke such sweet words that I believed he would surely take me for his wife." She firmly pressed a candle into the center of her bread. "Well," she sighed deeply. "I'm still a maid. I was a fool to have believed his false talk."

"Was Robert's manhood truly tiny?" asked Suzanna, her bronze skin glistening in the sunlight streaming through the open window.

I was stunned. "Why do you say that?"

She laughed heartily. "You use the word shrink, Isabella – *whether he can be a lover true or do intend to shrink.* 'Round here, we take that to mean a man cannot perform the act!"

"Death and Hell! That wasn't my intent, but what a blow to Robert's ego if all the maids in London interpret it your way."

"They are bound to," Suzanna concluded, nodding with absolute certainty.

We all giggled like school girls playing a trick on the braggart who prominently displays his bulging coxcomb to rouse women into heat.

"What did you say about fish?" Frances held the knife in her hand as she closed her eyes to remember the line. "*Thou didn't suspect no harm when thou upon the bait did look.* Did I get it right?"

"Aye!" I said, pleased that the line of verse struck a chord with her.

"How true you speak, Isabella! For was not Martin's good looks and sweet-talking tongue bait for me?"

"You're right to compare us to fish. For many men woo women for sport," chimed Suzanna as she filled her deep cuts in the bread with glue.

"When will you know if your poem will be printed?" asked Frances.

I breathed deeply. "When this work day is done. I must

hasten to Paternoster Row to receive the news."

Frances and Suzanna exchanged a knowing glance. "'Tis nearly five," said Frances. "Mistress Fergus is out with her brother and won't return till evening. Why don't you leave, and we'll set out these flea trenches, including yours, in every room of the house."

Suzanna agreed with an encouraging nod. "Aye, Isabella, and bring us back good tidings tomorrow."

I looked at the pair of them and considered myself blessed for the benevolent maidservants they were. Bidding them a heartfelt farewell, I hastily left. If my poem resonated with Frances and Suzanna, then it shall for all women. I prayed that Richard would have arrived at that same conclusion.

The shop door was locked when I arrived at Richard's shop. Whilst I waited for him to come to the door, I straightened the folds in my apron. My fingers fell upon something sticky. Fie! In my haste to finish the flea traps, I spilled glue on my clean linen apron. I tried to remove it with my nail but to no avail. When Richard unlocked the door, I stepped up too eagerly and tripped on the threshold.

He grabbed hold of me. "Steady there, Isabella!"

I put up my hands. "Careful! My apron is sticky with glue."

He laughed, holding me at arm's length. "My thanks for the warning. Maria would be truly vexed if I ruined this doublet she made me."

Indeed. It was a pleasing doublet, the color of seawater, with swirls of yellow thread along the buttons. Maria must have spent hours on it.

He closed the door and signaled for me to follow him. "Come, we'll discuss what I thought of your poem in my office."

I followed him, my mind ablaze with anxious thoughts. As I sat in his office, my back pressed into the chair, I hoped to hear him say, 'Isabella, you presented me with a flawless piece of work. Impressive work by one so young.' Instead, he fell into silence, his hands folded, eyes looking down at my writing on his desk. Zounds! Was he contemplating the right words to help ease the pain of his rejection? With clenched fists under my apron, I waited for Richard to begin. My heart skipped a beat when he smiled.

"You do understand, Isabella, that if I print and sell your poem, you must be willing to relinquish control to me."

I breathed. He was impressed and had nothing to fear from me. My penury purse didn't allow me to behave like Robert, who could afford to play the high-browed poet. And yet, even if I had been plentiful in purse, I would still yield to Richard, for I knew nothing about the business of making and selling books.

"I'm not Robert. I trust your judgment to make the necessary changes to sell my poem."

With a satisfied smile, he leaned back in his chair and placed his hands behind his head. "There were many things I liked about your poem. Mainly, you shun the ornate language of courtly poetry. 'Tis a style that's quickly falling out of fashion. My new breed of readers want writers who express themselves simply and directly as you do."

"I take it that you mean by my speaking plainly all women will understand my message."

"Aye, that's it. Something else I like is the young woman in your poem is not driven to despair by the lover who abandoned her. She steps back from her failed experience in love and offers sound advice, encouraging women to seek love cautiously. That works in our favor."

He rose from his chair and sat on the edge of his desk. "In my mind, the young woman in your poem is the voice of reason dispensing sound advice on spotting male deception."

"Women as rational creatures? Now, there's a notion not embraced by many." I clapped my hands gleefully, "I tell you, Richard, I'm honored to be the first to reverse that thinking."

"As am I in printing your poem," he concurred. "Men won't object to reading a poem written by a woman who offers prudent advice on seeking love, especially when prudence is the very trait the church encourages women to have."

A smile of admiration for Richard crept across my lips. His

defense for printing my poem aligned with the church's thinking, thus allowing little room for criticism. He returned to his desk and pointed to the stool next to it. "Come, sit by me. I will share my idea on how I will present your poem."

I moved with the speed of Hermes, for I was eager to hear his plan. He removed a poem from a nearby folder and placed it before me. "This poem is written by a bachelor who complains about a maiden breaking her betrothal promise without warning or explanation. My thinking is to pair this poem with yours in a pamphlet."

I picked up the bachelor's poem and read the first line with an exasperated laugh, *"Beware the feigned fidelity of inconstant maidens."*

"Well, now, Isabella, your poem will turn that notion on its head, won't it? Your poem casts the man as a temptress – a new role reversal."

"Thus, for the first time, we'll offer readers paired female and male-voiced complaints about love, with the female voice actually written by a woman. I wonder whose argument will win over the reader?"

Richard laughed. "I'm most keen to find out." He returned the bachelor's poem to the folder and brought mine out. "Now, let's look at changes I wish to make to your poem."

I sat still and prayed I would agree with his suggestions.

"From the start, why not remind your female readers of the one virtue women are told they must possess and is prized above all others?"

"May I?" I said, reaching for his inkwell and quill. The words spilled from my head onto the paper, and then I read them aloud. *"Ye Virgins that from Cupid's tents do bear away the prey, Whose hearts as yet with raging love most painfully apply."*

Richard rapped the table. "Do you see how the phrase, ye virgins, adds greater urgency to your message of self-protection and moves more effectively to your next stanza?"

I nodded slowly as I read the following lines of verse aloud: *"To you, I speak: for you be they, that good advice to lack.*

Aye. It's a good change."

"There's little else about your poem that needs altering. Oh. I could think of more examples of famous men who have betrayed women." He glanced at the hourglass with the blue sand that fascinated me on my previous visit to his office. "It's getting late. Why don't you come home with me, and we'll discuss a few more alterations to your poem."

Before I could answer, he added quickly. "Maria will be glad to see you and insist you spend the night. This morning, she made raspberry marmalade and remarked how much you liked it."

I remembered savoring every bite of Maria's marmalade on sweet wafers. That, coupled with seeing her again and the chance of a good night's sleep, was too tempting to refuse.

"Aye. I'd like that very much."

He gathered his belongings. "After we make the changes, I will consider how best to introduce you as an author to the reading public. And then, of course, there's the business of printing the pamphlet, but you need not worry about that. Leave all that to me."

My mind was spinning from this good turn of events. I never imagined that when Robert introduced me to Richard, he would someday be my printer.

"Richard, we may be at the beginning of a fruitful business relationship: me, a writer, and you, my printer."

He opened the door with a wide smile. "Well, now, Isabella. I believe you might be right about that."

28

Just Rewards

Something momentous happened a few weeks after my favorable meeting with Richard; on the first day of summertime, when Queen Elizabeth and her entourage left London for the Midlands, I found a note pinned to my door. My heart soared when I read it:

Dear Isabella,
Come with haste to my shop, for 'tis finished. I'll be here till dusk.
Your printer, Richard.

I knew, at once, that my poem was published and ready to be viewed. I slipped the note under my door and hurried down the stairs. Whistling a merry tune, I raced along Cheapside, weaving in and out of workers eager to get home for supper. The only hunger I felt was to behold my poem in print. I entered Richard's shop when the clock struck at half past six.

Two young lads, their identical brown caps perched atop their heads, were busy stacking reams of paper on the table next to the printing presses. Their voices, perfectly synchronized, asked, "Looking for Master Jones, miss?" Before I could respond, Richard bounded down the steps from his office, a bundle of books wrapped in brown paper in his arms. He was followed by John.

"Isabella! Good. You're here," Richard said, kissing both my cheeks. He then turned to the boys. "All right, lads, here's your last task for the day. Take this bundle to Mister Simeon, the bookseller six doors down at the sign of the rose. He's expecting them."

The boys nodded as the taller of the two grabbed the package.

"Make sure to close the door behind you when you leave."

"God grant you a good evening, Master Jones," they both said, their voices filled with respect.

Richard turned to me with the broadest smile, which could only indicate he was very pleased with the final printed copy of my poem. "I reckon this day will remain vivid in your mind for years to come," he said, signaling to John to give me the pamphlet he had in his hand.

I suddenly felt lightheaded. "I think I need to sit, or I shall faint."

John, ever the quick thinker, swiftly kicked a stool out from under a nearby table and guided me to it. I sat down, clutching the small pamphlet on my lap. It was of a delicate size, easily fitting into a pouch. The thought of carrying it with me always filled me with a sense of pride. I handled it with utmost care, the sixteen pages bound together by loose stitching on the side. My title, beautifully framed around the page's edge with a design resembling vines, graced the first page. I traced the interlocking swirls of the border with my finger.

"The border's design was John's idea," Richard said.

"I like it very much. And the woodcut of the rose? Was that your idea as well, John?"

John gave a modest nod, "Aye, Miss Whitney. I hope you approve?"

"It adds much beauty to the page," I said, impressed with his choice.

I read the title aloud, awed to see it set in print – "*An Admonition to all Young Gentlewomen and to all other Maids to Beware of Men's Flattery*. By Is. W. Joined to a Love letter sent by a Bachelor (a most faithful Lover) to an inconstant and faithless Maiden." My eye darted back to the abbreviation of my name. "You used my initials," I said, disappointed, for I wanted my full name affixed to my poem to add to the consternation of Robert and his aunt, Lady Bramwell.

"I thought it best to safeguard your identity," Richard explained. "Since your poem speaks of a maiden's experience in love, I thought it wise to use your initials for modesty's sake."

My parents would have thanked him for his good judgment, for I had written a poem about the perils of loving a man based on my experience.

"The accompanying poem by the bachelor also bears his initials," John added in earnest, turning the page to where the second poem starts and pointing to the author's initials.

Despite my displeasure at not seeing my full name below the title, I felt sure that all those who knew Robert and me as a couple would know that IS.W was indeed me, and the inconstant lover was Robert. Let him try to remove the stain cast upon his character in my poem.

I turned to the page where my poem began. In its entirety, it took up seven pages, front and back. My initials appeared at the top and bottom of each page. The words of my poem, set in bold, dark type, seemed to leap off the page, enticing maids of all ages to read my essential message: show prudence before surrendering your heart and body to a man, for many will use trickery to ensnare you and steal your heart. Resting my hand on the last page of my poem, I looked up at Richard.

"My thanks, Richard, for putting my poem first."

"Well, why not? I thought, let's hear what a woman has to say about love first."

"I'm sure the queen would agree with your sentiment!" I said, laughing, prompting Richard and John to join in.

"I think this occasion calls for a celebratory supper!" Richard declared. "What say you, Isabella? This Friday, let's meet at Ye Olde Cheshire Cheese."

"John, you must come too for your contribution to printing my poem," I urged.

Richard playfully grabbed John by his shoulders. "Of course, he should come."

"I would be most willing to escort you to the tavern from where your lodgings are," John said with a bashful smile.

I picked up the pen that rested beside the inkwell, jotted my address on a torn sheet of paper, and gave it to John.

"Till Friday then, Miss Whitney, at the hour of six," he said, stacking the reams of paper next to the presses.

He addressed me as Miss Whitney — by my troth! I will have to do something about that.

When I returned to my room, my dear cousin William was in my thoughts. He was so anxious about my well-being the day he departed, and now I had good tidings that would set his heart at rest.

Dearest cousin,
Good fortune visited me this week, for Richard Jones agreed to print and sell my poem. I saw it today in print and was overcome with joy. My identity is concealed safe for my initials and Richard's reference to me as a young gentlewoman. Accompanying my poem is another written by a bachelor, complaining of the inconstancy of his mistress. My poem is the first one a reader will lay their eyes on. How now? What do you make of my poem's prominent position? Richard set the two poems in a tiny booklet that fits in the palm of your hand. I hope to see young maids carrying it thusly, sharing the contents of my poem with their friends. As you see, all has turned out well. I thank the Lord every night for giving me a cousin with a benevolent heart. God keep you safe. Izzy.

☙❧

The celebratory supper for the publication of my poem was postponed, for John had fallen ill with pain in his stomach. Richard had been in constant touch with John, who was left in the care of his good mother. He was well enough to return to work within three days of her care, administering daily doses of balm, mint, and wormwood. We arranged to meet on the third Friday eve from the start of summertide. The meeting place was still Ye Olde Cheshire Cheese, and John would escort me.

I waited for John on a blissful summer eve. For the first

time since I moved back to London, I was dressed like a gentlewoman. I put away my apron and cap and wore a pretty gown with lace at its square-shaped neckline. A yellow hooded cape hung loosely about my shoulders.

I watched for John to emerge amongst the bustling crowd in Abchurch Lane, and I spied a lone male figure moving swiftly in my direction. I recognized the familiar swagger, full of bravado and purpose. God's blood! It was Robert! My stomach muscles tightened as they did when I first laid eyes on him in the library. Had he read my poem and now come to confront me about it? Pish. It mattered little to me if he was offended by my words. As he drew near, he flashed that winsome smile that once set my heart soaring.

"Well met, my dear Izzy!" he said most jovially.

In Robert's typical fashion, he was handsomely attired. His unbuttoned leather doublet revealed a white shirt with a diamond-shaped pattern, the silver thread adding a touch of elegance. His breeches, thigh-high, exposed the entire length of his legs in green silk hose. But there were changes, too. His beard was gone, and his once long locks had been shorn.

"Robert, your presence here is so unexpected," I managed to say, my tone masking my surprise.

He took hold of my hand. I noted that his pearl earring was gone. "I felt I had to congratulate you in person on your published poem. I'd thought it more personable to see you rather than leaving you a note – don't you agree?"

I withdrew my hand from his, a hint of annoyance creeping into my voice. "A note would have suited me fine, Robert." I moved away from him, feeling increasingly vexed by his surprise visit. "How did you know where to find me?"

He began in earnest, smiling. "I shall tell you. On Sunday last, I found myself at St. Paul's green and went to see Richard. I saw the title page of your poem glued to the wall of his bookstall. He couldn't stop boasting about your talent, which, I think, gave him much pleasure saying it to my face. Despite my insistence in knowing your whereabouts, he wasn't forthcoming. Thus, I went to the drapery shop where you presently work to speak with Mistress Fergus."

Fie! His aunt told him where I worked and no doubt relayed the tidbits of my conversation with her. "And Mistress Fergus readily told you where I live?"

"Nay, not at first, but I managed to coax it out of her," he said with a wink.

Good God! I cared not to hear the details of his dissembling to retrieve the information he wanted from Mistress Fergus. Robert excelled at being persuasive, impressing upon Mistress Fergus no doubt that he was the nephew of one of her most valued customers, Lady Bramwell in the Strand.

"I gather you read my poem?"

He nodded and touched his heart with a dramatic gesture. "Oh, Izzy, you have injured me so."

"Go to, Robert. You should be flattered that I included you in the company of such noteworthy scoundrels of love."

He moved toward me and began to recite the line from my poem that gave him offense:

"*For trail shall declare his truth and show what he doth think, whether he be a true lover or intend to shrink.* That was a hard hit, Izzy," he said with a furrowed brow. "Was it your intention to have maids laugh at my expense?" He moved closer and whispered, "I don't recall you complaining of my prowess in bed."

Marry! Suzanna was right. He read it as an insult to his manhood. What joy! He must have been the subject of much teasing by his friends and possibly his father. I ignored his complaint, opting not to soothe his pride over his manhood.

"Tell me, Robert, how do you find married life?"

"Tell me, Izzy, how do you like the single life?" He retorted in a tone of annoyance.

We were suddenly interrupted by the appearance of my upstairs burly and lecherous neighbor, who passed between us upon exiting the lodging house without uttering a pardon.

His shoulder forcibly brushed against Robert, causing him to step back. Serves Robert, right, I thought. Dressing in such finery would undoubtedly incite the ire of the ruffians around here.

Adjusting his cape, Robert scoffed, "I didn't realize how deep your ambition was to be a writer. You sacrificed the comfort of your family's home to live among ill-bred creatures."

"You always underestimated my resolve to be a writer. But Richard didn't," I said, striking a triumphant tone.

There was a long pause as we observed each other waiting to pounce upon the next critical remark.

"I notice that your long locks are shorn, the pearl earring in your lobe is gone — and your beard is gone too. You resemble your former self as a law student more than an aspiring balladeer."

He looked down at the ground. "Aye. I'm contemplating returning to Gray's Inn come September." Then he added quickly, "But nothing has been decided."

Of course. Robert didn't want to confess that his father had won the argument to stay in law school. A barrister was a far more suitable husband for the daughter of a viscount.

"How long will you remain in London?" he asked.

"A bit longer. I will write more poems now that Richard has agreed to print more."

"I tell you honestly, Izzy, when I read your poem, I was reminded of why I fell so deeply for you."

"Does your wife write poetry?" I shot back.

He laughed scornfully. "Nay, not at all." He moved so close that I could smell the scents of sweet almonds and nutmeg as he touched my shoulder with his gloved hand. "You're the only one I've ever met who can so exquisitely lay bare her soul in poetry. That's a very enticing trait, especially in a woman." He sighed. "How I have missed you, my Izzy."

Zounds! His audacity was unbearable. "Away with you, Robert. You must now find contentment in your wife's title and money."

Undaunted by my response, he stared at my dress and grinned. "Didn't I buy you that dress? I did. You wore it when we met Richard at George's Tavern in Southwark."

"An eventful night, to be sure, when I learned of your deceit. I'm wearing it to dine with Richard and John."

"John," he said with a derisive laugh. "Richard's pressman?"

"Pressman no more. He's a competent compositor. You'll see – he'll be a master printer like Richard in a year or two. Didn't you notice how impressive his design choices made my poem appear on the page?"

At that moment, in my praise of John, his soft and airy voice made his presence known and dissipated the strife that hung in the air between Robert and me.

"Good evening, Mistress Whitney," said John.

My eyes were glad of him. He appeared hale and hearty and was attired quite handsomely. Like my cousin William, he dressed modestly, sporting knee-length black breeches and matching colored hose. His white and grey doublet was fully buttoned, and there was a ruff about his neck and on the cuffs of his white shirt. He didn't pale in appearance next to Robert.

I stepped toward him. "John, you're looking well." I tilted my head in Robert's direction. "He was just leaving. Isn't that so, Robert?"

Slowly, Robert's mouth took on a wistful smile as he looked at John and me, standing shoulder to shoulder. "Fare you well, Izzy. God keep you safe," he said with a slight bow. And then, just as swiftly as he had arrived, he turned on his heels and walked away.

I watched Robert fade from view, my first great love, without a tinge of sadness. Aye. He had altered my life but no longer had a place in it.

I turned to John, "Shall we begin to make our way to meet Richard?"

"Let's proceed, Mistress Whitney," he said confidently.

"John, please call me –" I was about to say, Izzy, but my poem's warning, *try well before you trust,* made me pause. My affectionate familial nickname, Izzy, should only be uttered by those who prove true to me. For Izzy was a nickname spoken by those who bore me unconditional love, like my mother, father, siblings, William, and his family. And I had a deep sense that John would call me Izzy - not now, but in good time.

"Please, John, call me Isabella."

He nodded. "I enjoyed reading your poem, Isabella. It reminded me of *The Book of the City of Ladies* by Christine de Pizan.

My interest was piqued. "I have never heard of that writer. Tell me more."

"She was a poet at the court of the French king during the reign of our English king, Richard II."

"A poet, you say?" I said with interest.

"Aye, a poet. Like you, she used notable women from history as examples to defend women against men's derision. She went so far as to say that there should be schools for girls."

I clasped my hand to my heart - so surprised that a woman expressed such a sentiment in print. "How came you by this book?"

"My mother first read it as a young girl in France, long before it was translated into English, and insisted I read it too. 'Tis one of her favorite books."

Marry! I stopped and put my hand on his arm. "You read French?"

"My mother was determined that I learn her native tongue. I can speak and write in French as well."

"How fortunate you are to speak another language. Say something in French."

His piercing eyes locked with mine. "Vous devriez lire le livre, *La Ville des Dames*. You should read *The Book of the City of Ladies*," he said encouragingly.

My cheeks felt warm as I slipped my arm into his. "We shall read it together, John."

AUTHOR'S NOTE

About Isabella Whitney

I first discovered Isabella Whitney while conducting research for my Master's thesis on literacy and women in England during the sixteenth century. Isabella Whitney is credited as the first English woman believed to have written original secular poetry for publication in the mid-sixteenth century. Her feat was remarkable because it occurred when the acceptable writing endeavor for women was translations of religious works into English. She was in her late teens when her first volume of poetry concerning men-women relations was published. *The Copy of a Letter* (1567) with its adjoining poem, *The Admonition of the Author to all young Gentlewomen and to all other maids being in Love*, were love poems written in the personae of a jilted lover. Whitney presented an unconventional woman's perspective of how unfairly men treat women in love, which played a role in the debates on women's nature in the sixteenth century.

Whitney dared to challenge the hypocritical double standard on the behavior of the sexes in love at a time when the norm for women was to be seen and not heard. Another bold move for Whitney was to delay marriage in favor of writing during an age when a woman's sole purpose was to be a wife and mother. In one of her verse epistles addressed to her married sister, she wrote *Til some household cares mee tye, My books and Pen I will apply.*

Since there is scant information about her life, I wanted to tell the story of her journey from maidservant to unemployed domestic to early success as a poet through historical fiction.

I incorporated the rudimentary facts of her life into the storyline. She left her home in Chesire in her late teens to work as a maidservant in a prosperous household in London. Due to an unknown scandal, she lost her job. Many literary scholars believe the scandal concerned a failed romantic entanglement with a man, which became the impetus for her first collection of verses on love. The man's identity is not known. Rather than return home upon losing her job, she remained in London, facing economic difficulties, but determined to become a writer. Another consideration for the historical fiction route was my admiration for Isabella Whitney's gusty character. Her choice to defy the conventions of her day, both in her thinking and actions, impressed me. And I thought she would make an engaging literary heroine.

As this book reimages Isabella Whitney's life from maidservant to writer, I took creative liberties to fill the gaps in her biographical information. I agree with those historians who believe her job loss was due to a romantic entanglement with a man. I gave him the persona of Robert Barrington, the nephew of the widowed baroness who employed Isabella as a maidservant. Lady Bramwell is also my creation, as the identity of the woman Isabella worked for when she served as a maidservant in London is unknown. In my novel, Isabella's life takes a dramatic turn when she begins a relationship with Robert. He supports her interest in reading and writing, and through him, she meets the printer, Richard Jones.

Historically, Richard Jones was indeed Isabella Whitney's printer, and as in the novel, they established a successful professional relationship. Richard Jones was known for his publications of popular literature, mainly ballads, poetry, plays, and prose romance. A new literary format, the Herodian complaint form, made popular by Ovid's *Heroides*, was a hit with London's reading public. Always with his finger on the pulse of his readership, Jones looked to Isabella's poetry to satisfy the reading public. She was ready for it, having been well-versed in Ovid's works. As in the novel, Jones's idea was to pair Isabella's poem with two poems by men complaining of women's inconstancy in love. After her first volume of poetry was published by Richard Jones, he published and sold her second volume of poetry, *A Sweet Nosegay*, in 1573.

Although Isabella dreamed of becoming a professional writer, she continued to support herself by working as a domestic. It's believed that she married Richard Eldershaw, a physician, and had two children. There is no official record of Isabella Whitney's death.

About the *Querelle de femmes* or *the woman question*

The intellectual debate on the true nature of women began in the fourteenth century in Europe. The church propagated the idea that women had an inherent weak nature. It deemed women subordinate to men, which became the basis for excluding women from university or participating in public endeavors such as public speaking and writing. In her book, *The Book of the City of Ladies* (1405), Christine de Pizan, an Italian-born French poet in the court of King Charles II of France, defended women by showing the importance of women's past contributions to society. Her work is considered an early feminist work. The debate on the true nature of women arrived in England in the sixteenth century. It became a hot topic for men to write about and ushered in the pamphlet wars of attacks and defenses on women. The rise of the literate middle class and their keen interest in *the woman question* motivated many printers in London to increase their output on the topic.

About the Inns of Court

In sixteenth-century England, men interested in becoming barristers trained at one of the four Inns of Court: Gray's Inn, Lincoln's Inn, Inner Temple, and Middle Temple. Training to become a barrister was about seven years. Barrister was a sought-after position because of the opportunity to secure significant positions in government. During the reign of Elizabeth I, Gray's Inn rose in prominence. The Elizabethan era is considered the "golden age" for Gray's Inn, with Elizabeth serving as the Patron Lady. Gray's Inn became noted for the parties and festivals it hosted and student-based plays with Queen Elizabeth in attendance. Today, the Inns of Court are no longer the sole training ground for barristers; they continue to provide supplementary education. They are professional associations for barristers in England and Wales, to which all barristers must belong to one of the four inns of court.

About Theatre in the 1560's

Before Shakespeare's time, purpose-built playhouses in London and its suburbs had not been established. During the early reign of Queen Elizabeth I, actors and playwrights relied on aristocratic patrons. Notable aristocrats with close connections to Queen Elizabeth, such as Robert Dudley, Earl of Leicester, and his brother Ambrose Dudley, Third Earl of Warwick, maintained and protected their own company of players. Their companies performed in the provinces, as well as in London and at the court of Elizabeth I. The most profitable performance spaces were in the most prominent taverns and inns and the most spacious homes of wealthy merchants and noblemen in London and the provinces. All noblemen maintaining a private, liveried company of actors had to obtain a license before performing for public audiences. In 1574, Robert Dudley's troupe of players, Leicester's Men, received a royal patent from the queen's council, which allowed his actors to tour the country unmolested by local authorities.

EXCERPTS OF WORKS IN THE NOVEL

Isabella Whitney, *The Copy of a Letter with an Admonition by the Author, to all Young Gentlewomen,* (1567); *A Sweet Nosegay* (1573). *

Juan Luis Vives, *Education of a Christian Woman*, (1510) Edited and translated by Charles Fantazzi, University of Chicago Press, 2000.

A Ditty Delightfull of mother Watkins ale, reprinted in Joseph Lilly's, A Collection of Seventy-nine Black Letter Ballads and Broadsides, London, 1867.*

A Letter Sent by Maydens of London (1567). Handbook of the law of municipal corporations. Roger W. Cooley, 2010.*

*I have changed some wording in the original text to make it understandable to the contemporary reader.

ABOUT THE AUTHOR

Constance Briones is passionate about bringing to light the little-known stories of women and their contributions to history. She has a Masters in History focusing on women's studies, which informs her writing. For twenty years, Constance has taught an interdisciplinary study program in Language Arts and History in public schools. She is currently an educational docent for her city's historical society.

www.thehistoricalfictioncompany.com/hp-authors/
constance-briones

www.facebook.com/constancebrionesauthor

THANK YOU FOR READING
REVIEWS ARE APPRECIATED

www.historiumpress.com

www.ingramcontent.com/pod-product-compliance
Lightning Source LLC
Chambersburg PA
CBHW032237310726
48973CB00008B/2181